THE REGENCY LORDS & LADIES COLLECTION

**Glittering Regency Love Affairs
from your favourite historical authors.**

THE REGENCY LORDS & LADIES COLLECTION

Available from the
Regency Lords & Ladies Large Print Collection

LADY JANE'S PHYSICIAN

Anne Ashley

First published in Great Britain 1999
Large Print Edition 2010
Harlequin Mills & Boon Limited,
Eton House, 18-24 Paradise Road, Richmond, Surrey TW9 1SR

© Anne Ashley 1999

ISBN: 978 0 263 21058 3

Harlequin Mills & Boon policy is to use papers that are natural, renewable and recyclable products and made from wood grown in sustainable forests. The logging and manufacturing process conform to the legal environmental regulations of the country of origin.

Printed and bound in Great Britain
by CPI Antony Rowe, Chippenham, Wiltshire

Chapter One

1819

Having been instructed from a very young age in the correct behaviour expected of a person of quality, Lady Jane Beresford didn't betray her feelings by uttering a shriek of delight as her eyes caught sight of the milestone informing her she was nearing her journey's end, but contented herself with a faint, well-bred smile of satisfaction.

Most members of her social class would have applauded such restraint. Any forceful displays of emotion were considered vulgar in the extreme: behaviour all too often seen in those belonging to the lower orders. And how Jane envied them that at least! The lives of the poor might be hard and cheerless for the most part, but they were free to give full rein to their feelings whenever they chose, whereas...

She couldn't prevent the tiny sigh of discontentment from passing her lips. She would have been the first to admit that, being a daughter of the Earl of Eastbury, she had been spoilt and indulged from birth, given everything money could buy. Fine dresses and jewels had always been hers for the asking, so why did she feel so utterly dissatisfied with her lot? Why had she been experiencing, with increasing frequency, the need to break away from her highly privileged existence, and to loosen those constricting ties which bound her to certain members of a family whose sole ambition for the past four years had been to parade her on the *Marriage Mart* in the hope of finding her a suitable husband?

Lost in her far from pleasant reflections, she gave an almost imperceptible shake of her head. She didn't know what lay at the root of her seemingly ever-increasing dissatisfaction. All she did know was that there must be more to the life ahead of her than being married to some eligible gentleman, running his house efficiently and bearing his children. If there was not, then the future stretched out before her as desolate as a barren waste.

At least, she mused, trying desperately to take heart, by flatly refusing to accompany her father and mother on their trip to Italy, she had taken that first and so very important step down the road to blessed self-determination. Next month, when she attained her majority, she would be financially independent—free to live where and with whom she chose. She had made no definite plans as yet, but she felt little desire to remain in Kent. Large though the ancestral home was, there were times when it seemed grossly overcrowded, especially on those occasions when her only brother and his wife made one of their frequent and extended visits, or when any one of her married sisters descended on the family home, bringing spouse and progeny with her.

Coming out of her reverie, as the post-boys slowed down the team of horses to negotiate the gap between two massive stone pillars, Jane turned to her sole companion who had sat silently staring out of the window for most of the journey. "February is hardly the best time of year to go travelling any great distance, but I am so pleased I took your advice, Latimer, and accepted my cousin's invitation to stay at Knightley Hall."

"You seemed so disinclined to remain in Kent

or stay with any of your sisters, my lady," the abigail responded, casting her mistress an almost furtive glance. "You always speak so fondly of Lady Knightley. It seemed the obvious solution to your problem of where to stay whilst your parents were on the Continent."

"Yes, but remember we'll be in Hampshire a few weeks only. Then we'll be off on our travels again to stay with my aunt, Lady Templehurst, in Bath."

There was no response.

"I hope you do not find travelling too wearisome, Latimer?"

"Not at all, my lady."

And that was it, Jane thought, no more nor less, the barest minimum of conversation as usual. With that one exception, when Latimer had suggested accepting Sir Richard and Lady Knightley's invitation to stay in Hampshire, they seemed never to exchange more than a dozen words at any one time. How she missed dear old Fenwick! One could at least hold a decent conversation with her. She cast the maid a thoughtful look. No, Latimer most certainly wouldn't have been her first choice for a personal maid, but, she reminded herself, she had been given little say in the matter.

When her former maid had been forced to retire through ill health, Jane would have been quite content to have had one of the young servants employed in her father's ancestral home to look after her, but her mother would have none of it. Standards needed to be maintained and, without consulting her daughter, the Countess had taken it upon herself to find a replacement for Fenwick.

Jane's fine almond-shaped eyes narrowed as she studied her maid's attractive profile. Although Rose Latimer had been her personal maid for a little over two months, and had proved extremely efficient in her work, Jane, for some inexplicable reason, had been unable to attain anywhere near the same rapport with her as she had enjoyed with her former maid. She couldn't quite put her finger on what it was about Latimer that she didn't like, for the woman had most certainly never been found wanting in any way and had come, according to the Countess, with a glowing reference from Lady Fairfax, for whom Latimer had worked for more than ten years. But there was certainly an air of reserve about the attractive young abigail that seemed almost to border on—yes—resentment.

"Here at last!" Jane remarked, as the hired

vehicle came to a halt at the front entrance of a very imposing stone-built mansion.

Without waiting for a response, which she doubted she would have attained anyway, Jane stepped down from the carriage. After casting a cursory glance across the front aspect of the attractive Georgian building, she walked briskly towards the front door, which was opened before she had reached it by a very efficient young footman, resplendent in smart black and silver livery.

No sooner had she handed her fur-lined cloak to the manservant than Lady Knightley emerged from one of the rooms and came tripping lightly across the hall to embrace her warmly.

No one observing them together could have failed to notice the resemblance between the two young women—hair, eyes and build all ample testament to their kinship. No one could have failed to appreciate the depth of their mutual regard either, which was most strange in the circumstances. Although they had seen each other occasionally as children, when large gatherings of the Beresford family had been organised, it had been only during the past three years that they had met with any degree of frequency, and had swiftly become firm friends.

Jane had not infrequently pondered over this undeniable fact. Yet she would have been the first to admit that they had little in common. Her cousin's life revolved around her husband, their two small children and their niece, whereas she spent nearly all her time in society, engulfed in the social whirl, where she rubbed shoulders continuously with the cream of British aristocracy.

Holding her very welcome guest at arm's length, Lady Knightley cast an admiring glance over the very fashionable carriage outfit. "Green becomes you exceedingly well, my dear, but then you always did know precisely what suited you."

Jane's immediate response was to cast her very fine eyes over her relative's stylish appearance, thinking as she did so that Elizabeth had regained her trim figure remarkably quickly considering that she had less than three months before presented her husband with a second pledge of her affection, a son this time, who was destined to inherit this much admired country residence and the lion's share of his father's wealth.

"By your sublime air of contentment, Elizabeth, I must assume that both Louisa and baby Stephen are well, and that your darling niece, Juliet, is in fine fettle, too?"

Jane could never mention Juliet's name without remembering that dreadful morning, nearly four years before, when she had read an account in the newspaper of the tragic deaths of Sir Charles Knightley, his wife and their young son in a carriage accident. Blessedly, Juliet, little more than a babe, had been staying with relations at the time, and since the loss of her parents had been brought up by her uncle. Richard had never coveted the title, but had proved himself more than capable of stepping into his brother's shoes. He was a devoted guardian, and Jane knew that both he and Elizabeth looked upon little Juliet as their own child.

At mention of the children Lady Knightley's expression grew more serene. "Yes, they are all hale and hearty—thank goodness! You'll get numerous opportunities to visit the nursery during your stay, so I shall resist the temptation to behave like a proud mother by parading my offspring before you now."

"She'll take a chill and become too ill to visit anyone if you leave her standing in this draughty hall for very much longer," a faintly sarcastic, but very attractive, deep masculine voice unexpectedly remarked, and Jane turned to see her cousin's very personable husband framed in a doorway.

Sir Richard Knightley was one of the few gentlemen with whom Jane had always felt completely at ease. Without the least hesitation she moved smilingly towards him and found herself enveloped in a pair of strong, muscular arms.

From the very first time they had met, a few months after his marriage to Elizabeth had taken place, she had liked him and had taken little notice of the wicked stories circulating at the time about his hurried marriage being a complete failure. One glance at the couple had been sufficient to convince her, if not those malicious Society tabbies whose chief object in life was to circulate spiteful untruths, that Sir Richard Knightley was very much in love with his pretty young wife, and she had glimpsed nothing during the intervening years to make her doubt her first impressions and change her mind.

As Sir Richard disengaged his welcoming hold, she looked up at his smiling face. He was undoubtedly a very attractive man, handsome enough to send any young girl's heart a'fluttering, but it was his intelligence and easy charm of manner which had, and still did, attract Jane. His being married, of course, placed him outside that category which she termed "The Predatory

Male', a species which she continued to keep at a discreet distance. Three highly successful Seasons, where she had been courted and flattered by dozens of eligible bachelors, and some not so eligible, had not turned her head, as might well have been the case with a less sensible young woman. Instead, her success had had the opposite effect. She had become, perhaps, a trifle too cynical, and most certainly never accepted any stranger at face value.

Unfortunately the air of cool reserve she tended to adopt whenever in the company of strangers, most especially those of the male gender, had earned her something of an undeserved reputation. Certain sections of Society considered her a trifle aloof, haughty, even, but Sir Richard knew this was far from the truth. As far as he was concerned she was the most convivial member of his wife's family—a warm and very caring young woman, whose manners were unimpeachable.

Entwining her arm through his, he took welcome charge of their guest by escorting her to a chair placed near the fire in the comfortable and very elegantly furnished drawing-room. "I trust there was no last-minute hitch before your parents set off on their trip to Italy?" he enquired, handing her a glass of Madeira before seating himself beside his wife on a nearby sofa. "I must confess I was more than just a little surprised when we received your letter accepting our invitation. Elizabeth and I were firmly convinced that you would want to sample the delights of Venice and Rome."

"What a shallow, frivolous creature you must think me! Just goes to show how wrong one can be," Jane quipped, before she suddenly became aware of the Knightleys' rather elegant attire. "I must say you both look as fine as fivepence! I do not imagine for a moment that you put on all your finery in my honour. Expecting other guests, are we?"

"Yes, you impertinent little wretch!" Richard responded good-humouredly.

"A small dinner-party, that is all. Nothing grand, I assure you," Elizabeth put in, before her cousin and husband could indulge in one of their light-hearted bantering exchanges. "I arranged it before I knew you would be staying with us, Jane. It will be my first social event since giving birth to Stephen, and I'm rather looking forward to it. But you mustn't feel obliged to join us if you feel disinclined or tired after your journey. Richard and I will quite understand."

"Dear me! Do you think me such a poor

creature as to be overset by a few hours' journey in a carriage? Of course I shall join you!"

"I'm so glad!" Elizabeth exclaimed with evident pleasure. "You see, I've invited Lord Pentecost and his mother. It would be difficult to exclude them, their being such close neighbours," she went on, raising her voice slightly in a valiant attempt to drown her husband's derisive snort. "Lady Pentecost is not well liked, as you know, Jane. And I'm afraid poor Perry has become very withdrawn since his father's demise. I was wondering if you'd mind very much if I placed him next to you at the table? You always did get along so well together."

Jane stared down into the contents of her glass, seeing images from the past when she and Lord Pentecost had been children and had indulged in some mischievous prank. "I haven't seen dear Perry since he came into the title. I shall enjoy catching up on all his news."

She cast a surreptitious glance in Richard's direction, and could only assume by his dour expression that he wasn't experiencing much delight at the prospect of having the new Lord Pentecost and the Dowager as his guests. "You both know, of course, that the Dowager Lady

Pentecost is a friend of my mother's, and Perry was a frequent visitor to our home when he was a boy. What you are not perhaps aware of is that at one time my darling mama seriously considered the prospect of marriage between us."

Richard's dark brows rose, ample confirmation that he, like Jane herself, considered the mere idea as ludicrous in the extreme. They simply would not suit.

"Mama is not always very wise, Richard," she remarked with a faint half-smile. "But there was never the remotest chance of a union between our families. Not only would I never consider the idea, even though I like Perry very well, but my father would never countenance such a match."

She sighed, and there was an unmistakable flicker of sadness in her lovely grey-green eyes. "Papa, like so many other misguided souls, considers poor Perry half-witted. To call him so is to do him a gross injustice, believe me. He's immensely shy, has little self-confidence, and will do almost anything to avoid a quarrel, but he's certainly no fool, and is a completely different person when away from that odious mother of his." She looked across at her interested listeners steadily. "Believe me, there are very few I would rather have placed next to me at the dinner-table."

On learning that the party had been arranged for early in the evening, Lady Knightley being one to keep strictly to country hours when residing in Hampshire, Jane didn't delay in going up to the charming bedchamber allocated to her for the duration of her stay, and, within a relatively short space of time, dressed in a very stylish evening gown of dark green velvet, she rejoined her host and hostess.

As Jane had been drilled from a ridiculously young age in the gentle art of polite drawing-room conversation, neither Richard nor Elizabeth experienced the least qualms in leaving her to her own devices when their guests began to arrive. It wasn't very long before the drawing-room was humming with voices raised in cheerful discourse, and Elizabeth was on the point of abandoning her position near the door when a tall, loose-limbed man, with over-long and slightly waving light brown hair, came striding purposefully into the room, and checked her intention of rejoining her husband by taking her roughly into his arms and planting a smacking kiss on her cheek.

Completely unruffled by the unpolished greeting, Elizabeth gazed up at the late arrival with an un-mistakable depth of affection in her eyes. "Well, well, well! Wonders will never cease. I cannot in all honesty say that I was expecting you to grace our rather informal little gathering with your august presence, Dr Carrington," she teased him.

"Little baggage! You know full well that I never refuse an invitation to dine here without a very good reason," he responded with all the blunt in-formality of a long-standing friendship.

He turned his head, and Elizabeth watched those clear, alert grey eyes of his scan the room. She had known Dr Thomas Carrington for many years and looked upon him as a dear and much loved surrogate brother, but, being a young woman of sense, this did not mean she was blind to his faults. Tom had always possessed a rather brusque manner which, it couldn't be denied, oc-casionally bordered on the downright rude, and he had an acid tongue which he never made the least attempt to sweeten when in the presence of the fair sex. In fact, more often than not, it was the ladies who succeeded in rousing his somewhat peppery temperament, especially those who were forever making far too much of trifling ailments.

His blunt manners certainly did little to endear him to many members of her sex, but those females who called upon his services with good reason were without exception extremely satisfied with his undeniable abilities, and many would not hear a word said against the man who was universally acknowledged as being a very fine physician.

He had lived in the area almost as long as she had herself and, therefore, was acquainted very well with nearly everyone present. So she knew, by the sudden frown which creased his high, intelligent forehead, the instant his keen gaze had fallen upon the stranger in their midst.

"Who is that over there talking with the Pentecosts?" Although Elizabeth had not infrequently twitted him over his seeming indifferent to the ladies, there was little that escaped his notice and, like any other red-blooded male, he certainly admired a pretty face and trim figure. "A relative of yours?" he added, instantly perceiving the resemblance.

"Yes, my cousin, Lady Jane Beresford. Don't you recall my telling you that we were expecting her to stay with us for a short while?"

"No, can't say I do remember." He tut-tutted.

"Another aristo, eh? I think the French had the right idea, there, trying to cleanse their land of the scourge. Still," he went on, ignoring the fulminating glance he received, "one must be fair and keep an open mind. After all, you and Sir Richard are quite acceptable."

Elizabeth's expression turned to one of combined affection and exasperation. She had heard his derogatory views on her social class too many times in the past to be offended by anything he might say and, truth to tell, in many ways she agreed with him. But what would her well-bred cousin make of him? she wondered. There was no denying that Lady Jane Beresford was the epitome of a lady of quality, accustomed to every attention and courtesy, whereas Tom was not precisely renowned for playing the chivalrous gallant, and had never been known to put a guard on his tongue, no matter how refined the company might be.

She was spared the unnerving task of making the introductions quite so early in the evening by the sudden appearance of her very efficient butler, who announced that dinner was served, and she promptly secured the offices of the good doctor to escort her into the dining-room. Unfortunately, there was little she could do to prevent her casual-mannered friend, who had never been one to stand on ceremony, from indulging in a slight breach of etiquette by nodding his head in acknowledgement as Jane, on the arm of her childhood friend Lord Peregrine Pentecost, passed his chair. He received what could best be described as a frosty stare in response, and followed her progress down the length of the table with a decidedly disapproving frown.

"Haughty little madam!" he muttered as he seated himself on his hostess's right. "There may be a certain similarity between you in looks, Lizzie, my love, but that's about all. That little minx needs taking down a peg or two and taught a few basic manners."

Elizabeth almost choked. "I hardly think you're in a position to criticise, Dr Carrington," she remarked, coming immediately to her cousin's defence. "You're not precisely overburdened with a surfeit of good manners yourself."

His shapely brows rose in exaggerated surprise. "And when have you ever heard me being deliberately rude to anyone without good reason, may I ask?"

"Frequently!" she responded without preamble.

"Whereas my cousin is extremely polite as a rule, most especially to those less fortunate than herself. I have never heard her talk down to anyone, not even the lowliest servant."

"Well, that's something, I suppose," Tom responded fair-mindedly and, under the pretext of reaching for his glass of wine, leaned forward and cast a smiling glance at his friend's cousin who, at that precise moment, happened to be gazing absently at the simple, but very effective, flower arrangements adorning the table. Their eyes met and held briefly, before Jane turned away, her finely arched brows almost meeting in a severe frown above the bridge of her decidedly aristocratic little nose.

Although Dr Carrington wasn't to know it, her far from approving expression had nothing whatsoever to do with his actions, which, had he but known it, would have amused rather than annoyed her. She had not noticed his nod of acknowledgement when she had entered the dining-room. Truth to tell, she was only vaguely aware of his existence, for her thoughts were centred on her childhood friend and the drastic changes she had perceived in him.

Elizabeth had most certainly not exaggerated

when she had remarked on the fact that Lord Peregrine Pentecost had altered during the past year. He had come into the title upon the death of his father almost twelve months ago. He had just attained the age of three-and-twenty at that time, and one might have supposed that this new status would have boosted his self-esteem. Sadly, though, this had not proved to be the case. In fact, during the short time Jane had been conversing with him, she thought that he seemed more withdrawn than ever, almost in an enclosed world of his own.

"Perry, what's wrong?" she asked gently, and was dismayed to see him start so violently that he almost dropped his fork. "Is there something troubling you?"

He seemed to debate within himself, but if he did, just for one moment, consider confiding in her he certainly thought better of it, for he merely said, "No, I'm fine." But the smile which accompanied the assurance nowhere near reached his kindly blue eyes. "And delighted to see you again after such a long time. I didn't realise you intended visiting Hampshire."

"For a few weeks only, Perry. I could, of course, have stayed with one of my sisters whilst the Earl and Countess are abroad, or remained with my brother and his wife, who have once again in-stalled themselves in the ancestral home, but I find the over-protective attitude of my family a little trying at times, as you know."

This drew a spontaneous chuckle from him which was a relief to hear. "Yes, I recall clearly that when you were a little girl your family always tended to treat you like some fragile doll, which was quite foolish when one comes to consider it. You were such an intrepid little thing, always game for any lark. I suppose, though, it's only natural for them to concern themselves about you, your being so much younger than the rest of them. I certainly wish I had brothers and sisters."

"I thought you looked upon me as a sister, Perry?"

He appeared to consider this. "Yes, I suppose I do in a way… Certainly as a dear and trusted friend. You're one of the few people I feel completely at ease with, Janie. You're always so open and honest, and say precisely what you think, at least to me, but I can never recall your saying anything deliberately hurtful. Hetta's rather like that too."

"I think we've known each other for far too long not to be completely truthful with each other." She cast him a thoughtful glance. "Who, by the way, is Hetta?"

Realising instantly, by the sudden guarded look which took possession of his fine, aristocratic features, that on this occasion, at least, she had been a little too inquisitive, Jane prudently changed the subject, and within a relatively short space of time had her friend conversing easily again.

Elizabeth wasn't slow to perceive how relaxed the young baron appeared in her cousin's company, and as soon as the ladies had returned to the drawing-room, leaving the gentlemen to enjoy their port and brandy, she didn't hesitate to take Jane to one side and thank her for putting a guest, whose introversion could be a little trying at times, at his ease.

Jane waved one slender white hand in a dismissive gesture. "As I've mentioned before, Perry's fine when he's out of reach of his mother's pernicious influence." She frowned slightly as she cast a surreptitious glance in the formidable Lady Pentecost's direction. Even as a child she had never liked the woman, and failed to understand how her mother could look upon such a scheming, tattle-mongering harridan as a friend.

She then cast a sweeping glance over the other ladies present, most of whom were completely unknown to her. "Is there a lady here by the name of Hetta?" she asked, focusing her attention briefly on a slender girl of about seventeen, whose bright golden ringlets danced about her very pretty face each time she moved her head, and whose china-blue eyes always fell shyly before any continued scrutiny.

"No, my dear. There's no one here with that name. In fact, the only Hetta I know is Miss Henrietta Dilbey, the local squire's niece. She came to live with him several months ago after her mother died."

Jane regarded her cousin steadily. "Why haven't they been invited here tonight? Not up to snuff?"

Elizabeth couldn't help chuckling at this blunt enquiry. Although Lady Jane's manners were faultless in public, as Lord Peregrine had remarked, she did not mince words with those whom she knew well. "No such thing! The squire is well respected in these parts, and his niece is a charming young woman. Unfortunately the poor man is suffering from the gout at the moment, and Hetta sent me a very prettily worded letter declining the invitation. And now that I have satisfied your curiosity, Cousin, you can do something for me, and entertain the ladies on the pianoforte while we await the arrival of the tea things."

Jane complied, if not with enthusiasm precisely, then with a complacency born of vast experience at being asked to display her undoubted talents.

From the tender age of ten, when she had first shown signs of superior musical gifts, the Countess of Eastbury had encouraged her youngest offspring to entertain the other members of the family for short periods during the evenings. It certainly had been a far from rare occurrence for Jane to display her skill on more formal occasions, when high-ranking personages had been staying at the ancestral home, and it had been quite the norm for her to play a selection of country dances when the younger members of the Beresford household had wanted to enjoy an impromptu romp.

Consequently, after the tea trolley had been removed, it never occurred to her to demur when a unanimous request for her to play again was raised. Seating herself once again before the very fine instrument placed in the corner of the room, she entertained the ladies by playing a popular tune of the day, and then acquiesced further by agreeing to accompany Elizabeth in a duet.

It was while the cousins, each acknowledged as having been blessed with a well above average singing voice, were halfway through performing a hauntingly lovely ballad that Sir Richard led the gentlemen back into the room. He, of course, had been privileged to hear Elizabeth and Jane perform together quite frequently, but Dr Carrington, trailing in the rear, had not been so fortunate and was instantly captivated by the flawless performance.

Tom would have been the first to admit that he had not infrequently passed rather uncomplimentary remarks about what he stigmatised as insipid after-dinner entertainment. Listening to what Society considered to be an accomplished young lady displaying a modicum of skill on the pianoforte or harp did not rate highly in his assessment of an enjoyable evening. Generally he avoided such gatherings like the plague, but found himself now, quite surprisingly, unable to draw his attention away from the charming vista in the corner of the comfortable drawing-room.

He had always considered Elizabeth, with her well-proportioned figure and finely boned face, a fine specimen of womanhood, but it was the female whose fingers moved with undeniable skill over the instrument's keys who captured his attention.

At first glance, the resemblance between the

cousins appeared quite marked, but, after closer inspection, he could perceive several very discernible differences: Lady Jane's hair was, he decided, rather more liberally streaked with auburn tints, her large almond-shaped eyes were a little greener than her cousin's, the shapely mouth a little fuller; and there was most definitely a more distinctive aristocratic line to the nose. There was no denying that both had been blessed with delicate high cheekbones, and there was certainly a similarity in those softly rounded chins, but it would have been quite wrong, he decided finally, to suggest that they were alike as two peas in a pod.

When the rendition came to an end both ladies, refusing all entreaties to perform again, moved away from the instrument to permit another of the female guests to display her musical talents. Elizabeth was on the point of steering her cousin in the direction of a footman, who was bearing several glasses of wine on a silver tray, when she noticed her good friend the doctor heading in their direction.

At any other time it might have occurred to Elizabeth to wonder why her friend, who could never be described as a sociable animal, should actively seek an introduction to an aristocratic young lady with whom, on the surface at least, he couldn't possibly have anything in common. He had seemed quite indifferent to the several young ladies she had brought to his notice during the past three years, in the hope that one might capture his interest and persuade him to venture down the matrimonial path, and all her well-meaning efforts had been in vain.

She had come to the conclusion that Dr Carrington belonged to that group of unfathomable males who from birth were destined to remain confirmed bachelors, and she only hoped, after making the introductions and moving away to mingle with her other guests, that for once in his life Tom could manage to control the provocative side of his nature and behave like a perfect gentleman. But she didn't hold out much hope.

Unaware of the slight concern her relative was experiencing on her behalf, Jane withdrew her hand from fingers that were strong and yet surprisingly gentle, and found herself being closely scrutinised by a pair of thickly lashed and rather penetrating grey eyes.

Somewhere in the recesses of her mind memory stirred, and she vaguely recalled being told about a doctor for whom Elizabeth had a warm regard. "Am I right in thinking that you and my cousin have known each other for some considerable time, Dr Carrington?" she asked, in an attempt to break the uncomfortable silence which followed their hostess's departure.

"Yes, we have, ma'am," he responded in the most attractive deep, throaty voice. "We lived together in Bristol for several years before she married Richard."

Jane blinked up at him, wondering if he realised just what might have been inferred from that admission. She knew enough about her cousin's upbringing to be certain that nothing untoward had occurred between Elizabeth and this young doctor, and only innate good breeding prevented her from bursting out laughing at such a verbal blunder.

"Er—yes. I recall now that my cousin went to live with her maternal grandmother shortly after her father died. I assume, Dr Carrington, that you must have resided there also?"

Tom regarded her much as he might have done some half-witted child. "Didn't I just say so?" he remarked, in a voice betraying slight impatience, and Jane, unaccustomed to being spoken to in such a fashion, experienced a rare spasm of irritation.

"No, sir. You did not. In fact, you almost made it sound as if you and my cousin—" Only just managing to check herself in time, she didn't know whether to feel amused or piqued at the ease with which she had nearly been led into uttering something so indecorous. "Yes, yes, of course you did," she finished in some confusion, not knowing quite what to think of her cousin's friend.

In this, at least, they were in perfect accord, for Tom most certainly didn't know what to make of her. She was undeniably strikingly lovely, but that, he very much feared, was all she had to commend her. There had been a great deal of in-breeding over the years in these old aristocratic families, which had led to the inevitable, tragic consequences. It was common knowledge that many mansions dotted about the land possessed a secret, well-locked room where a family member was hidden away from prying eyes. He wouldn't suggest for a moment that Lady Jane might end her days by being kept firmly under re-straint, but from their short conversation so far he suspected that there wasn't very much in her upper works.

"How long do you intend staying here with the Knightleys?" he asked, deciding it might be wise to keep their conversation, brief though he intended it to be, on simple topics.

"Until mid-March. Then I shall be journeying on to Bath." Jane was of a similar mind—much better to converse only on mundane subjects. "I do enjoy travelling about this land of ours, don't you, sir?"

"I can take it or leave it," he returned dampeningly. "But I hardly think this season, when the weather can be so confoundedly unpredictable, is the best time to go careering about the country, ma'am. Damned foolish if you ask me!"

It was as much as Jane could do to stop herself from gasping at such impudence! How dared this person presume to censure her actions? Never before could she recall experiencing such a surge of animosity towards a virtual stranger, and almost felt a sense of relief when she noticed the Dowager Lady Pentecost crossing the room in their direction.

"Ah! So you are becoming acquainted with the good doctor, Jane, my dear," remarked the Dowager, whose reputation as a vicious tabby had been well earned. "He has made something of a name for himself in these parts."

As an ill-mannered bore, no doubt, Jane thought nastily. But years of being schooled in polite behaviour could not be so easily forgotten, and she satisfied herself by responding with honeyed sweetness, "And, no doubt, it is well deserved."

Tom's eyes narrowed fractionally, but the Dowager detected nothing amiss and her thin-lipped mouth twisted into that falsely ingratiating smile which had always managed to set Jane's small white teeth on edge.

"I assure you, dearest Jane, that one hears nothing but excellent reports about him wherever one visits in the locale."

"You exaggerate, ma'am," Tom countered, his tone making it abundantly obvious, to one of his listeners, at least, that either he was bored with the topic of conversation, or far from enamoured with the company in which he now found himself.

"If it wasn't for the fact that Clarence Fieldhouse, another very worthy physician in the area, has been our family doctor for many years," Lady Pentecost went on, just as though he hadn't spoken, "I would have no hesitation in calling upon Dr Carrington's services." Once again the tight-lipped mouth curled into its unpleasant smile. "However, unlike many others you see here tonight, Jane, I believe in remaining loyal to those who have served my family well."

"I applaud your sentiments, ma'am," Tom took the opportunity to say as she paused for breath. "Loyalty is always to be commended. So long as it is not mistaken for bigoted idolatry." And with that, and the briefest of nods, he swung round on his heels, leaving the Dowager almost quivering with indignation, and the Earl of Eastbury's youngest daughter still not knowing quite what to make of him.

For a few moments Jane studied his elegant, long-striding gait as he headed across the room in their host's direction, and was unable to suppress a grudging half-smile of admiration. Dr Carrington might be abrupt to the point of rudeness, but one couldn't help admiring someone with sufficient pluck not to balk at indulging in a verbal battle with the formidable Lady Pentecost—and, furthermore, coming out the clear victor after one rapier-tongued gibe. Yes, he had certainly risen in her estimation, she was forced to admit, although whether or not that was sufficient reason for her even to consider liking him a little was quite another matter.

Chapter Two

"How wonderful to see you up and about so early, Jane," was Lady Knightley's pleasant greeting as her cousin, bright-eyed and impeccably groomed as always, entered the breakfast parlour the following morning. "I trust you slept well, and have fully recovered from the rigours of yesterday? Both Richard and I thought you were utterly splendid remaining downstairs with us throughout the entire evening."

Slanting a faintly mocking glance at her cousin, Jane seated herself opposite, wondering as she did so whether living for such long periods in the country might not be having some adverse effect on her cousin's mental powers.

"My dear Elizabeth, a day's journey by carriage and attending a party which ended just after midnight is hardly likely to overtax such a hardened socialite as myself who, I might remind you, is quite accustomed to retiring as late as four in the morning."

Elizabeth couldn't help smiling at this. "Yes, I do tend to forget that your lifestyle is vastly different from my own," she admitted wryly. "I really don't know where you get your energy from, my dear. I find a fortnight in the capital more than enough, and cannot wait to return to the peace and quiet of the country to recuperate."

Reaching for the coffee-pot, Elizabeth poured her cousin a cup of the freshly made brew. She had been granted little opportunity for private conversation the previous evening, her duties as hostess having kept her fully occupied, and, although she was very well aware that Jane had absolutely no difficulty in mixing with strangers, she could not help wondering how her impeccably mannered cousin had coped with one or two of the guests.

Curiosity got the better of her and she found herself saying, "I'm certain you must have found some of those present last night rather peculiar characters, to say the least, Dr Carrington to name but one. He's a particular friend of ours, but I know his manner can be—well—a little odd at times."

Years of practice held her in good stead, and Jane succeeded without much difficulty in suppressing a rather wicked smile before refreshing herself from the contents of her cup. Odd was hardly how she would have described him. Downright rude was much nearer the mark! But in view of the fact that the doctor was a close friend of the family's she refrained from speaking her mind, and merely made some vague response, before tactfully changing the subject by politely requesting the loan of a mount in order to explore the estate.

The morning looked set to remain dry and the unfamiliar countryside beckoned. Nevertheless, knowing that Elizabeth was eager to display the youngest members of the Knightley family, Jane paid the first of what was destined to be many visits to the nursery during her stay. Consequently, quite some time had elapsed before she returned to her bedchamber in order to change into her riding-habit so that she might indulge in her favourite form of exercise.

As she had no intention of riding beyond the estate, Jane dispensed with the services of a groom and set off across the park in the direction of the home wood. Although it was cold, with a biting wind sweeping the country from the east, the sky was virtually cloudless and the weak February sun was doing its best to brighten the landscape. There was no denying, though, that parks, no matter how grand, never looked their best at this time of year, and Sir Richard's acres were no exception. Trees still bare of their greenery could hardly be described as an awe-inspiring sight, and the few evergreens doing their best to add splashes of colour didn't improve the woodland setting enough to increase her desire to explore the area in any great depth.

She had just encouraged Elizabeth's mare to cross a shallow brook, choked with twigs and decaying leaves, and was on the point of turning onto a track which would eventually lead, she hoped, to a different part of the estate, when she distinctly heard a trill of feminine laughter, quickly followed by a deeper masculine rumble.

Apparently she wasn't the only one out exploring the woods that morning, she mused. In all probability it was nothing more sinister than a pair of innocent locals taking advantage of a short-cut across Sir Richard's land. Many of the country folk living in the village near her father's estate did precisely the same thing, and they never did any harm. Her father certainly didn't object to his lands being used for such a purpose and she doubted very much that Richard, kind-hearted soul that he was, would object either.

In any event, she had absolutely no intention of playing the informant, and was about to be on her way, when she distinctly heard a very familiar voice exclaim, "Oh, Hetta! You do say the drollest things!"

The next instant Lord Pentecost, accompanied by a lady whose slender form was swathed in a voluminous grey cloak, appeared from behind a dense clump of pine trees. Leading their mounts, and deep in conversation, they seemed oblivious to Jane's presence, and for a few moments she was able to observe them undetected. She was a little too far away to see their expressions clearly, but any fool could tell by the bursts of spontaneous laughter that floated across in the air that they were very much at ease in each other's company.

Feeling suddenly intrusive, and yet knowing that she couldn't possibly go on her way without being observed, Jane decided to delay no longer in making her presence known. Digging her heel into the mare's flank, she rode slowly towards the happy couple, eventually attracting her childhood friend's attention.

"Why, Janie! What a delightful surprise!"

Lord Pentecost certainly sounded genuinely pleased to see her, but Jane experienced the uneasy feeling that he would have been far happier if their paths had not crossed. She had no wish to force her company on her friend and his companion if they preferred to be alone, but at the same time felt that it would appear abominably rude if she went on her way again without exchanging a few pleasantries first. So, kicking her foot free of the stirrup, she slipped to the ground and covered the last few yards on foot, noticing as she did so that her friend was scanning the area of wood behind her rather keenly, as though he was expecting to see someone lurking behind a tree.

"Out and about on your own, Janie?" At her nod of confirmation, he seemed to relax slightly and did not delay in introducing her to his companion, Miss Henrietta Dilbey.

Jane found herself being regarded very warmly by a pair of soft brown eyes before a tiny hand reached out to capture hers. "Perry mentioned earlier that you were staying with the Knightleys. He has talked of you so often that I was hoping we should meet during your visit." The greeting, spoken in a soft and pleasantly mellow voice, sounded sincerely meant, and Jane found herself instantly drawn to Lord Pentecost's charming companion. "The one thing he didn't tell me, though," she went on, releasing her gentle clasp, "was how very pretty you are."

Jane could quite easily have returned the compliment. A dainty creature of below average height, Miss Dilbey possessed the most delicately featured elfin face, framed with a riot of bouncy chestnut curls. At first glance she appeared little more than a child, but the directness of her gaze and her dignified, self-assured air gave Jane every reason to suppose that they were quite possibly much the same age.

"Hetta came to live in the area several months ago," Lord Pentecost remarked, drawing Jane's attention to his fine aristocratic features and bright golden locks.

No two people could have complemented each other more, she decided. Perry, lean and of moderate height, possessed a shoulder perfectly situated for the diminutive Miss Dilbey to rest her head, should the notion ever take her.

"Yes, I recall my cousin remarking on it yesterday evening, Perry," Jane responded, turning her attention once again to his companion. "You reside, I understand, with your uncle, Miss Dilbey?"

"Yes. He very kindly invited me to live with him after my mother passed away last year…" her sweet, bow-shaped mouth curled into a tender little smile "…although insisted would be more accurate, I suppose. He decided that I had endured sufficient hardship because of what he termed my father's folly and my mother's stubborn pride, and would not hear of me finding a position as a governess or paid companion."

"Papa was a dear man, my lady," she went on to explain as they began to walk slowly onwards, leading their mounts, "but was not very wise when it came to business matters. Mama was a proud woman and refused all offers of help after Papa died. She sold our lovely home in order to pay off outstanding debts and we were forced to take rented accommodation. We could no longer afford the luxury of servants, and it was only by exercising the strictest economy that we managed to get by."

"I think you are quite remarkable to remain so cheerful after all that has happened to you," Perry announced, regarding Miss Dilbey with evident respect, but the lady would have none of it.

"Nonsense, Perry! I have been more fortunate than most. Many gently bred females are forced to find some genteel occupation in order to live, but I have been blessed with a kindly uncle. He spoils me quite dreadfully, and I'm ashamed to say I like it very much."

Jane experienced more than a twinge of admiration for the down-to-earth Miss Dilbey, too, and couldn't help wondering whether she would have remained quite so cheerfully resigned to her fate if she had suddenly found herself in a similar situation.

No, she didn't think so, she decided, after giving the matter a moment's consideration, and feeling more than just a little ashamed of herself. Through no fault of her own, Henrietta Dilbey's circumstances had been much reduced after her father's demise, and yet she had, it appeared, remained cheerful, accepting her lot with good grace—whereas she, Lady Jane Beresford, the daughter of a wealthy peer of the realm, having always been able to demand every comfort and luxury, had been for some considerable time completely dissatisfied with her life.

Really, it wasn't shame she ought to be feeling, but disgust, she thought, trying desperately to shake off her sudden feeling of despondency. What on earth was the matter with her? She had everything money could buy, so why was she experiencing, increasingly, these moods of utter discontentment? What was it that she wanted, expected from life that she didn't already have?

Successfully suppressing a heartfelt sigh, she forced herself back to the present, and began to notice how completely relaxed her childhood friend appeared. She couldn't ever recall hearing Perry converse with quite so much confidence. All at once he seemed an entirely different person—quite the self-assured gentleman and blissfully contented with life. But she swiftly came to realise that it was merely a façade.

"I'm afraid this is where I must leave you both," he said as they emerged from the wood onto a narrow road. "I promised Mama that I would escort her on a visit to a neighbour, so I had better not be late, otherwise I'll only receive one of her scolds. I would very much appreciate it, Janie," he went on, turning to look directly at her, "if you wouldn't mention meeting with me this morning. Mama would be sure to hear about it, and then I would be subjected to an inquisition each time I wished to go out, with her demanding to know where I was going and whom I intended to see." He sighed. "I have few pleasures in life, and should like to retain the ones I have for as long as possible, you see."

Jane most definitely did not see—not at all; but she gave him her assurances, none the less, before he mounted his horse and rode away in the direction of his estate.

"You look slightly disapproving," Henrietta remarked, smiling faintly. "And if it's the sight of Perry, a fine horseman by anyone's standards, mounted on that deplorable slug, I cannot say I'm surprised. If I had my way that would be the first of many changes I would make, and encourage him to purchase a mount more worthy of his capabilities."

Jane, in fact, hadn't noticed his mount, but now that her attention had been drawn to the beast she couldn't help but agree. "But the unsuitability of his mount was not what was perplexing me, Miss Dilbey," she freely admitted. "It was why Perry should imagine that his mother could dictate how he should go on."

There was a moment's silence before Henrietta said, "I should have thought that you, having been acquainted with the family for many years, would have been in a better position to answer that than I, my lady. I have lived in the area not much above six months, and have met Lady Pentecost on very few occasions, but even I have come to the conclusion that she is a most unpleasant and domineering woman."

"Well, yes. She's always been that," Jane responded with a dismissive wave of her hand. "But Perry's no longer a child. He's all but reached the age of four-and-twenty…master in his own home, surely?"

"Is he, my lady?"

There was something in Miss Dilbey's suddenly hard, almost disgusted expression that sent a shiver of apprehension feathering its way down the length of Jane's spine, so when her companion suggested that they ride for a while she didn't hesitate for a moment. Evidently Henrietta was privy to certain information concerning the young Lord Pentecost, and Jane was still sufficiently interested in the welfare of her childhood friend to try to discover just precisely what was causing him so much disquiet. She wasn't left in ignorance for long.

"I never met Perry's father," Henrietta began. "He died a few months before I came to live with my uncle, but common report would have me believe that he was very like his son, shy and retiring, preferring the solitude of his library to paying calls on friends and neighbours, although he was, by all accounts, a frequent visitor to my uncle's home. According to Uncle Silas, the late Lord Pentecost played an excellent game of chess. Perry is like him in that way, too." She paused for a moment to stare straight ahead, before surprising Jane by asking how much she knew about the Pentecost family's history.

"Not very much, I'm afraid. Perry's father married quite late in life. He'd turned forty. Lady Pentecost was not precisely just out of the school-room, either, but she did, by all accounts, come to the marriage with a substantial dowry, which went some way, I suppose, to compensate for her unfortunately domineering nature."

Miss Dilbey betrayed her rather mischievous sense of humour by chuckling at this wicked observation, but then became serious again. "Have you ever heard mention of insanity in Perry's family? Am I correct in thinking that the late Lord Pentecost's brother died a lunatic?"

"Perry's father did have a brother, certainly," Jane concurred, but with a mild look of surprise. "I do know that he died young, but I cannot recall ever hearing that he was insane." She cast Miss Dilbey a searching glance. "Who told you such a thing?"

"Perry himself. But I'm not certain who told him," Henrietta admitted. "And, of course, it is the great fear that he may succumb to madness himself that is causing him such mental anguish. Today he was in a rare cheerful mood, my lady, but I have seen him in such despair that he can hardly bring himself to utter a single word."

For several moments Jane was too stunned even to speak, her mind a whirl of discordant thoughts. "But Perry isn't mad, merely shy—unsure of himself."

Henrietta nodded in agreement. "And it is hardly surprising in the circumstances," she remarked, the light of battle suddenly flashing in the depths of her attractive brown eyes. "How could one expect the poor man to be self-assured and decisive when throughout his life he has been under the influence of his mother, a dictatorial creature who, I do not doubt, has continuously ridiculed his every action and criticised his every word? And his father has done little to improve his son's lot. What on earth possessed him to make such a ridiculous will?"

Jane had been staring straight ahead down the unfamiliar lane, digesting everything that was being said, but the reference to the late Lord Pentecost, who, she was very well aware, had been very fond of his sole offspring, drew her head round.

"I cannot believe he disinherited Perry. Besides, the estate must have been entailed."

"Oh, yes. The land and title are Perry's, right enough, but he is unable to touch so much as a penny of his father's private wealth until he attains his thirtieth birthday, or in the event that he marries." Miss Dilbey's expression clearly betrayed her deep concern. "From what Perry tells me, I understand that his choice of wife will not be his alone. He must marry a female of good birth, and then only with his mother's full approval, in order to attain his inheritance."

A sigh escaped her. "One must suppose, in view of the fact that he was very fond of his son, that the late Lord Pentecost acted out of the purest of motives, but he certainly did his son no favours by insisting that Lady Pentecost must give her consent to any marriage."

"No, indeed," Jane agreed, clearly seeing now her childhood friend's unfortunate predicament, and cast a thoughtful glance in her companion's direction. "You show a deal of concern for Perry's welfare, Miss Dilbey. You are obviously very fond of him."

"Yes, I am," she freely admitted, "but I'm trying desperately to be sensible and not to allow my regard to deepen."

Jane had already come to the conclusion that Henrietta, for all her diminutive size, was not one to boggle at plain speaking, and therefore didn't hesitate to say, "Because you believe Perry's choice would not find favour in his mother's eyes?"

Henrietta's spontaneous gurgle of laughter was answer enough, even before she said, "As I've already mentioned, Lady Pentecost and I have found ourselves in each other's company on very few occasions, but already we have had—how shall I phrase it?—differences of opinion. The Dilbey family is an old and respected one, but even if I were an heiress I still do not believe I would find favour in her eyes, simply because I am not a cowering female whom she could dominate."

Although she didn't doubt Henrietta's sincerity for a moment, Jane found the latter observation rather perplexing. After all, a marriage between Perry and herself had once been fervently hoped for, and Jane would hardly have described her own disposition as pliant—although, she supposed, she would have more than met Lady Pentecost's high ideals in every other respect.

Her eyes narrowed as she tried to recall that occasion, nearly two years ago, when her mother, during a quiet evening at the ancestral home, had suggested a union between the two families. After Jane's blunt refusal ever to consider such a thing, the subject had never once been raised again.

She didn't doubt for a moment that the Countess had passed on her daughter's sentiments. But, surely, if Lady Pentecost had truly desired the match, she wouldn't have accepted defeat so easily? Now that she came to consider the matter, something about the whole business just didn't ring true. Perhaps it had not been Lady Pentecost who had desired the match, but her husband, in failing health, who had wished to see his son suitably married.

"So, you believe Lady Pentecost hopes for a daughter-in-law whom she could dominate, as she does her son?"

"There are times, certainly, when I think just that, but then at others…" Henrietta shook her head, looking and sounding genuinely perplexed. "There is a very wealthy family by the name of

Boddington living not far from here whose eldest daughter, Louisa, is both pretty and biddable—admirably suitable for Perry's wife, you might think, and yet I cannot in all honesty say that I have witnessed or heard anything to suggest that Lady Pentecost is desirous of a match between them. In fact, I have been present on two occasions when she has said something intentionally derogatory, it seemed to me, about her son, which only succeeded in showing Perry in a very poor light.

"Truth to tell, I don't know how that scheming woman's mind works. I wouldn't be in the least surprised, though, to discover that she doesn't wish her son ever to marry. After all, she rules the roost at Pentecost Grange. And as long as Perry remains a bachelor she will continue to enjoy her comfortable existence."

She gave a sudden whoop of laughter. "Oh, dear, would you listen to me? I'm getting as bad as Perry with all my suspicions. He's certain the servants at the Grange spy on him. I don't know whether this is true or not, but I do know that Lady Pentecost pensioned off many of the older servants shortly after her husband's demise, and had the audacity to replace them with persons of entirely her own choosing."

Knowing only too well how autocratic the Dowager Lady Pentecost could be, Jane was not in the least surprised by this snippet of information. "Oh, she did, did she?"

"I'm afraid so. And from what Perry tells me they are completely loyal to her. It must be dreadful living in that house, fearing that your every movement is being watched. It is little wonder he asked you not to mention seeing him. He must cherish his moments of freedom away from the place, and those ever watchful eyes."

"But that is just it, Miss Dilbey—he isn't ever free. He's shackled to his mother by the will his father made and by his own dark fears…. Yet shackles, Miss Dilbey, can be broken."

Jane was silent for several thoughtful moments before she enquired, "Has Perry discussed his concerns over his health with anyone else? With his doctor, perhaps?"

"I'm not certain, but he may well have done so. Unfortunately, Dr Fieldhouse is a particular friend of his mother's. So, if Perry did consult him, I would imagine that the Dowager is very well aware of the fact." Henrietta's sigh was clearly one of exasperation. "I do wish Perry would seek Dr Carrington's services. Unlike Dr

Fieldhouse, Thomas Carrington is highly respected in these parts."

"So I have been led to infer," Jane responded, with such a decided lack of interest that Henrietta, always sensitive to a person's sudden change in mood, looked at the Earl's daughter sharply.

"Was the good doctor amongst those at Lady Knightley's dinner-party yesterday evening, by any chance?"

Jane's far from approving look spoke volumes, and Henrietta frankly laughed. "Oh, dear. Evidently he didn't make a very favourable impression. He's my uncle's physician, so I have come into contact with him on several occasions. His manner can be a little curt at times, but I don't dislike that. He's a plain-spoken man, but a trustworthy one, and a very fine doctor."

"That, too, I have been led to infer," Jane responded with a grudging half-smile as she focused her attention on the road ahead. Then, returning to their former topic of conversation, she said, "As a rule I'm not one to interfere in matters that do not directly concern me, but Perry's a friend of mine, and I couldn't with a clear conscience turn my back on him when he's quite obviously in need of support. And you've certainly told me enough to make me feel decidedly uneasy about several matters concerning him.

"I think the first thing to be done is to try to discover more about Cedric Pentecost. Although Perry must be certain that his uncle was insane, I'm not convinced at all, for I feel sure I would have learned about it. I don't expect it will be an easy task uncovering the truth. Cedric Pentecost has been dead for a number of years, but there are surely some people still living in the district who must remember him?"

Henrietta nodded in agreement. "I thought of doing precisely the same thing, only I decided it would appear rather odd if a virtual stranger started asking questions about someone who had been dead for more than a quarter of a century. Besides which, Perry told me all that he did in the strictest confidence. The last thing in the world I want is to start spreading rumours. The poor man has enough to contend with without people gossiping about him behind his back."

"Well, quite! Be assured, though, that I shall be discretion itself," Jane pledged. "However, if you've no objection, it might be wise to take the Knightleys into our confidence. My cousin Elizabeth is no fool, and she has a fondness for

Perry." She didn't add that Sir Richard did not think quite so highly of the young baron, but even he, she felt certain, could be persuaded to discover what he could about Perry's uncle.

They had by this time ridden some considerable distance. Richard's wood had been left far behind, and they were surrounded by open fields. Henrietta, drawing her mount to a halt as they arrived at a crossroads, turned to Jane with an apologetic smile.

"This, I'm afraid, is where we must part company. I'm sorry I've taken up so much of your time this morning. You must think it most odd that a complete stranger should confide in you in such a way, but I've been at my wits' end, just not knowing what to do for the best. It really was a godsend your coming here."

"Do not build up your hopes, Miss Dilbey. I'm not certain that there is very much I can do to help, though I shall certainly pay a call at the Grange, and try if I can to have some private conversation with Perry." She glanced about her at the unfamiliar countryside. "You, however, are in a position to help me by disclosing the quickest way back to Knightley Hall. Needless to say, I haven't a clue where I am."

Henrietta obliged, and soon afterwards they parted company, with Jane setting off in the opposite direction. She had ridden no more than a couple of hundred yards when she became aware of her mount's slight limp. Kicking her foot free of the stirrup, she slipped to the ground. The shoe appeared to be intact, but it was clear that something was wrong. So she decided to make things more comfortable for the animal by leading the mare across a field which, if Miss Dilbey's directions turned out to be accurate, ought to bring her out on the road leading to Knightley Hall's main gateway.

Keeping half an eye on the mare, to ensure that the discomfort was not worsening, she set off across the pasture, her mind dwelling on the unenviable situation in which her friend Perry now found himself. So deep in thought did she become that she failed to notice that the middle of the field was absolutely peppered with rabbit holes, until the inevitable happened and she suddenly found herself in an inelegant heap on the damp grass.

It was only when, cursing her clumsiness, she tried to rise to her feet again that she realised she had not come through the unfortunate episode unscathed. Her right ankle began to throb painfully, and by the time she had reached the road on the far side of the field she was finding each step an excruciating effort.

A milestone set in the grass verge made a convenient resting-place while she considered her plight. Knightley Hall's main entrance couldn't be that far away, she felt certain, but it was pointless shying away from the fact that it wouldn't be an easy task getting there. She was just debating whether to press on, regardless of the pain, or stay precisely where she was in the vain hope that Richard, who had gone out early that morning to the small market town nearby, might come bowling along the lane in the very near future, when she detected the distinctive sound of hoof-beats.

Horse and rider were a little too far away for her to see them clearly, but she felt sure that, although it was most certainly a tall and powerfully built man, it wasn't Richard, who, according to Elizabeth, had gone out in his curricle. It certainly wasn't advisable to accost complete strangers in isolated spots, yet there were occasions when the strict rules of conduct governing the behaviour of young, unmarried females were best ignored. And this was definitely one of them, she decided, as the traveller drew steadily nearer, and she realised with a feeling of relief that the gentleman astride the sturdy cob was not a complete stranger after all.

"Good morning, Dr Carrington," she said hurriedly as he doffed his hat in acknowledgement, and she experienced the dreadful suspicion that he had every intention of simply riding by and leaving her to her own devices. "I'm afraid I've been rather foolish, and am in need of your help."

Drawing the gelding to a halt, he at last dismounted and regarded her healthy complexion in silence for several moments. "What seems to be the trouble, ma'am?" he enquired, with such a marked lack of interest that it was on the tip of her tongue to tell him not to bother to concern himself and be on his way, but sense prevailed.

"I've hurt my right ankle. I'm certain it's only sprained, but it is rather painful," she explained, managing to control her rising ire at his continued, impassive regard. "Elizabeth's mare developed a limp, and so I decided to walk her across the field back to the Hall. Unfortunately my foot managed to find its way into a rabbit hole."

With a decidedly unsympathetic air, he knelt down in front of her and began to loosen the laces of her right boot. "It would appear that you and Elizabeth's mount are well matched." He tutted. "A pair of right clumsy fillies!"

Totally unaccustomed to receiving even the mildest insult, Jane was momentarily lost for words, and by the time she had formulated something cutting to say in response to the far from accurate observation the doctor's attention was fully occupied in trying to remove her calf-boot. So, she merely contented herself with casting him a frosty glare which went completely unnoticed. However, she was forced to concede that, although Dr Carrington's manners were acerbic in the extreme, his touch could not have been gentler as he examined the injured ankle.

"Yes, it's only sprained," he confirmed, "but you're going to need to rest it as much as possible for the next couple of days." He did take the trouble to glance up at her then, and could easily detect the glint of disapproval in the lovely grey-green eyes, and assumed this stemmed from pique at being forced to remain housebound.

For some perverse reason, for he certainly didn't consider himself a vindictive person, Tom gained a deal of wicked satisfaction from the knowledge that her freedom would be drastically curtailed, if only for a short period. Like most members of her social class, she was undoubtedly accustomed to doing precisely as she chose, when she chose, and he didn't consider that it would do her a mite of harm to learn that she could not have everything her own way all the time. If nothing else, it would teach the pampered little madam to look where she was putting her feet from now on, he mused, successfully suppressing a smug grin as he turned his attention to her mount.

"Like yourself, she's not badly injured," he remarked, after raising the mare's foreleg to examine the hoof. "There's a stone wedged in there. Unfortunately I've nothing about me to prise it out—" his impatient sigh was quite audible "—so it looks as if I'll be put to the trouble of escorting you back to the Hall myself."

Put to the trouble…? Jane could hardly believe she had heard correctly. Why, it was tantamount to telling her that she was nothing more than a confounded nuisance!

She felt her hackles rise, a rare experience for her, and couldn't resist saying, in retaliation, "Please do not put yourself out on my account,

Dr Carrington. I'm certain I shall manage to hobble back…eventually."

"I dare say you could," he agreed, with infuriating calm, "but it would show a marked lack of good sense, not to mention a sad want of conduct, for you to make the attempt, in view of the fact that I've been kind enough to offer my services, don't you agree?"

In rapidly mounting frustration, Jane allowed him to help her to her feet, and was in the process of deciding whether he was being deliberately provoking, or was merely too dull-witted to recognise sarcasm, when he further confounded her by lifting her effortlessly high in the air. She experienced a fleeting moment of sheer helplessness before being settled on the cob's back, and was astonished to discover that she didn't dislike the sensation in the least.

"For heaven's sake relax, girl!" Tom admonished in his usual forthright manner as he eased himself into the saddle behind her, and slid one arm about her trim waist in order to grip the reins, while stretching out with the other to grasp those of Elizabeth's mare. "You're perfectly safe. I'll not let you fall."

The assurance did little to ease those strangely

disturbing sensations rippling through her. Thomas Carrington might well be a pillar of the community and a much respected physician, but Jane found it impossible to see him in that comforting light when his strong, muscular leg was resting against her thigh and his broad expanse of chest was pressed so firmly against her slender back that she was almost too frightened to breathe lest he detect the loud thudding of her heart. There was no doubt about it—he certainly belonged to that most intriguing of species: the dangerously attractive, all-powerful male—domineering, menacing and most definitely best avoided.

Although Jane's pulse remained annoyingly erratic throughout the mercifully short ride back to the Hall, at least the embarrassed hue had faded from her cheeks, and she accepted with real gratitude the doctor's supporting arm as she limped towards the house.

"Is your mistress at home, Medway?" Tom enquired when they finally stepped into the front hall.

"Yes, sir. She's in the nursery," the butler responded, casting the Earl's daughter a look of sympathy.

"In that case be good enough to lead the way to

Lady Jane's bedchamber, and then go along and inform your mistress that her cousin has met with a slight accident."

Evidently believing her incapable of walking further, and allowing her no say in the matter, anyway, Tom swept her into his arms and went striding up the stairs in the butler's wake. Although Jane was slender, with little or no superfluous fat on her anywhere, the feat could not have been an easy one, and yet she noticed that he wasn't even breathing particularly heavily when he entered the bedchamber and placed her down on the very comfortable bed.

She refrained from comment when he calmly deposited himself down beside her, and once again eased her foot gently out of the calf-boot, but when, without so much as a by-your-leave, he raised her skirts and attempted to roll down her stocking she decided his liberty-taking had gone quite far enough.

"Don't be ridiculous, girl!" he admonished, slapping her restraining hand away none too gently. "I'm a physician, and quite accustomed to seeing bared limbs every day of the week."

"Be that as it may, Dr Carrington, but I really think my maid or Elizabeth ought to be present while you carry out your examination," she argued, in a vain attempt to bring to his attention the gross impropriety of the situation.

"I don't doubt one or the other will be here presently," he responded, secretly amused by this becoming display of maidenly modesty, even though it was completely wasted on him. "In the meantime let me assure you that your virtue is quite safe. I'm not in the habit of ravishing innocent young damsels—at least, not in the forenoon, or when I'm carrying out my duties as a practitioner, that is."

By the flashing look of annoyance she cast him, it was evident that she was unaccustomed to being teased, but whatever response she might have made was held in check by the sudden appearance of the lady of the house, who swept into the room demanding to know what had occurred.

"Thank heavens you happened along, Tom!" Elizabeth remarked with real gratitude when she had been regaled with the short list of her cousin's misfortunes. "The poor girl might have been stranded there for hours. It isn't a particularly well-used road."

This timely reminder that she hadn't even been gracious enough to offer her own thanks pricked

Jane's conscience. She was on the point of rectifying this sad lapse in good manners when her rescuer succeeded in destroying any feelings of gratitude she might have felt.

"Yes, most opportune!" he said. "But is the chit appreciative...? No, not a whit! I was forced to endure a stony silence throughout the entire ride back here, and since our arrival she's been glowering at me like an infuriated kitten. There's ingratitude for you! Why, it's enough to destroy the good Samaritan in any upstanding citizen."

Succeeding yet again in curbing a smile at the fulminating glance he received, Tom rose from the bed. "Have a cold compress put on that ankle, Elizabeth. It isn't a particularly bad sprain, but she'll need to rest it for a couple of days. Besides," he added, as his parting shot, "a couple of days in bed will do her the world of good. Give her the opportunity to study a book on civility."

Jane had been hard-pressed to contain her temper since first meeting up with him, and never more so than now. "Well, really!" she exclaimed the instant he had left the room. "He has the cursed impudence to suggest that I need to read a book on etiquette!"

Never before could she recall feeling so exasperated with anyone, and for the first time ever did not attempt to conceal her feelings of ill-usage. "He may be a friend of yours, Elizabeth, but I shall take leave to inform you that he is the most ill-mannered creature it has ever been my misfortune to encounter!" she announced, giving full rein to her temper, and was then further incensed when her cousin's only response was to dissolve into whoops of laughter.

Chapter Three

Tom contemplated the flickering shadows on the low ceiling of the bedchamber before transferring his gaze to the woman lying silently beside him. Her glossy dark brown locks, framing her face, were in some disorder, and her eyes were closed, but he sensed that she wasn't asleep.

After their pleasurable activities between the sheets, the bedcovers, not surprisingly, had become entangled and seemed to have knotted themselves around the swell of her hips. She made no attempt to cover herself, but then, why should she? She had nothing of which to be ashamed. She was a fine figure of a woman by any standards: full-bosomed and curvaceous. She had bared her charms for him on too many occasions during the past couple of years or so for her to feel the least self-conscious of her nakedness in his presence. There was no denying that she had made an excellent mistress, both passionate and loyal, but after what she had disclosed this night there was no way that their mutually satisfying liaison could continue.

A sigh escaped him. Poor Margaret, a young widow with a son to raise, certainly hadn't enjoyed an easy life, though she had, he supposed, been more fortunate than many of her class. Squire Dilbey, a good-hearted man with rigid principles, had not evicted her from this cottage when her husband had died, as many other members of the landed gentry would undoubtedly have done, but had allowed her to remain, and at a reduced rent.

Tom recollected clearly that it had been in his capacity as a physician that he had first come into contact with the very attractive young widow. Margaret had been left very low after a particularly virulent bout of influenza and her young son, Ben, naturally anxious over his mother's weakened state, had walked the four miles to Melcham to seek the doctor's help, a luxury they could ill afford. Ben had paid off the debt by doing odd jobs at Tom's rented house. Even at the young age of eleven, Ben had proved himself a good little worker, and Tom had continued to employ him ever since to help around the house and tend the small garden.

That, too, he supposed, would cease in the very near future, if Margaret went ahead and married the blacksmith. It would certainly benefit her son if she did. The blacksmith, a widower with two young daughters, certainly needed a woman about the place. Ben would benefit from learning a good trade, and his mother would no longer be forced to work those long hours, sewing by the light of a candle in order to put some food on the table.

Tom looked down at her again with a touch of regret in his eyes. Margaret Ryan was certainly no whore, but he supposed he had treated her as such during these past years, visiting this cottage whenever the mood had taken him, and paying for his pleasures by depositing some coins on the dresser before he had left each time. Fond of her though he was, as far as he was concerned their long association had been little more than a business transaction, and there was no denying that she had been grateful for the extra money. Perhaps he had been selfish to use her in such a way, but nothing, he told himself, could be changed by suffering pangs of conscience now.

Swinging his feet to the floor, he quickly scrambled into his discarded clothes and went almost silently over to the door. Force of habit sent his hand into his coat pocket to draw out his purse, but then he checked himself, remembering clearly her request.

"This time just for love," she had said, before pressing her full, rounded breasts against his chest and drawing him down onto the bed. He doubted very much that the passionate interlude which had followed had very much to do with that emotion—not on his side, at least—but he would not insult whatever feeling she might have experienced by paying for his pleasures this time, and quietly he left her, knowing instinctively that she wanted no words of farewell.

Wrapping his cloak more tightly about him against the frosty evening air, he collected his mount from the small stable, and took one final glance back at the cottage as he made slowly for home.

There was no doubt in his mind that he would miss Margaret Ryan, but if it was the security of marriage she now felt she needed, then he wouldn't selfishly try to stand in her way. After all, there could never be any question of a marriage between them. Without doubt she had the power to satisfy him physically, though certainly not mentally, or in any deeply emotional way. But then, he reminded himself, no female had ever ignited that elusive, loving tenderness in his breast, not even Elizabeth whom he had always cared for above any other woman.

He arrived at the road leading to Knightley Hall, and instinctively drew his mount to a halt, recalling clearly the chance encounter with Elizabeth's cousin that morning. How he had ruffled that aristocratic little madam's feathers! That dagger-look she had cast him before he had left the bedchamber still had the power to amuse him even now. Unless he mistook the matter, there was a great deal of fire beneath that ice-cool reserve of hers— a great deal more to that young woman than mere physical beauty, he decided, with a complete turnabout of his former opinion. She, he didn't doubt for a moment, could certainly stimulate him mentally.

Although he had been careful not to show it, the prickly little darling already attracted him physically, but he was sensible enough to realise that there would be little point in getting to know her better. She was as far above his touch as…as he was above Margaret's.

God, how he hated this class distinction! It placed insurmountable barriers between people, but there was little point in trying to pretend that it didn't exist. Lady Jane Beresford belonged to the cream of aristocracy, whereas he, in her eyes, was no doubt nothing more than a struggling country practitioner, worthy of a polite exchange of pleasantries, but little more. No, there was no future in trying to get to know the lovely Lady Jane better. And it might prove dangerous for his peace of mind, he decided, urging his mount homewards, for him to try to do so.

The following day Jane was relieved when Dr Carrington did not pay a return visit to the Hall and see how her injury was progressing. The ankle remained badly swollen, and Elizabeth was all for summoning her friend back, but Jane wouldn't hear of it, declaring that it would be a waste of the doctor's time, and that the swelling would subside if she rested.

Perversely, though, during her second day in bed, she began to feel piqued that Dr Carrington hadn't been sufficiently interested in her well-being even to send a note to inquire how she went on, but put these feelings of irritation down to the fact that she was already heartily sick of the forced confinement.

Thankfully, by the third day she deemed her ankle sufficiently recovered to risk a venture out of doors. Her two days of inactivity had given her ample opportunity to dwell on that very enlightening conversation with Miss Dilbey, and, although she didn't doubt for a moment Henrietta's sincerity and genuine concern, Jane still felt the need to talk to Perry first, before committing herself to doing anything on his behalf. Not that she thought there was very much she could do by herself, but for the time being, at least, she decided it would be wisest to keep her own counsel, and not to confess her feelings of unease to others.

Consequently, Jane left the Hall without informing either her host or hostess where she was bound. Evidently Richard held her in no way responsible for the slight injury to his wife's mare, deeming it an unfortunate occurrence that could have happened to any rider, and raised not the smallest objection to her borrowing one of his prized geldings. He did, however, insist that this time she took the sensible precaution of being accompanied by a groom. This was an edict that proved very beneficial, for the young stable-lad had been born and bred in the area, and was able to escort her to her destination in very good time.

Since Perry had usually visited them, it had been eight years since Jane had accompanied her mother on her one and only short visit to Pentecost Grange. In truth, she had no very clear recollections of her stay, but had to own as she entered the grounds that the moderately sized Restoration mansion, set in its acres of open parkland, was very pleasing to the eye. Any woman would be more than content to be mistress of such a fine house. If Lady Pentecost was, indeed, very reluctant to relinquish her position to another, then no one could blame her for that—providing, of course, that she didn't resort to underhanded stratagems to retain her position which would be detrimental to her son.

Still doing her level best to keep an open mind, Jane approached the front entrance and was admitted by a small, shifty-eyed individual in a suit of black cloth, who she presumed was the butler. If he turned out to be one of those servants recently employed by Lady Pentecost, Jane could quite understand Perry's unease, for on first impressions she wouldn't trust the man an inch.

"Is your master at home?" she enquired, taking a moment to gaze about her before looking back at the servant to discover a most disrespectful expression on his thin, sharp-featured face.

"And which master would that be, miss?" was his eventual surly response.

All Jane's proud aristocratic breeding came to the fore and she cast her eyes over him in a glance of such icy contempt that he visibly blanched. "You would do well to keep a civil tongue in your head when you address me, my good man. Now, inform Lord Pentecost at once that Lady Jane Beresford is here to see him!"

"The young master is not at home at present," he responded, sickeningly obsequious now, "but the mistress is receiving in the drawing-room."

Jane hardly gave him time to announce her before she swept regally past into the room. She took a moment to cast a quick glance at the gentleman sprawled at his ease in the chair by the hearth, for all the world as though he owned the place, before turning her attention to the formidable matron seated on the sofa.

"Why, my dear! What an unexpected pleasure!"

"Unexpected, ma'am?" Jane quizzed, very much on her guard. "You must surely realise that

Mama would not be best pleased if I was not courteous enough to pay one of her oldest friends a visit whilst I was residing so close by."

Lady Pentecost appeared highly delighted by the explanation, so it was perhaps just as well that she didn't realise that Jane considered her mother somewhat unwise when it came to her choice of friends. Jane's expression, however, gave nothing away, nor did she betray her utter contempt for Sir Willoughby Wentworth when at last he managed to ease his massive bulk out of the chair in order to take her hand in an over-familiar grasp.

"You know my brother, of course. He's staying with us for a short while."

"Yes, we've met before on several occasions, ma'am," Jane responded, successfully withdrawing her hand from the obese baronet's podgy-fingered grasp before accepting the invitation to sit on the sofa.

"And we have another guest staying with us for a few days," Lady Pentecost informed her, with an infuriatingly self-satisfied smile. "The Honourable Simon Fairfax called unexpectedly yesterday to offer his belated condolences on my husband's sad demise. He was journeying to Bristol to stay with friends, but I managed to persuade him to remain with us for a few days. And he's promised to return to us next month to attend my spring ball. I do trust that you will still be here, dear Jane. I should be most disappointed if you were to return to Kent and not honour us with your presence. My little spring gathering is considered quite an event hereabouts."

"I'm not returning to Kent, but shall be journeying on to Bath to stay with my aunt, Lady Templehurst, for a while. I shall be delighted to attend." Whether she gained much pleasure from the event remained to be seen, but she realised that it was to her advantage to see as much of Perry as possible in order to gain a clear idea of what kind of life he was leading here at the Grange. "And shall you be remaining here for your sister's party, Sir Willoughby?"

"Oh, aye, aye! Must lend my support. Play the host, don't you see?"

"No, sir. I'm afraid I do not see." Jane raised her finely arched brows in exaggerated surprise. "Surely, as master of this house, that role falls to Perry?"

"Well, ordinarily, of course it would." Lady Pentecost hurriedly intervened. "But I'm afraid dear Perry hasn't been himself of late, almost permanently locked in a world of his own. Surely you observed that at the Knightleys' dinner-party the other evening? It would be quite heartless of me to expect him to host such a large party, when his uncle has very kindly offered his services."

So, Henrietta had certainly not been fanciful when she had suggested that all was not as it should be here at the Grange. How very cunning the odious Lady Pentecost was to feign consideration for her son as her reason for not wishing him to take his rightful place at her side during the forthcoming event. Whereas, if the truth be known, the real reason was possibly an attempt to undermine further his position as master of this house. After all, it would show Perry in a very poor light if he were to appear unequal to the task of playing host at his own spring ball. And hadn't Henrietta suggested that Lady Pentecost seemed to revel in making her son appear inadequate in front of others?

Jane's eyes narrowed speculatively as she glanced in the formidable Dowager's direction. Perhaps it just might be possible to persuade Lady Pentecost that she wouldn't be precisely basking in approval, either, if it was seen that her son's role had been taken by another. Social position was all-important to her, and this, Jane realised with lightning clarity, might just prove to be the chink in the formidable lady's armour.

"I certainly did perceive a difference in him, ma'am. But—" she shrugged "—it was only to be expected in the circumstances. Some people take longer to get over a bereavement than others. His father's death was a great loss to him, as you above anyone else should know."

"Indeed, yes," Lady Pentecost agreed, if a touch warily. "And it is simply because he is not himself that I feel it would be grossly unfair to expect him to host my spring ball."

The possessive *my* did not go unnoticed, but Jane wisely chose to ignore it. "Your consideration does you great credit, ma'am, and it is only natural that you should wish to protect your son." She took a significant moment to glance at the wall behind Lady Pentecost at a very fine portrait by Sir Joshua Reynolds of a former mistress of the Grange. "Unfortunately there are those in Society who would not view your actions in that very commendable light."

"I'm afraid I do not perfectly understand you," Lady Pentecost responded, visibly bristling. "I think you must explain precisely what you mean."

"Oh, come, ma'am! You must recall, surely, the way the Dowager Lady Merrivale insisted that her son host her ball the year before last. The Viscount, like Perry, is not fond of large social gatherings. But at least Perry does not stammer! It cannot be denied that the young Viscount's speech impediment caused some merriment during the proceedings, but the general consensus of opinion was that the Dowager was quite right in persuading her son to do his duty. And that was far more of an ordeal for the young Viscount than Perry shall be forced to endure. Lady Merrivale's ball was, after all, held during the height of the Season with five hundred guests present, not a small country affair where one is surrounded by friends and neighbours."

She waited a moment for Lady Pentecost to digest fully what had been said, before adding, "Nevertheless, knowing Perry as I do, I doubt he will relish the prospect, but better that he make the attempt than relinquish the role to another, and have malicious rumours circulating that you were too selfish a mother to offer him your support."

It was quite evident by Lady Pentecost's suddenly thoughtful expression that she had not considered this possibility, but Jane was sensible enough to realise that it would be unwise to expound on the topic further and thereby risk arousing suspicions in that far-from-obtuse lady's mind. She was, therefore, heartily thankful when an interruption occurred, and she turned her head to see Perry, accompanied by the strikingly handsome Simon Fairfax, enter the room.

"Hello, Janie. How nice to see you again!"

"I thought it time I paid a visit to the Grange. And I did have a particular reason for wishing to see you, Perry."

She rose from the sofa and, without enlightening him further, offered her hand to the blond-haired, blue-eyed Adonis standing beside him. Many considered Mr Fairfax the most handsome man on the social scene by far, and there was no denying that he was well favoured in both face and form. His address was polished and his appearance was always faultless, but for some obscure reason that Jane herself had never been able to understand she had never quite liked him. Nevertheless, her innate good manners came to the fore and she betrayed none of her slight reservations about him as she politely enquired after his parents.

"They are both quite well, my lady, although I

did suspect that my father was about to succumb to one of his frequent bouts of gout." His teeth flashed in a sportive smile. "Consequently, I decided to make myself scarce by paying a visit to some friends of mine residing near Bristol. My father is not at his best at such times."

"And I am so glad you decided to visit us here," Lady Pentecost put in, looking remarkably well pleased at having such a handsome gentleman residing with them, if only for a few days.

"I could not pass so close by without enquiring how you go on, ma'am, and offering my belated personal condolences on your loss."

Although Lady Pentecost appeared to find nothing amiss in these disclosures, Jane most certainly did. Perry's father had died almost a year ago. Wasn't it leaving it rather late to express one's sympathy now? Added to which, the Fairfax estate was situated in Berkshire, and the main post road from London to the west of the country was more than twenty miles' distance from Pentecost Grange. Simon Fairfax had hardly been passing close by if his intention had been to visit Bristol.

"Did you say you wished to see me?" Perry asked, breaking into Jane's puzzled thoughts.

"Oh, yes, I did." She cast him a bright, wickedly impish smile. "Sir Richard happened to mention over breakfast this morning that he might be selling one of his hacks, and I instantly thought of you and wondered whether you might be interested?"

"It isn't the grey, is it, Janie?" he asked, with all the excited interest of a schoolboy.

"Yes, it is, as it happens."

"Oh, by Jove! He's a prime un!"

"Very likely," his mother put in with a decidedly disapproving sniff. "Sir Richard, as we all know, is quite renowned for the horseflesh he keeps. But I hardly think you are in need of a further mount."

Jane didn't know which irritated her more— Lady Pentecost's lofty assumption that her word was law, or Perry's submissive attitude to his mother's every whim. By his crestfallen expression it was plain that he wouldn't even attempt to force the issue, but Jane was made of sterner stuff.

"What a pity! You would have looked as fine as fivepence on that grey, Perry. Although..." she paused to affect a puzzled expression "...Sir Richard did seem disinclined to offer the animal to you."

The grossly false admission had the desired

effect and Lady Pentecost's chin rose sharply. "And why, pray, did he seem reluctant?"

"Well, ma'am, for some obscure reason he didn't seem to think Perry was up to handling the gelding."

"What!" Sir Willoughby, looking positively indignant, eased his large bulk upright in the chair. "You may tell Sir Richard from me that if he thinks that about the boy then he's far out. My nephew has his faults, plenty of 'em. But I'll give the lad his due—he's got a fine seat on a horse." He turned his disapproving gaze in his sister's direction. "This is what comes, Sophia, of keeping rubbishing job horses in your stable. You could at least see the boy was decently mounted!"

"It wouldn't hurt, surely, just to take a look at the grey?" Mr Fairfax remarked suavely, breaking the silence which followed the baronet's unexpected outburst. "I certainly wouldn't object to casting my eyes over Sir Richard's cattle."

Lady Pentecost, admitting defeat with bad grace, announced pettishly that Peregrine might do as he liked, and Jane would have felt extremely grateful to Simon Fairfax for his support if she hadn't gained the distinct impression by the look he cast her that he, at least, was perfectly well aware of what she had been about.

"That's settled, then!" Unable to hold that penetrating, blue-eyed gaze, she turned to her friend. "It is time I was on my way, Perry. I'll tell Sir Richard to expect you in the morning."

Delaying only for the time it took to make her farewells and to secure Perry's escort to the stables, Jane left the uncomfortable atmosphere of the drawing-room, almost sighing with relief as she stepped outside the house.

"I don't think you were being perfectly truthful back there, Janie, were you?"

"About what, Perry?" she enquired, all wide-eyed innocence.

"About Sir Richard. You see, he let me try that grey of his a few months back, when we met up by chance along one of the lanes. He told me I handled the horse very well."

"No, I wasn't being truthful," she admitted at last. "But it turned the trick, did it not?"

"Oh, aye! That's why I never said anything at the time. Thought it might work. You see, Mama doesn't care what she says about me herself, but she doesn't like it when she discovers that others have been saying unflattering things about the family."

Jane cast him a look of approval. No, there really wasn't much wrong with his understanding. She then changed the subject by remarking on his mother's evident delight at having Mr Fairfax under their roof.

Perry's sudden frown betrayed his feelings clearly enough, even before he said, "Don't like the fellow very much, Janie. Although I've been acquainted with him for several years, he's never been what I'd call a particular friend." He shook his head. "Dashed odd the way he turned up that way. Suppose he must have had his reasons for visiting, but I don't believe for a moment that it was because he wished to offer his condolences over my father's death. Dashed smoky, if you ask me! Wish Mama hadn't asked him to stay."

No, Perry certainly wasn't the fool many people took him for. It was just a pity that he didn't exert his authority a little more, Jane decided, and echoed her thoughts aloud.

"Not much point in doing so really," was his rather lethargic response, and she experienced more than just a twinge of annoyance of his apathy.

"Oh, for heaven's sake, Perry! You are master of this fine estate, and it's high time you accepted the responsibility. You're more than capable of running this place, and making your own decisions. You know you are."

"Yes, I do know. Trouble is, though, I might start to enjoy it too much, and then when the time came for me to give it up…"

As his soft voice trailed away, Jane looked at him closely and reached out her hand to touch his arm as she quickly discerned the look of helpless desolation in his kindly eyes. She realised she would be betraying the fact that Henrietta had confided in her, but felt she had little choice, and said, "Perry, you surely don't truly believe there is something wrong with you mentally, do you? Why, it's preposterous!"

"Is it, Janie? I suspect you certainly thought so at one time, otherwise why did you flatly refuse to entertain the notion of a marriage between us?" There was a decidedly quizzical lift to his left brow. "Oh, yes, I heard all about it. Mama told me."

Jane realised that little would be gained by trying to deny it and, quickly deciding that attack was her best form of defence, gave him back look for look. "Well, don't try to pretend that you were not mighty pleased that I did quash the idea. You've admitted yourself that you look upon me as the closest thing you've ever had to a sister. Why, we virtually grew up together. How on earth could I possibly view you in the light of a prospective husband? I never have, and I never shall.

But that does not mean that I have ever suspected that there is something wrong with you mentally. I can only wonder at your mother putting such a ridiculous notion into your head!"

"It wasn't Mama… It was my father."

"Your—your father?" Jane was stunned. "When did he tell you? What did he tell you?"

"It was a few days before he died," Perry answered, his eyes firmly fixed on his acres of rolling parkland. "He said he was very concerned about me because I reminded him so much of his brother. I'd never heard him talk about Uncle Cedric before, so it came as a very great shock to me. He said that it was a blessing that he died when he did, because he feared he would have had to be placed in an asylum."

"But, Perry, that doesn't mean that your father considered you might end the same way," Jane rushed to assure him. "Remember your father was very ill when he told you this and, maybe, was a little confused himself." She searched wildly for something else to say—anything which might put his mind at rest. "Have you discussed this with anyone else?"

"I told Hetta, of course. It was she who told you, wasn't it?"

Jane nodded, not attempting to deny the fact.

"Mama confirmed it was true, but said I wasn't to worry…said that she would always look after me."

Yes, I just bet she did! Jane thought angrily, certain now that Henrietta's suspicion that the Dowager was taking advantage of the situation was well founded.

"I spoke to Dr Fieldhouse, too, some months ago," Perry added.

"And what did he say?"

"He told me that I had been a weak child who had suffered from convulsions—and an over-heated brain."

"Well, and what of it? Many small children are similarly afflicted. It doesn't presuppose that they will go mad in later years."

"Perhaps not," he conceded. "But you cannot deny, Janie, if you're honest, that I'm not perfectly normal. Mama is forever telling me so. I never feel easy in the company of strangers. I become ridiculously tongue-tied and always manage to say the wrong things."

Jane couldn't forbear from smiling at this. "Believe me, Perry, you are certainly not unique in that. Practice at small talk is all that is required to overcome that particular difficulty. And you know yourself that you behave completely differently when in the company of friends. There is no trying to get away from the fact that you are, basically, a very reserved person, but that doesn't mean there is anything seriously amiss with you mentally."

Jane did her best to reassure him further as they continued their stroll towards the stables, but this was no easy task when a seed of doubt had been sown in her own mind. Had it been Lady Pentecost who had initially enlightened him about his uncle, Jane would certainly have suspected some ulterior motive and dismissed the revelation out of hand. However, the late Lord Pentecost was an entirely different matter. He had been touchingly fond of his sole offspring, and would never have said or done anything deliberately to hurt him.

It might well be, as she had suggested, that Perry's father had been confused in his mind during his final days. Nevertheless, as she had told Henrietta Dilbey, she knew little of the Pentecost family history, and was even more ignorant on the complex subject of insanity. But for the sake of her friend she was determined to discover all that she could about both!

Chapter Four

For a few seconds Tom ignored the rapping on the door and continued to study the notes on his desk. Then he remembered that his housekeeper had stepped out to take a few provisions to a sick old lady living nearby, and hadn't returned as yet.

There were times when the door-knocker was never still, but he would far rather not have a moment to himself, seeing an endless stream of patients, than sit idly twiddling his thumbs, his skills as a physician wasted simply because the vast majority couldn't afford a doctor's fees. He had made it a policy never to press for payment and this custom had certainly been beneficial to the poor folk of Melcham and those living in the surrounding area who were, now, not afraid to call on his services. It was true that payments were not always prompt, nor were they always paid in the coin of the realm; it was not uncommon for him to discover the odd rabbit or game bird, or even a sack of vegetables, on his doorstep.

Wondering who, or what, might be awaiting him this time, he opened the door, and instantly recognised, by the lustrous russet-coloured curls peeking beneath the rim of the elegant beaver hat, precisely who had surprisingly called, even before she drew her attention away from the busy main street and turned to face him.

"Why, Lady Jane! This is an unexpected pleasure!" He moved to one side, allowing her to enter the narrow passageway, and noticed at once the slight limp as she made her way into his consulting-room. "Your ankle is still giving you some trouble, I see."

"What…? Oh, no, not really. I suppose I've exercised it rather more than I should today. No, that isn't why I'm here," she explained, seating herself on the chair placed by the desk. "Although it does remind me that I owe you payment for your services, Dr Carrington."

He sat down behind his desk and regarded her in silence for a long moment, suddenly wondering why it was that he found it virtually impossible to view her in the light of a patient. There was no denying the fact that she was an exceptionally lovely young woman, but he had treated scores of pretty females during his professional career, and had never found the least difficulty in viewing any one of them as just another being in need of his professional help. So what was it about this young woman that set her quite apart from all the rest?

"I believe I mentioned that I experienced the whim to play the good Samaritan that morning. There will be no charge."

"Very generous of you, Dr Carrington. However, unlike so many, I can afford to pay and would prefer to do so," she responded, wondering why he was regarding her in that peculiar and most disconcerting way—his gaze so intense, it seemed as though he was continually assessing her. It was impossible to know precisely what he was thinking, but she guessed by the slight narrowing of his penetrating grey eyes that her last remark had not pleased him overmuch.

"You see, I find I'm in need of your help again, Doctor, and it would be quite wrong of me to expect all your services to be free of charge," she continued, in an attempt to placate him. Whether she had succeeded in her aim was difficult to judge, so she decided it might be wise to come straight to the point of her visit. "How knowledgeable are you on the subject of insanity? Have you come across many cases during your professional career?"

She couldn't have astounded him more if she had just confessed to being a man. It crossed his mind to wonder whether she might not be indulging in some mischievous prank in retribution for his rather uncalled-for remarks the other day, but he doubted whether such a refined, aristocratic young lady would demean herself by resorting to such tactics. Besides which, those lovely eyes of hers, never wavering for a second, gazed across the desk at him in all seriousness, betraying, if anything, only a deep-seated concern.

"During my training in London I did undertake to visit one or two asylums housing the mentally unbalanced, certainly. I have come across the rare case during my professional career, and have seen many examples of the natural deterioration of the brain in the elderly, but I have no specialised knowledge on the subject of mental illness, save that I could recognise certain, very obvious symptoms."

The deeply worried look did not diminish, and he experienced the most overwhelming desire to comfort her, to reassure her that she had nothing whatsoever to fear, but without knowing specifically what was troubling her his well-meaning intentions might do more harm than good.

"What, precisely, is concerning you, my lady? Have you been suffering from severe headaches of late? Have you, perhaps, suddenly found yourself in a place and had no notion how you got there? Do you hear voices, or see strange visions?"

For a few moments Jane was too stunned to speak and it took a monumental effort to stop herself from gaping across the desk at him. The implication of his impertinent questions was abundantly clear: he had the temerity to suppose that she was here on her own account. Never before had she been so insulted, and only her genuine concern for Perry prevented her from informing the presumptuous individual seated opposite precisely what she thought about him.

"We appear to be at cross purposes, Dr Carrington," she told him with careful restraint. "My unease of mind, if I may phrase it so, is not on my own account. Perhaps it might save further misunderstandings if I asked the questions."

Amused by the all too evident resentment at what he considered his quite natural assumption, and experiencing a grudging regard for her praiseworthy self-control, he decided that the more he saw of Lady Jane Beresford, the more he liked her. He suspected that deep down she was a very restful young woman, who would be as happy sitting quietly by a fireside, plying her needle or reading a book, as she would be attending the grandest ball. He suspected, too, that she possessed hidden depths, hitherto untouched, and experienced a strangely powerful desire to be the one to peel away all those layers of highly polished aristocratic reserve and reveal to the world the real essence of the woman beneath.

Leaning back against the chair, he gave her his full attention, more than willing to satisfy her curiosity by answering any questions she might pose, but before she could even open that delectable mouth of hers to commence her inquisition there was a thunderous pounding, as though someone was trying to kick down his front door.

Jane, understandably startled, watched in some concern as the doctor stalked from the room. She could only assume that the perpetrator of the clamorous interruption was either inebriated, or in desperate need of help. A hurried exchange of voices filtered down the passageway, before Dr

Carrington came striding back into the room, followed by a huge giant of a man, who must have stood easily six feet six in his stockinged feet, holding an injured youth in his massive arms.

Her presence having been forgotten completely, Jane rose from the chair, uncertain what to do. In the circumstances it wasn't likely that the doctor would be free to give her his attention for some time, and she wondered whether she ought not to slip quietly away, yet hesitated in doing so if there was a chance she could be of some help.

Calling over his shoulder, Tom requested a basin of water and some clean towels. He had addressed himself to the burly individual, who had removed his misshapen hat and now stood twisting it nervously round and round in his large, work-roughened hands. However, one look at the man's sickly pallor was sufficient to inform Jane, at least, that for all his great strength his constitution was weak when it came to the sight of blood.

"Why not take a seat?" she urged him, indicating the chair she herself had just vacated, and he cast her a look of real gratitude. "You sit there whilst I get the basin. No doubt Dr Carrington will wish to ask you some questions."

Having no idea of the layout of the house, Jane

took a minute or two to locate the spacious kitchen. She managed to find the items she needed without any difficulty, and as luck would have it there was a clean apron lying over the back of one of the chairs. Remaining only for the time it took to remove her hat and jacket and roll up the sleeves of her silk blouse, she slipped the apron over her head, and then quickly returned to the consulting-room.

"Where did you find him, Sam?" she was in time to hear Dr Carrington ask.

"On the Pentecost estate. I were out there in the cart delivering some work I'd finished doing for 'em. Young Ben 'ere had been lying in the woods there all night, seemingly. It were lucky he managed to crawl as far as the road, otherwise I'd never 'ave seen 'im."

"You young fool!" Tom growled, addressing himself to the boy whose face was contorted in agony after the removal of his boot. "You're damned lucky it was Sam who found you and not the gamekeeper."

Placing the bowl and the clean towels down on the table by the doctor's elbow, Jane looked down at the badly torn flesh on the boy's right leg, and knew without being told what device must have caused the injury. Her father was very much against the use of mantraps. He would not entertain the employment of such evil devices anywhere on his land, and, now that Jane was seeing for the first time the results of resorting to such inhuman poaching deterrents, she could well understand her father's staunch opposition.

"You're lucky, young Ben, that the trap was faulty and didn't spring fully closed!" Tom announced, after he had washed away some of the blood, and could see better the extent of the injuries. "Otherwise your ankle would have been crushed. As it is, it's still a damnable mess!"

Jane felt sorry for the boy, who could not, she guessed, have been much above thirteen. He was receiving scant sympathy from the good doctor, and perhaps he really didn't deserve very much. There was little doubt in her mind that Ben had foolishly been breaking the law during the night, even though the dreaded word 'poaching' had been avoided being mentioned thus far.

"Is there no one who ought to be informed about what has occurred?" she asked, and received a strange look from Tom, who seemed suddenly to be aware of her continued presence, before he glanced briefly over his shoulder.

"Yes, I suppose Margaret had best be told without delay. Would you see to that, Sam? Try not to alarm her. The ankle isn't broken, but I'd like to keep him here for a few days to keep an eye on it."

"Aye, I'll do that, Dr Carrington." The huge man eased his large bulk up from the chair and went across to the door. "I've a mind to take m' belt to the young varmint for the needless worry he'll cause 'is dear ma."

"Loath though I am to deny you, my friend, that pleasure I intend shall be mine!" Tom announced, casting the boy a look which boded ill for him once his injuries had healed.

"It—it's the fust time I ever done it, Dr Carrington," was Ben's nervous response as Sam's heavy footsteps could be heard retreating down the passageway. "And I only went along for a lark."

"I'll fetch some fresh water." Jane hurriedly picked up the bowl and tactfully left the room before Tom gave vent to the wrath all too obviously bubbling up inside him. By the time she returned poor Ben looked decidedly chastened, and she could only guess at the peal which had been rung over him. "Is there anything else you need?"

"There are some rolled-up bandages in that

drawer over there," Tom responded, nodding in the direction of a tall cabinet. "You'll find some laudanum in the cupboard, and will you also bring me that bottle on the far right on the bottom shelf?"

Once the injury had been cleaned, and the leg bandaged up, Tom carried the boy out of the room. Jane could hear the sound of his footsteps above as she tidied the consulting-room and returned the bowl and soiled towels to the kitchen. She had just rolled down her sleeves and was about to put on her jacket when Tom came striding into the kitchen, his face as black and forbidding as a thundercloud.

"Now you've seen, firsthand, the needless suffering your class seem to delight in causing, Lady Jane Beresford! That boy was damned lucky not to lose part of his leg. I've been forced to amputate more than once before." He ran impatient fingers through his thick, slightly waving hair, while his eyes, hardened by biting resentment, swept over her in a look of undisguised contempt. "It might so easily have been yet another young life ruined, and for what...? Stealing some paltry rabbit or pheasant. I hope you feel damned proud of yourself and your rapacious kind!"

Never before had Jane met with such open hostility. It seemed almost as if he hated the very ground she walked upon, but she knew this couldn't possibly be true. What harm had she ever done him, after all? His wrath over the boy's injury was understandable, but why was he venting his anger on her? She desperately wanted to defend herself, to try to explain that not all people of her social class were insensitive to the suffering of those less fortunate than themselves, but her throat was suddenly numb and the words refused to come.

Whatever else he might have hurled at her, unjustified or not, was destined to remain unspoken, for the door-knocker could be heard again, and he swung round on his heels, leaving her prey to a maelstrom of conflicting emotions, not least of which were anger and a deep feeling of hurt.

With hands that were far from steady, she reached for her hat and went out into the passageway in time to see him wrapped in an attractive woman's arms. He was doing his best to comfort her with reassuring words, spoken in a voice totally at variance with the one he had used only moments before. Jane guessed that the woman was the injured boy's mother, and her evident distress was only natural, but she sensed a familiarity between them, an almost lover-like intimacy.

They passed by her without a word, and mounted the stairs, but Jane had no intention of awaiting the doctor's return and let herself quietly out of the house. Hurt and anger still gnawed deep inside her, but these feelings wcrc overshadowed by the sudden surge of a quite different emotion, one she had never experienced before and one which she feared to name.

By the time Jane was dressing for dinner that evening she had managed to place the unfortunate events of the morning into perspective. She still felt profoundly hurt by Dr Carrington's verbal assault, but, being a young woman blessed with a great presence of mind, she refused to dwell on the unwarranted abuse, and had been able to concentrate her thoughts on the far more pressing problem of how best to help her friend Perry. There was no doubt in her mind at all now, after her visit to the Grange, that he was in dire need of someone's help.

"Yes, that will do very nicely, thank you, Latimer," she remarked, after the last curl had been pinned into place. She studied her reflection for a moment, and then rose from the stool in order to collect her shawl.

"Oh, by the by, I had the unexpected pleasure of coming face to face with the son of your former employer. Apparently he's staying with the Pentecosts for a few days and should be riding over with Lord Pentecost tomorrow morning to look over one of Sir Richard's horses."

As it was a rare feat, indeed, to raise any sort of response from the taciturn maid, Jane was rather surprised when Latimer immediately enquired, "Tomorrow morning, did you say?"

"Yes, that's right." Jane glanced across the room at her then, but rather too late to glimpse the sparkle which, for one unguarded moment, flickered in the maid's dark eyes, a strange mixture of euphoria and anticipation. "Why? Were you hoping to see him?"

"Of course not, my lady." Latimer looked flustered for a second or two, but quickly regained her composure. "I—I cannot deny I was fond of him. Master Simon was always kind to me. He—he's such a thoughtful gentleman."

"So I have been led to infer. I must confess, though, Latimer, this benevolent side to his character comes as a complete surprise to me. I've met him on numerous occasions in the past and had always considered him a young gentleman too busy in the pursuit of his own pleasures to give his fellow man more than a passing thought."

A decidedly furtive glance was cast in her direction, but as Jane was busy arranging the shawl about her shoulders she missed this, too. "Tidy up here, Latimer. I shan't need you again today."

As her parents were highly social creatures, it was rare for Jane to sit down to dinner with less than a dozen people present. It made a pleasant change, therefore, to dine with just her host and hostess for company. The meal was delicious and Jane was tempted into sampling nearly all the varying dishes, but the conversation for the most part went over her head, with her answering any questions directed at her in monosyllables. Elizabeth exchanged a meaningful look with her husband, and because Richard was fond of his wife's young relative he didn't linger over the port, but joined the ladies in the drawing-room to take tea.

"Have you something on your mind, Jane?" he asked, coming straight to the point. "You seemed in a world of your own during dinner."

She smiled as she watched him take the seat opposite, touched by his genuine concern. "Yes,

I have, Richard, and you may be able to help," she told him, and at once had his full attention. "What do you know about Perry's family? Were you well acquainted with his father?"

"Was anyone?" It seemed a glib response, yet there was nothing in his demeanour as he settled himself more comfortably in the chair to suggest that he was anything other than serious. "He was a man who preferred his own company. He was amiable enough whenever our paths happened to cross, but he certainly wasn't a man for socialising very much. He always struck me as someone who would have been perfectly content to be a recluse."

He had told her no more than she already knew herself, so Jane didn't dwell on his response, but went straight on to ask what he could tell her about the late Lord Pentecost's brother.

"Not very much, I'm afraid. He died young. I was still in short-coats at the time." Richard frowned in an effort to remember. "I believe he fell from his horse while riding over the estate. Don't think he ever regained consciousness."

Jane didn't attempt to hide her astonishment. "His death was a direct result of a riding accident?"

"Yes… Yes, I'm certain I'm right, but I don't

recall all the details." He regarded her keenly. "Why the sudden interest, Jane?"

"Because Perry has been led to believe that his uncle died a lunatic, Richard. And he has this morbid fear that he, too, will succumb to madness."

"Good gad!" Richard couldn't have looked more astonished. "Well, it's the first I've heard of it. Although, if there was madness in one's family, one would certainly refrain from advertising the fact."

"Well, quite!" Elizabeth agreed, before frowning heavily. "But Perry isn't mad, merely very shy."

"That is precisely what I think, Cousin. But if a person is told often enough that he isn't normal, it isn't inconceivable that he may one day come to believe it himself."

Jane then went on to relate the disturbing conversation she had had with Perry that morning. "Now, had it been Lady Pentecost who had told him about his uncle I would be inclined to dismiss the whole thing, but it wasn't. And I have a dreadful suspicion that she is playing on poor Perry's fears."

"In what way?" Richard asked, pausing in the act of taking a pinch of snuff.

"Oh, I don't know," Jane responded, feeling suddenly weary after the unpleasant events of the day. "Perhaps I'm merely being fanciful because I don't like the woman and wouldn't trust her an inch. But I hadn't been at the Grange more than five minutes before she made a point of saying that Perry had been behaving rather strangely of late."

"Now you mention it," Elizabeth remarked, her frown returning, "she said something very similar to me the other week when we came upon each other in Melcham."

"From what I can gather she has remarked on her son's state of mind to several persons hereabouts. But that isn't all. That great barrel of blubber Sir Willoughby Wentworth is at present staying at the Grange. And looking for all the world as though he owns the place! But what really made me fume," she went on, when her listeners had managed to control their mirth at her unflattering description of the baronet, "was the way that odious woman had the sheer effrontery to suppose that she could forbid Perry from purchasing that grey of yours.

"Which reminds me, Richard. I owe you an apology," she added, having the grace to look shamefaced. "I'm afraid I intimated that you considered Perry unequal to handling the gelding—which was sufficient, of course, to force Lady

Pentecost to do an abrupt about-face. Dear Perry, though, saw through my little stratagem at once."

"Then he certainly isn't the slow-top most people take him for. But it really is up to him to be more assertive in his own home."

"I know, Richard." She sighed. "Perry is by nature very easygoing. That doesn't mean I think him incapable of making decisions. On the contrary, I'm certain he could quite easily make a success of running that estate of his—it's whether or not he'll make the attempt. I very much fear that, while he has this dark cloud hanging over him concerning his late uncle's mental state, he's going to continue leaving everything in his mother's hands."

"As Elizabeth will no doubt tell you, I never concern myself over other people's troubles," Richard announced, after a moment's intense thought. "But what I am prepared to do is talk to some of our older neighbours who might remember Perry's uncle. In the meantime, if you are determined to help your friend, you could do no better than consult Thomas Carrington. He, I don't doubt, will be able to answer any questions on the subject of mental health."

"I had already considered that," Jane confessed,

looking and sounding decidedly nettled. "I paid a call on him this morning, as it happens. Unfortunately my visit was not well timed and his attention was required elsewhere."

She decided against enlightening them as to the events which had taken place at the doctor's house. Poaching was, after all, a serious crime, and she had no intention of spreading the story abroad and risk bringing more trouble to young Ben.

"I must say that I do not think your doctor friend improves on further acquaintance," she remarked drily, forcing both Elizabeth and Richard to suppress smiles. "However, for the sake of my friend, I suppose it behoves me to beard the lion in his den just one more time."

Chapter Five

Although Jane had made it abundantly clear that she was far from enthusiastic at the prospect of making a return visit to the doctor's premises in Melcham, she was determined to do so, and directly after breakfast the following morning, with the same trusty young groom to accompany her, she set off in the direction of the small market town.

February was rapidly drawing to a close and the damp, depressing days which had plagued most of the month seemed to be a thing of the past. There had been a noticeable rise in temperature, too, during the latter half of the week, and, although Jane wouldn't have said that it was precisely mild for the time of year, the flora seemed to have responded to the degrees of extra warmth and wild primroses abounded everywhere.

From a very young age she had always taken a

keen interest in her surroundings, and invariably discovered something whilst out and about to capture her notice, no matter where she happened to be, and today's venture abroad proved no exception. As they reached the outskirts of Melcham her attention was quickly drawn to a moderately sized house, which she had failed completely to observe the day before, her mind having still been dwelling on that most unpleasant interlude with Dr Carrington.

Drawing her mount to a halt, she peered through the high black railings that partially shielded the pleasant grounds from the busy street, and studied the charming dwelling that was constructed in the same warm, creamy-coloured stone as the Knightleys' Georgian mansion. It nowhere near approached the grandeur of Knightley Hall, but it was just the kind of house that would suit her very well.

She had been for some months seriously considering the possibility of setting up her own establishment. It wasn't that she didn't love her family dearly, because she most definitely did, but she couldn't deny the fact that she had little in common with her mother, whom she considered on occasions quite light-minded, and who never seemed completely happy unless she was presiding over a house full of guests—and the mere thought of making her home with one of her sisters was enough to send her into a decline. As the youngest member of the family, she was still looked upon as a child, and she found her sisters' over-protective attitude claustrophobic and their well-meaning but unsought advice faintly irritating.

In less than a month she would have attained her majority, and would be financially independent. She was very much looking forward to the freedom her substantial inheritance would give her, and a house like this one, large enough to invite guests to stay, but not so large as to make most of the rooms superfluous, would suit her admirably.

The curtains drawn across the ground-floor windows led her to suppose that the house was not occupied at the present time. She was just debating who might possibly own the charming property—a successful lawyer or prosperous merchant?—when out of the corner of her eye she glimpsed a tall figure striding along the road in her direction, and was astounded to discover that her heart, for some inexplicable reason, seemed to be trying to pound its way out of her chest.

"Why, Lady Jane!" Tom doffed his black beaver

hat with all the practised ease of a Bond Street beau. "It must have been fate that decreed we should meet up unexpectedly this way."

Jane looked down from her horse at his ruggedly handsome and smiling countenance in some confusion. Really, he was a most disconcerting man! The last time he had spoken to her it had been with something akin to loathing in his voice, and yet here he was, not twenty-four hours later, looking and sounding genuinely delighted to see her. What an enigma the infuriating creature was, to be sure!

"Well, it so happens, Dr Carrington, that I was on my way to see you," she told him, seeing no reason to deny the fact.

"Life is full of coincidence, is it not? I myself had every intention of paying you a visit today," he further confounded her by confessing. "And as the weather, too, appears to be favouring us, shall we make the most of it by enjoying a short stroll?"

As Jane could think of no earthly reason to refuse, she allowed him to assist her to the ground, and then watched as he turned to her groom who, for some reason best known to himself, was taking an active interest in the proceedings.

"Be good enough to take Lady Jane's mount to

my home. I'm sure my housekeeper will be only too happy to furnish you with a tankard of ale and a slice of her delicious apple tart whilst you await our return."

Thus dispensing with the groom's undesirable presence, Tom returned his attention to Jane, who was regarding him with a mixture of curiosity and suspicion. "Yes, very well done of me, wasn't it? Now you can safely ring a peal over my head for the disgraceful way I behaved towards you yesterday, without anyone else listening."

Jane was completely taken aback. It had certainly occurred to her that he must have a specific reason for desiring privacy, but never in her wildest imaginings had she supposed that his actions had stemmed from such unselfish motives. Evidently he had suffered pangs of conscience over his outburst and wished to make amends. She would not have supposed for a moment that this rudely abrupt individual, who had seemed from their very first meeting to delight in being deliberately provoking, was capable of such gallantry. Life was full of surprises!

Rapidly increasing confusion had an adverse effect on her natural poise. Falteringly, she made a less than lucid attempt to try to assure him that it had never for an instant crossed her mind to allude to that particular incident and that she harboured no ill will, but he cut in abruptly.

"Then you are being far more gracious than I have any right to deserve, ma'am!" His anger was all too evidently directed at himself. "I was completely out of order! My boorish behaviour was totally inexcusable and I can only beg your forgiveness."

This generous apology, spoken with such sincerity, touched her deeply. She had not infrequently bridled at his curt manner and less than gentlemanly behaviour, but for some inexplicable reason she attained no satisfaction whatsoever at seeing him standing before her, if not precisely humbled, then clearly betraying a disgust of himself.

"On the contrary, Dr Carrington, there was some excuse for your outburst," she surprised even herself by responding. "You were naturally concerned about that boy, who had been quite cruelly and needlessly injured. And over that, at least, we are in complete accord. I, like my father, abhor the use of mantraps and believe their use should be outlawed. But that does not mean I approve of poaching. The persons involved in such activities have scant regard for their victims. In most instances the animals suffer a protracted and painful death. And there are those who would say that the boy suffered no more than he deserved."

"You, unless I much mistake the matter, are not amongst their number?"

He was looking at her so intently that she would have found it impossiblc to lie, even had she wished to do so. "No," she admitted, hardly aware that he was slipping her arm through his as they commenced their stroll. "I am not."

A sigh escaped her. "Heaven knows, we've had our fair share of bad harvests already this century, Dr Carrington, and I for one could not blame a man for breaking the law in order to put some food in his children's bellies. Sadly, though, this frequently isn't the case. Throughout the length and breadth of the land organised gangs of poachers steal vast amounts of game, and not in order to feed their families, but merely for gain. Even so, I consider the penalties for such activities far too high, yet I can also sympathise with the many landowners who regularly have their stocks depleted."

"Against all the odds, my lady, I am beginning to think that you and I have more in common than I would ever have believed possible."

Jane was frankly startled by the softly spoken admission, and more so when she suddenly realised that they were strolling arm in arm, for all the world like a pair of lovers, along the private drive of the house she had been admiring a little earlier.

"Oh!" she muttered, growing quite pink with embarrassment as she quickly extricated herself from his gentle hold. Then, perversely female, promptly wished she had not done so, for there had been something highly comforting in the feel of the latent strength beneath the sleeve of that loose-fitting jacket. Never before could she recall being so acutely aware of the powerful aura a gentleman, well favoured in both face and figure, could exude, and felt attracted whilst at the same time faintly intimidated by it.

"Why are we here, Dr Carrington?" she asked, trying desperately to quell the strange sensation in the pit of her stomach which threatened to ripple its way through every part of her. "You should have said that you were making a professional call, and I would willingly have awaited your return at your house."

"Rest easy, ma'am. I am not here in any professional capacity, merely keeping an eye on the place in the absence of its owner, a friend of mine," he explained, extracting a key from his pocket to unlock the front door. "His mother had been ill for some time and passed away several months ago. Since her death, John has been travelling extensively throughout Europe. In his last letter he informed me that, although he intends returning to England in the spring, he has no intention of living here, as he owns a house in London, and wondered whether I would consider purchasing this property. He knows I've always liked the place."

"Really?" Jane's ears pricked up at this. "And are you going to buy it, Dr Carrington?"

"I cannot deny that I'm very tempted, and yet I keep asking myself whether I really need a house of this size, charming though it is. Come and take a look around," he invited, throwing wide the door to allow her to step into a far from spacious but adequately sized hall. "And whilst I take you on a guided tour you can tell me why you wished to see me today."

Although it was hardly considered correct behaviour to enter an unoccupied abode with a gentleman who was a virtual stranger, it never entered Jane's head for a moment to demur. Not only did it grant her the chance to discuss her concerns with the doctor without fear of interruption, but it offered the golden opportunity to inspect a dwelling that she herself might well consider purchasing.

"I wished to continue the discussion we were having yesterday, before your time was taken up by more pressing matters." She waited until he had thrown back the curtains to enable her to see the front parlour more clearly, before asking, "How is the young lawbreaker who was responsible for bringing our conversation to an end yesterday progressing?"

"In some discomfort—which is no more than the damnable young fool deserves!" he growled, making not the least attempt to put a guard on his tongue in her presence. "I still don't think he realises just how lucky he's been. If it hadn't been for Sam finding him, he might well have been dragged before the local magistrate by now with a prison sentence looming. I've been trying to drill into him that it wouldn't have mattered a whit to the authorities that he hadn't been actively poaching. Just his being there would have been sufficient to condemn him."

He was still experiencing a deal of anger over Ben's escapade, but at least today he had his feelings well under control. Raising his eyes, he watched Jane move with all the fluid grace of a born dancer about the room, and was reminded yet again how grossly unfair he had been to vent his ill humour on her.

She had unselfishly done everything humanly possibly to help when Ben had been carried into the house, yet something inside him had snapped when he had walked back downstairs to the kitchen, and had seen her standing there, rolling down the sleeves of that expensive silk blouse before slipping her arms into the jacket of her stylish riding-habit. Why, that outfit alone would have kept a poor family adequately nourished for several weeks!

There was no denying the fact that Lady Jane Beresford epitomised everything he considered most unjust in society. She belonged to the class that had altogether too much of everything; she belonged to the class that unfairly governed this land, passing laws to protect their privileged positions to the detriment of the majority; she belonged to the selfish class that kept the poor downtrodden, forcing them to toil long and hard in order to eke out a meagre existence.

He wasn't so prejudiced that he wouldn't accept

that there were many just and caring members of the aristocracy, who wished for change and to see a fairer distribution of wealth—Richard, to name but one—but these, sadly, were definitely in the minority. A ruthless determination to retain their way of life at any cost was all that mattered to most of Lady Jane's kind. So why was it, he wondered, that he felt strangely drawn to this young woman? Was it merely a strong physical attraction he felt, or something far more profound?

Thrusting these rather disturbing thoughts aside, he tried to recall the gist of their conversation the previous day. "If my memory serves me correctly you were experiencing some concern over the mental state of…a relative of yours, perhaps?"

"No, not a relative, Dr Carrington." She hovered for a moment, uncertain, then decided only complete honesty would serve. "I'm worried about a friend of mine, Lord Pentecost."

She saw his dark brows suddenly snap together before he turned and led the way out of the room, and couldn't forbear to smile. "I'm tolerably certain that Lord Pentecost is not precisely basking in the sunshine of your approval at the moment, but—"

"That's putting it mildly," he interrupted, opening

the door to a spacious drawing-room. "Hardly surprising in view of what occurred yesterday."

"Indeed, no. But I doubt Perry was responsible for having those inhuman contraptions placed on his land," Jane responded, in defence of her friend, and without further ado went on to disclose Lord Peregrine's fears. "And because he has been told that he is very like this uncle he is now convinced that he will end the same way."

"If his uncle's condition was an isolated case, then I should say that was most unlikely." As her concern for the young baron was abundantly obvious, he would dearly have liked to terminate the discussion on that optimistic note, but knew it would be an insult to her intelligence to do so. "However, if there had been other instances in past generations, then I'm afraid there may be some cause for concern. Do you happen to know for a fact that any of his ancestors suffered a similar condition?"

"No, I'm afraid I don't know, and unfortunately I'm not really in a position to find out, either. I certainly wouldn't dream of asking his mother," she confided, looking and sounding decidedly hostile. "I have the dreadful suspicion, you see, that she's taking advantage of Perry's fears."

"No, I'm afraid I don't see," he returned with that innate bluntness which so characterised him. "In what way is she taking advantage?"

"Because he's convinced himself that he hasn't any kind of a future, he leaves the running of his estate to his mother. I also believe that he considers marriage out of the question—which, of course, ensures that the Dowager remains mistress at the Grange."

She regarded him solemnly, much as an enquiring child might who was eager for knowledge, but who was a little afraid of learning some unpalatable truth. "You must have come into contact with Lord Pentecost from time to time, Dr Carrington. Have you ever suspected there might be something more seriously wrong with him than extreme diffidence?"

"No, I have not," he replied, and the prompt assurance instantly erased much of the concern in her eyes, but he could see that she was still not completely reassured. "Why doesn't Lord Peregrine have a talk with Dr Fieldhouse? He, I understand, has been the family's physician for years. He might know a little of their history and would be in a position to allay any fears."

By her sudden frown he knew that this suggestion, for some reason, didn't meet with her approval. He had scant regard for Dr Fieldhouse himself, considering him a bigoted fool for refusing to employ more modern methods of treatment, and a disgrace to their profession for offering his services only to those who were in a position to grease his palm with shining gold coins.

"Or he could, of course, pay me a visit. I would be more than happy to see him, and if I considered there were grounds for concern I could furnish him with the name of a colleague of mine in London who is more of an expert in this particular branch of medicine."

"Would you do that, Dr Carrington?" She regarded him with real gratitude. "I should feel so much easier if you were to speak with him."

It quite amazed him to discover that he was more than just a little willing to comply, if not to alleviate the young baron's concerns, then certainly to restore this young woman's peace of mind.

"I shall be happy to do so," he assured her, feeling highly gratified by the warm look of approval she cast him. "But you must remember that he is to all intents and purposes Dr Fieldhouse's patient and it would be quite unethical for me to call at Pentecost Grange merely at your behest. However, it is quite another matter if Lord Peregrine, himself, should decide to consult me."

"Of course, yes…yes, I'll have a talk with him." She didn't attempt to disguise the immense feeling of relief she was experiencing. No matter what her personal opinion of Thomas Carrington might be—and she was still far from certain whether she liked him or not—she felt, like so many others, that one could put complete faith in him as a physician.

She was about to express her sincere thanks for his invaluable help in the matter, when for the first time she became embarrassingly aware of precisely where they were standing. So engrossed had she become in their conversation that, apart from the first couple of rooms they had entered, she had taken precious little interest in her surroundings, and had been blissfully unaware that at some point they had re-entered the hall and had climbed the carved wooden staircase to the upper floor.

"Oh, dear," she muttered, staring in some alarm at the bedchamber's most prominent feature. "I really don't think it is at all the thing for us to be alone in here, Dr Carrington." His immediate response to this gross understatement was to roar with laughter which, quite naturally, only succeeded in adding to her discomfiture.

"My dear young woman, if seduction had been on my mind I would have made use of the large sofa in the drawing-room, and not waited to ravish you in the comfort of a four-poster bed!"

Then suddenly it wasn't amusing any more. There she stood, an exceptionally lovely and infinitely desirable young woman, a matter of a few feet away. It would be a simple matter to reach out for her and begin to satisfy that ever increasing desire in his loins, but iron control kept his arms firmly by his sides and stilled his eyes from wandering over the delectable virginal body just begging to be awakened to the untold joys of lovemaking.

Had it been any other young woman standing there perhaps he might not have attempted to retain such a rigid hold on his baser instincts. But this was no ordinary young woman, and no man possessed of any degree of honour should consider soiling innocence and, furthermore, innocence of such high quality.

No, the Lady Jane Beresfords of the world were not for the likes of him. Much safer to consort only with those females of his own class, or those like Margaret Ryan who knew the rules. Lady

Jane was well above his touch and destined for some wealthy aristocrat, who would sample the sweet reward of his patience on their wedding night, and not before. The truth was a bitter pill to swallow, but better to begin treatment now before the undesirable and highly threatening condition which he preferred not to name could take a firm hold.

"Forgive me, ma'am. In my professional capacity I see a great many females in just such surroundings, which, of course, is quite in order, but my doctor's mantle, never left off for very long, makes me tend to forget the social niceties at times."

Feeling suddenly extremely foolish for making such an issue of it, Jane led the way out of the room and down the stairs to the hall. As he had quite rightly pointed out, he was a doctor and, as such, would adhere to the rigid codes of conduct when dealing with members of her sex. The trouble was, though, that for some inexplicable reason she was finding it increasingly difficult to view him in the light of a practitioner and, unless she was very much mistaken, just for one unguarded moment, his view of her had been far removed from that of a patient.

"This is a fine house, Dr Carrington," she remarked, in an attempt to break the uncomfortable silence which was threatening to lengthen between them. "If you should decide not to acquire it, I think the owner will have little difficulty in getting it off his hands."

"That's true enough," he agreed, gazing almost wistfully about the charming hall. "I cannot help asking myself, though, what the deuce I would need six bedrooms for?"

She chuckled. "Well, at the moment you don't, of course. But I should think it highly likely that you'll marry one day, and when you've a wife and a growing family you might be glad of the extra space."

The instant she had spoken she sensed a change in him, even before she turned to see his eyes glinting like chips of ice, sharp and dangerous. "We had best not tarry here longer, ma'am," he announced, his tone as coolly unfriendly as his expression.

She followed him outside, wondering what on earth she had said or done now to put him so suddenly out of temper. He really was the most unfathomable creature!

When Jane arrived back at Knightley Hall it was to discover that Lord Pentecost had called, but had ridden back out again almost immediately with the master of the house, and that her cousin was at present in the drawing-room.

Deciding to change out of her habit before joining Elizabeth, Jane smiled to herself as she headed across the hall towards the staircase. She was delighted that Perry had made the effort to view the grey. It proved that he had far from lost complete interest in every aspect of his life; more importantly, it offered her the opportunity to speak with him again, and confess what she had taken it upon herself to do on his behalf.

She had almost reached the head of the stairs when she chanced to turn her head and saw her personal maid hurrying across the hall in the direction of the kitchen area. Even from this distance she could see that Latimer appeared far from her usually composed self: her face looked decidedly flushed and she was twitching at the folds of her gown as though she felt she was in some slight disorder.

A few moments later she caught sight of a tall figure emerging from the front parlour. Blond head bent, as though immersed in his own thoughts, he didn't notice her, and Jane followed his progress across the chequered floor of the hall. Unless she was very much mistaken, Latimer had been coming from that direction, too. If this did turn out to be the case then it seemed more than likely that she had been ensconced in that sunny little room with Simon Fairfax. How very odd! she mused. What on earth could Simon have wished to impart to a former employee that he could not have said in front of Elizabeth in the drawing-room?

Once in her bedchamber she didn't delay in summoning her maid, and whilst being assisted into one of her very fashionable morning gowns, an elegant but practical creation in dark blue velvet, she asked in a light, conversational way how long Sir Richard and Lady Knightley had been entertaining their morning callers.

"I didn't know they had any, my lady. I've been fully occupied since you rode out earlier with pressing several of your gowns in the laundry."

The response came easily enough, and Jane might not have given the matter any more thought if she hadn't chanced to glimpse a smugly satisfied smile, quickly suppressed, reflected clearly in the tall mirror standing in the corner of the room.

Now, what possible motive could there be for telling such a deliberate lie? she wondered, collecting her fringed blue shawl before leaving her room. Was she such a dragon of a mistress that her maid feared to mention that she had passed a few innocent pleasantries above stairs with the son of her former employer? By her own admission, Latimer had been happy working for the Fairfax family, and if she did still harbour a secret *tendre* for the handsome son—well, what of it? She wouldn't be the first attractive young woman in service to indulge in foolish fantasies. But that didn't alter the fact that her maid had been far from truthful, and Jane had to admit that she resented this.

If and when she did set up an establishment of her own, she felt she would need people about her whom she could trust implicitly, and she had to own that there had always been a certain something about Latimer that she had never quite liked. There was no denying, though, that it would be totally unjust to use this morning's insignificant occurrence as a means of being rid of her. Quite contemptible, in fact! No, she wouldn't make up her mind just yet whether to keep Latimer or not; she would wait until they returned to Kent before finally making a decision. Then, if she still felt she would be happier with a new personal maid, she would grant Latimer plenty of time in which to find a new position.

She entered the drawing-room to discover that Sir Richard and Perry had returned, and to find the handsome Mr Fairfax, now seated beside her cousin on one of the elegant sofas, doing a sterling job of entertaining his host and hostess with a lively résumé of the latest town gossip.

Jane was delighted to hear that Perry had made up his mind to have the grey, and was even more pleased to learn that he had accepted Sir Richard's kind invitation to spend a quiet evening at the Hall playing chess some time. It was precisely this sort of thing that might help him to acquire an interest in life once more, which hopefully might lead to his taking a more active part in the running of his estate. However, she didn't envisage any significant changes taking place until he was freed from that burdensome mantle of fear that permanently shrouded him.

She was naturally eager to tell him of the conversation she had had with Thomas Carrington earlier, but was forced to wait until both gentlemen had taken their leave of the Knightleys and she accompanied them out to the stable yard. Her opportunity came when Mr Fairfax, who evidently had not done so on their arrival, began to inspect Sir Richard's fine string of horses, but Perry's reaction to her disclosures was far from enthusiastic.

"I don't see what good it would do talking to him, Janie. Like most people round here, he probably thinks I belong in a sanatorium already."

"People don't think that, Perry. At least Sir Richard and Elizabeth most certainly do not, and neither does Dr Carrington. He gave me every reason to believe that if your uncle's case was an isolated one, then you have nothing to worry about. Do you happen to know if any of your ancestors were similarly afflicted?"

He shook his head. "Father never spoke about his family very much. I could always ask Mama, I suppose. Perhaps she might know."

"No, don't do that," she responded a little too urgently, and he looked at her sharply.

"Why ever not?"

Jane swiftly sought some plausible reason for his not doing so. "Well, because it might upset her if she discovered just how concerned you were. It would be much better if you tried to discover the truth yourself."

He seemed to accept this, and after a few

moments said, "Well, I don't suppose it could do any harm to have a talk with Dr Carrington, and I shan't mention anything to my mother. She wouldn't like it, you see. She hasn't a good word to say about him."

Jane resisted the temptation to retort that the Dowager Lady Pentecost rarely uttered a good word about anyone, but prompted by rising frustration and anger couldn't prevent herself from saying, "It's high time, Perry, that you began to take control of your own life. How on earth do you imagine your neighbours…your servants… anyone will ever respect you when you continually kowtow to your mother's every whim? For heaven's sake, learn to stand on your own two feet!"

With that she stalked back towards the house, already bitterly regretting her harshly spoken words, but knowing they had needed to be said. Sir Richard had been so right: Perry must learn to assert himself. There was little she or anyone else could do to help if he wasn't prepared to do something to help himself.

Chapter Six

"Now," Jane remarked as she took her seat opposite the Knightleys in their well-sprung travelling carriage, "Caroline Westbridge is that charming lady you introduced me to at your dinner-party. If my memory serves me correctly, she is your nearest neighbour, a widow and, I believe, has one son who is at present up at Oxford."

"What a memory you have!" Elizabeth was genuinely impressed. "I must have introduced you to a dozen or more strangers that night. How on earth can you remember such details?"

"Practice, Cousin." Jane's lips curled into a wry smile. "I was instructed from an early age, and had an excellent teacher in my darling mama. She instilled in me how very important it is to remember the smallest details about a person, so that one has something to fall back on if the conversation should ever flag. Added to which, there are those who, on first encountering, always make a favourable impression." She didn't add that there were also those who most certainly did not, her mind's eye conjuring up a clear image of a ruggedly handsome face, with its square determined jaw, almost hawk-like nose and clear, intelligent grey eyes.

She hadn't seen Dr Carrington since their meeting in Melcham the week before, but that hadn't prevented him from intruding into her thoughts rather too frequently for her peace of mind. She had repeatedly told herself that this simply stemmed from her concerns over Perry, whom she had also thought about often, and whose hurt expression after her ill-tempered outburst had continued to prick her conscience.

Something certainly had needed to be said by someone, that was for sure. Perry simply couldn't possibly go on as he had been doing, living from day to day and allowing others to make his decisions for him. But was she in any better case herself? Hadn't she always been guilty of precisely the same thing: kowtowing to the wishes of her family and living an undeniably pleasant but, none the less, meaningless existence, where the pursuit of personal pleasure was the only thing that mattered? Even now, when she had seriously considered the possibility of setting up her own establishment, she still remained far from certain that it was what she truly wanted—was far from sure that she would be any happier being her own mistress than she was now.

Really, she was hardly in a position to criticise poor Perry, she inwardly chastised herself. At least he had some excuse for behaving the way he did, with the dreadful prospect of insanity looming on his life's horizon. What excuses could she make for being miserably discontented, for being gripped by this ever increasing lethargy? She owed Perry an abject apology for ripping up at him that way. No doubt he would be amongst those at Caroline Westbridge's dinner-party this evening, and with any luck she would be able to have a few minutes' private conversation with him.

Unfortunately she was denied the opportunity to make her peace. On arriving at Mrs Westbridge's charming Tudor manor house she was informed by Caroline that, because Lady Pentecost was a little out of sorts, the family would not be attending. Jane was naturally disappointed to learn this, but brightened almost at once when she saw that Henrietta Dilbey was amongst the guests.

She seated herself without invitation beside Henrietta on the sofa, and, after exchanging a few pleasantries with Miss Dilbey's uncle, whom she found a very likeable and jovial man, she turned to Henrietta. Without further ado, she explained what she had been doing on Perry's behalf since their encounter in the wood.

"Strangely enough I'm rather relieved to hear you say that you feel all is not as it should be up at the Grange," Henrietta admitted. "Although I have never for one moment suspected that there might be anything seriously wrong with Perry mentally, I must confess there have been occasions when I've thought him slightly neurotic over certain things—this obsession he has that people are spying on him, to name but one."

"Over that, I think he has every reason to be concerned," Jane didn't hesitate to inform her. "The butler at the Grange is a most unpleasant fellow and, I understand, is one of those servants recently employed by Lady Pentecost. He's a surly, shifty-eyed little rodent, and I wouldn't trust him an inch. That doesn't alter the fact, though, that Perry should be master in his own home." She studied the delicately painted figures on her exquisite pearl-encrusted fan. "And I'm afraid I told him so in no uncertain terms."

Henrietta smiled. "Yes, I know. He rode over to the house the other day to show us the grey. That is most definitely a step in the right direction. It was so good seeing him suitably mounted!"

Jane's sombre expression remained, and Henrietta sensed the reason behind it. "You were perfectly right, you know, to say what you did," she assured her gently. "Perry must stand on his own two feet. I must confess there have been numerous occasions when I have wanted to scold him for precisely the same reason. We can only hope that he possesses the good sense to listen to your advice, and also makes the effort to visit Dr Carrington."

Jane looked at her sharply. "Do you suspect there's a good chance he might not?"

"I'm not sure," she was honest enough to admit. "Maybe he's afraid of having his worst fears confirmed. He was certainly in a very subdued frame of mind when last I spoke with him, I know that. It's such a pity he has decided to absent himself from this gathering tonight."

A sudden commotion by the door drew her attention and she glanced across the room, her eyes widening in astonishment. "Oh, but surprise, surprise! Dr Carrington has not done so. And he's looking as fine as fivepence, too! What on earth has come over him? I know Mrs Westbridge is a particular friend, but it's most unusual for him to accept a dinner invitation. It seems only your cousin is able to prise him away from his work and persuade him to enjoy an occasional evening out."

Miss Dilbey was not the only one to raise a brow as Dr Carrington, whose unsociability was renowned, strode across the large drawing-room in his hostess's direction, but Jane was oblivious to the many startled expressions bent in his direction. She returned her attention to her fan and put it to good use on her suddenly glowing cheeks, deciding that she must be ailing for something to have suddenly grown overheated this way. After all, it wasn't as though she was unused to seeing a fine physique displayed to perfection in a pair of tight-fitting pantaloons, which covered well-muscled limbs without so much as a hairline crease, and a masterpiece of tailoring expertly encasing a pair of superior shoulders.

Sir Richard was one of the few whose expression remained impassive. It was not completely unknown for Tom to enjoy an evening in genteel company, but it was certainly not a common occurrence. Caroline Westbridge was a charming and well-liked person, and Tom had struck up a friendship with her and her son soon after moving into the district, so he didn't give the young doctor's arrival a second thought until later, when, seated at the dinner-table, he happened to catch a pair of penetrating grey eyes, giving little away, it had to be said, steadily regarding a certain lady. If she was aware of the attention she was receiving she certainly betrayed no sign of it. In fact, she seemed in a strangely subdued frame of mind.

"You're very quiet this evening, Jane. Something troubling you?"

If the truth be known she was unhappy over several things, not least her foolishly immature reaction at Dr Carrington's unexpected appearance, but she had no intention of admitting that.

"I was hoping to see Perry here this evening, Richard," she responding, gaining some comfort from the fact that it wasn't a lie. "I'm afraid I'm suffering from a surfeit of remorse. I was rather sharp with him when he came over to the Hall to purchase your grey."

"He looked in fine trim to me when I came

across him exercising his new acquisition yesterday. The lad's got an excellent seat on a horse, I'll give him that."

"Was he out on his own?"

"Yes. I understand their guest has at last moved on, but is expected back next week for the ball." He reached for his wine glass and fortified himself from its contents before saying, "Loath though I am to indulge in vulgar gossip, am I right in thinking that Lord Fairfax is struggling to keep the creditors from his door?"

"It's certainly a rumour going about, and it wouldn't surprise me if it turned out to be true. He's an inveterate gambler and a notorious womaniser." She kept her voice low, but there was no mistaking the censure it contained. "You might have supposed that a man who won't see his sixtieth birthday again would have preferred the quiet comfort of his own fireside, rather than…than expending what little energy he still possesses in the pursuit of frivolous and ruinous pleasures that he can ill afford."

Richard much admired the delicate restraint. Evidently she would have liked to be far more unreserved and scathing. "Perhaps he is looking to his son to restore their fortunes. There's no denying that Simon Fairfax is a handsome devil." He cast her a surreptitious glance, remembering clearly the way Simon had looked in her direction when he had paid that visit with Perry to the Hall. Unlike Tom's prolonged but benign scrutiny, Simon's unguarded look had been penetratingly hard and calculating. Richard hadn't liked it at all, and it had left him with an acute feeling of disquiet—foreboding, almost.

"No doubt he's on the lookout for an heiress, Jane."

She found herself instantly responding to the thread of warning in his deeply resonant voice. "Well, it certainly won't be me, Richard. I have found myself in his company on numerous occasions during the past three London Seasons. There's no denying that he's extremely pleasing on the eye, but I find his elegant charm rather too studied for my taste. Added to which, there are all the signs, inadequately concealed to a person who can lay claim to any depth of perception, that he'll turn out to be as debauched as his father."

Richard couldn't help smiling at this ruthless dissection of the man's rather imperfect character. She could, he didn't doubt, have said a great deal more to the Honourable Simon Fairfax's discredit, but she had said sufficient to make her estimation of him quite plain, and to allay the slight fear he had been harbouring that she might be susceptible to a handsome face.

No, Elizabeth's young cousin was certainly no fool, he mused. She didn't accept people at face value, which was no bad thing. However, he couldn't help wondering whether the imperfections she so easily perceived in members of his sex might not be, in part, the reason why such a lovely young woman, favourably blessed in face and form, had chosen thus far not to marry.

If she were waiting for *Mr Perfection* himself to cross her path before she would even consider taking the matrimonial plunge, then he feared she was destined to end her days an old maiden aunt. But, no—Jane had far too much common sense to believe that such a paragon of all the virtues existed. He suspected, though, that she was certainly looking for something in a prospective husband that she had thus far failed to find in any one of those many dashing young sprigs who had paraded before her during her Seasons in London.

Without conscious thought, he fixed his gaze on an immaculately attired form seated a little further down the table, and a notion occurred to him—so novel that he almost dismissed it as ludicrous, but not quite. Reaching for his glass, he took a further fortifying swallow. It was high time he invited his good friend the doctor to a quiet family dinner again, with perhaps a hand or two of cards afterwards. Yes, he mused, the evening might prove most enlightening.

The following evening Jane was in her bedchamber studying her reflection in the tall pier-glass, wondering why she was taking so much trouble over her appearance. After changing her mind three times, she had finally selected to wear the green velvet gown she had donned for the dinner-party on the evening she had arrived at the Hall. The dress suited her very well, its rich dark colour emphasising the green in her eyes and the glorious rich red highlights in her russet locks. On any other occasion her appearance would have satisfied her, but it certainly didn't now.

Really, she must be quite mad to take such pains over her appearance, she reflected, simply because that odious Dr Thomas Carrington might, just might, condescend to come to dinner. She couldn't understand why Elizabeth and Richard, a most discerning couple, thought so highly of him. He was abominably rude! Why, he'd barely taken the trouble to speak to her at Caroline's dinner-party, and the few words he had forced himself to utter could hardly have been described as flattering.

She had been conversing again with Henrietta, who had just disclosed her uncle's plans to take her to London for a few weeks in the spring, when Richard had brought his friend across to the sofa on which she had been sitting.

"Add your entreaties to mine, Jane, my dear," he had said. "I'm trying to persuade Tom to join us for dinner tomorrow evening and, later, make up a foursome at whist."

"Oh, yes, do, Dr Carrington," she had responded, a completely unforced and quite dazzling smile curving her lips. "It would be such a pleasant, relaxing evening."

"I'm sure it would, ma'am," he had responded, if not slightingly, then certainly with a distinct lack of enthusiasm. "But even the prospect of enjoying an evening in your distinguished and charming company could not induce me to neglect my patients, should there be any in need of my services."

Odious man! she thought angrily, more vexed

with herself, if the truth be known, for still feeling unaccountably hurt by his far from gallant response. He was so confoundedly rude most of the time that she couldn't understand why she should have imagined, on the morning he had shown her round that pleasant house in Melcham, that she quite liked him. Foolish beyond measure! She most definitely didn't like the infuriating creature… No, not a whit!

Annoyance added an extra sparkle to her eyes and a becoming flush to her cheeks, both of which intensified as she swept into the drawing-room to discover the person whom she was desperately trying to convince herself that she never wished to see again sprawled at his ease in one of Sir Richard's comfortable chairs. He had reverted to his casual form of attire: loose-fitting jacket, a clean but abysmally tied cravat, slightly creased unmentionables and, of all things, top boots, which she took, for some inexplicable reason, as a deliberate insult to herself.

Tom, more amused than irritated by her ill-concealed look of staunch disapproval at his far from appropriate attire, rose to his feet. "I must ask you to excuse my appearance, ma'am. I received an urgent summons from one of my patients late in the afternoon, and rather than run the risk of arriving late for dinner I didn't return to my house to change, but came straight here."

She raised one slender white shoulder in a nonchalant shrug. "So long as my cousin does not object... No doubt, though, she is far too gratified that you have condescended to accept her dinner invitation to dwell unduly on any social niceties—or lack of them."

Elizabeth was astonished. Never before had she heard her cousin speak in such a haughty, ill-natured fashion to anyone. She didn't for a moment suppose that Tom's casual appearance had instigated such blatant hostility, and could only assume that he had, at some point in the not too distant past, said or done something to offend Jane—which, knowing him as she did, wouldn't have surprised her in the least.

She cast a pleading glance in her husband's direction, hoping for support, but all he did in response was to stroll across the room in the direction of the decanters. Men were simply useless at times! Unless someone could restore Jane's normally sunny humour, the evening promised to be an unmitigated disaster.

"Come and sit by me, Jane," she invited, patting

that portion of sofa beside her. "I haven't seen you since your visit to the Dilbeys this afternoon. Did you have an enjoyable time?"

"Yes, very." And her completely unforced smile went some way to lessen her cousin's fears of impending doom. "I like Hetta very much," she admitted, betraying the fact that she and Miss Dilbey were now on familiar, first-name terms. "She's a charming person."

"I couldn't agree more," Richard said, handing her a glass of Madeira. "She's a level-headed young woman who, as you quite rightly pointed out, has an abundance of charm, and would make any man a good wife."

"Had you anyone particularly in mind?" Jane quizzed him.

"No, my dear. It has always been my policy never, I repeat never, to meddle in other people's private affairs—unless, of course, they concern me in some way. In fact, only one person has ever induced me to disregard this excellent maxim."

Even Tom betrayed mild surprise at this admission. "Good Lord, Richard! Who on earth possesses the strength of character to steer you off the straight and narrow?"

"The fair Lady Jane, no less."

"Me?" Jane experienced a deal of pleasurable satisfaction at learning this and, ignoring Dr Carrington's tut-tut of disapproval, asked, "And how, pray, did I induce you to do that?"

"Your deep concerns over a certain someone's well-being, m'dear." He smiled at her instant expression of understanding. "I rode over to see General Sir George Lansdowne this morning. He's a crusty old rogue who'll talk endlessly about his years in the army if you give him half a chance. He's well into his eighties, and has lived in Lansdowne House, which is less than a mile from the Grange, all his life. I thought if anyone could tell me about the Pentecost family, then he could."

"And did you discover something of interest?" his wife prompted, when he paused to sip his wine.

"Not a great deal, I'm afraid. It was as I told you, Jane. Perry's uncle died as a direct result of a riding accident."

She frowned slightly. "So we still don't know whether he was mentally deranged at the time."

"As I've mentioned before, I've never heard tell of it, although Lansdowne did seem to think that Cedric had been unwell for several weeks, and that was why the late Lord Pentecost had brought him back from Oxford. He couldn't, however, recall any of the details." Finishing off his wine, he placed the empty glass on the mantelshelf behind him. "If Perry wishes to learn more, then it's really up to him to make his own enquiries."

"I expect he'll do just that," Tom announced unexpectedly, drawing all eyes to him. "He came to see me this morning," he went on to explain, "and we had a long talk. He has given me every reason to suppose that from now on he intends to call upon my services, should the need arise, and, therefore, I'm not prepared to betray a doctor-patient confidentiality by discussing the matter further...except to say that it is my considered opinion he has little to worry about."

Jane felt all her pent-up animosity towards him ebbing away. Dr Carrington hadn't needed to say anything, and she suspected the only reason for disclosing as much as he had was purely and simply for her benefit, to ease her burden of worry.

"That ought to prove most interesting," Elizabeth remarked, with an impish smile, "if you are ever called upon to visit the Grange."

Tom didn't pretend to misunderstand. He had made no secret of the fact that he had scant regard for Lady Pentecost. "If I am summoned by Lord Pentecost, then of course I shall go."

"I wonder if you'll now receive an invitation to their spring ball?"

"Highly unlikely, Elizabeth, if the Dowager has any say in the matter, and I certainly shan't lose any sleep over once again being deliberately excluded. Besides which, it's immaterial anyway. I'm intending to travel into Wiltshire next week to spend some time with the eminent surgeon William Dent, who, you may recall, was rewarded with a knighthood for his services during the Peninsular War."

"Oh, dear. We shall be thin of enjoyable company in the near future. Jane intends to leave us then, too." Elizabeth turned to her cousin with a look of entreaty. "Are you sure you cannot postpone your departure another week? It seems you've been with us no time at all."

"I should love to," Jane responded, touched by her cousin's genuine affection. "But I'm afraid it's impossible. I promised Lady Templehurst that I would be with her on my birthday."

"In that case, of course you must go. I know how very fond you are of our aunt Augusta."

Elizabeth fell into a reminiscent mood. "I haven't set eyes on her for years, not since the day of my father's funeral. I recall being terrified of her as a child, but I suspect that beneath that crusty exterior beats the heart of a very kindly soul. She never forgets to send me a little something on my birthday. I really must make the effort to visit her or, perhaps, invite her here. Do you think she would come, Jane?"

"I'm certain she would. She's well into her sixties now, but apart from a little rheumatism she's healthy enough, and is quite able to travel long distances, though it's rare these days that she does so. And she's always had a soft spot for you. She frequently asks after you, and I know for a fact that she always preferred your father to mine."

Elizabeth was shocked. "Never tell me she said so to your face?"

"Aunt Augusta, as you very well know, has never been one to hide her teeth. Nearly every member of the family is somewhat in awe of her, even my father. Heaven knows why!" She cast a fleeting glance in Tom's direction. "The only way to deal with ill-tempered people is to stand up to them, do you not agree, Dr Carrington?"

He hadn't missed the wickedly provocative glint in her eyes, and was very well aware that the veiled gibe was directed at him. "In most cases, yes," he responded, successfully suppressing a smile. "But it is not always advisable to instigate wrath in the elderly. I can offer you a case in point. Not long after I had set up my practice in Bristol, I had a patient who was renowned for his innate bad temper. You remember him, Elizabeth, I'm sure—that cross-grained old curmudgeon, Josiah Peacemore. A most inappropriate name! Well, to cut a long story short, he worked himself up into a passion and suffered an apoplexy which took him off."

"Really, Dr Carrington?" Jane was all wide-eyed innocence. "This didn't possibly happen directly after he had sustained a visit from you, by any chance?"

"Little baggage!" he muttered, sending both Jane and Elizabeth into such paroxysms of mirth that neither saw the tender look which accompanied his far from polite response. But Richard most certainly noticed it. It told him much of what he wanted to know, and made him feel faintly uneasy.

Chapter Seven

Sir Richard's light travelling carriage was a masterpiece of the coach-maker's art. The generously padded interior cocooned its occupants in velvet luxury as, hardly so much as swaying, it bowled along the narrow, twisting lanes.

It was quite dark by now, so Jane didn't try to pierce the gloom in a vain attempt to take one of her last chances to view this delightful part of England. How she would dearly love to see it in late spring and summer when the countryside was at its most glorious! How she wished, now, that her visit had not been quite so short! Elizabeth and Richard could not possibly have made her feel more welcome, and she had no desire to bring her pleasant stay with them to an end, but she knew she must. A promise was a promise, and she was a female who believed in keeping her word, so she must leave for Lady Templehurst's house in Bath the day after tomorrow.

It was rather a pity, though, that she had been denied their company on her penultimate evening in Hampshire, but it couldn't be helped. Elizabeth, having succumbed to a slight chill, had spent the past two days closeted in her private apartments in an attempt not to pass on the infection. The children, as far as Jane was aware, were thankfully betraying no symptoms, but poor Richard most certainly was.

He had woken that morning with a sore throat and a blinding headache. Ever the considerate gentleman, though, he had still been more than willing to escort her to the Pentecosts' ball, but she wouldn't hear of it. The sensible place for him was by his own fireside. Besides which, there had been no real need of his added protection. With the highly competent head groom tooling the equipage, the trusty young stable-lad who had accompanied her on her many exploratory rides sitting beside him on the box, and with her maid to bear her company, she was safe enough.

"When, precisely, do you intend commencing your journey to Bath, my lady?" Latimer asked, breaking the silence which had ensued since taking their seats in the carriage.

"I've arranged for the post-chaise to be at Knightley Hall directly after breakfast the day after tomorrow. I wish to arrive in Bath in good time for dinner."

Even though she still remained far from certain that she would retain Latimer's services for very much longer, she had no intention of making what might well turn out to be the maid's last few weeks in her employ uncomfortable by behaving coolly towards her, and so enquired pleasantly, "Are you looking forward to embarking on the second stage of our travels, Latimer?"

"Yes, my lady, I am," the maid responded, betraying for the first time ever a modicum of enthusiasm to continue conversing.

As Jane was destined to discover to her cost, this ought to have made her suspicious, but she didn't give the rare display of animation a second thought, except to say, "I hope you haven't been too bored during our time here in Hampshire?"

"Not at all, my lady. I have found sufficient work to occupy me." Latimer's attractive dark eyes flickered with something akin to regret as she stared levelly across the carriage at the Earl of Eastbury's daughter. "No one could ever accuse you of being an exacting mistress and I enjoyed the several walks I was able to take across the estate. But I must confess that I'm more than ready, now, for a change."

They had by this time joined the line of carriages waiting to deposit their passengers at Pentecost Grange's impressive colonnaded front entrance. When it came to their turn to alight, Jane parted company with her maid in the spacious hall—she to make her way to the large salon where the ball was being held, Latimer to join the other abigails in a room on the upper floor, where they would no doubt pass their time indulging in idle gossip, if not called upon to make lightning repairs to accidental tears in their mistresses' expensive gowns.

As Jane drew near the entrance to the large salon she saw Perry standing beside his mother near the door. Appropriately attired in full evening garb, a long-tailed black coat and black satin knee-smalls, he looked remarkably composed in the circumstances. Like his father, he had no great fondness for the large occasion and was most certainly not overburdened with a surfeit of small talk either, so Jane was rather surprised, not to say relieved, when he managed to extract a chortle of amusement from the lady at the head of the small queue of guests waiting in line to greet the host and hostess.

"You look to be bearing up remarkably well," she quizzed him, when at last she reached the head of the queue.

"I wouldn't go as far as to say that, Janie," he returned, with a smile of such real warmth that she was certain he felt no animosity towards her for her scathing remarks at their last meeting. "I understood that Uncle Willoughby was to lend Mama his support, but then it was insisted upon that I perform my duties."

"I'm afraid, Perry, that my influence might be to blame for that," she admitted, drawing him aside a little so that his mother could not overhear. "If I'm not very careful I stand in the gravest danger of turning into an interfering old harridan. But I simply couldn't bear the thought of Sir Willougby usurping your position."

"Oh, so it's you I've to thank for this, is it?" But his look of mock severity didn't fool her for a moment. "I'll have a thing or two to say to you later, my girl. And don't forget to save me a dance."

How wonderful it was to see her childhood friend coping, if not superbly then at least adequately enough, with what for him must surely be a considerable ordeal, Jane mused as she wandered into the large salon, which was already quite crowded with what she supposed must represent the cream of Hampshire society. It was no use supposing that Perry's disposition would ever change to that extent and, in truth, she wasn't so very certain that she wished to see any great transformation in him. However, there could be no doubt that a weighty burden had been lifted from his mind and she would always be grateful to a certain doctor for bringing this about.

Her thoughts were echoed by Miss Dilbey, who, having been looking out for Jane's arrival, had meandered her way round the groups of elegantly attired and chattering guests towards her quarry.

"Although he's considerably easier in his mind now that he's spoken to Dr Carrington," Henrietta confirmed as they made themselves comfortable on two vacant chairs placed by the wall, "he's still determined to visit the specialist in London when he goes there in the spring."

How very interesting! Was Perry's real motive for journeying to the capital merely to attain a second opinion about his mental health, or was the underlying reason, perhaps, a desire not to be parted from his good friend Miss Dilbey? What a pity, Jane mused, that she herself had more or less decided to forgo the Season this year. It might have proved most interesting to see how things progressed between the two of them, now that Perry's mental health was no longer a bar to a closer relationship developing.

She cast Hetta a quick appraising glance. She was still in half-mourning and wearing the same pearl-grey gown that she had donned for Caroline Westbridge's party the previous week. The colour suited her well enough, but Jane sincerely hoped she hadn't inherited her mother's stubborn pride, and would permit her uncle to buy her some new dresses when she went to London in the spring. Her uncle was certainly no pauper, and it would be nice to see Hetta dressed in more vibrant colours once her period of mourning came to an end.

"And how has the Dowager Lady Pentecost taken this evident change we perceive in her son? Does she know he intends to go to London?"

"Oh, yes. He's told her that, but hasn't explained the reason why." Hetta grinned wickedly. "She was not best pleased to hear that he had consulted Dr Carrington, though. And Perry was far from happy to discover that she had somehow managed to find out about the visit, and promptly insisted on sending his new practitioner a belated invitation, which, as you can imagine, didn't go down too well with his darling mama."

Jane raised one white shoulder in a dismissive shrug. "She ought to be mighty well pleased, then, that he didn't accept."

"Oh, but he did!"

Jane didn't attempt to hide her astonishment as she gazed about the room in vain for a glimpse of Tom's tall figure. "But he told me he was travelling into Wiltshire."

"Be that as it may, he's here. He came with Mrs Westbridge's party. I thought I saw him accompanying her into the room set out for cards a little earlier."

A delicious feeling of euphoria washed over Jane. Their leave-taking after that most enjoyable dinner at Knightley Hall a few evenings before had been swift and slightly formal, considering the camaraderie which had rapidly grown between them after the initial frosty start. At Richard's behest, Tom had called to examine Elizabeth the previous day, but Jane had been out enjoying her daily ride and had missed seeing him—a circumstance that had caused her more disappointment than she cared to admit.

A tall figure suddenly appearing before her sent her pulse rate soaring, but a feeling of acute disappointment swiftly followed to restore her to normality when she raised her eyes to those of Simon Fairfax.

"Good evening, Lady Jane. Will you do me the singular honour of partnering me in the next set of country dances which is now forming?"

How polished the address! What an abundance of elegant charm this tall, blond-haired Adonis oozed! Surely she must be the envy of nearly every young female in the room. So why was it, Jane wondered, placing her fingers on the immaculate sleeve of his long-tailed coat as he guided her to the area designated for dancing, that he, and all those dashing young blades like him, never caused the least fluttering in her young breast? Why was it that she would much rather be in the company of a certain gentleman whose manners were more often than not less than perfect, and whose frequent acerbic remarks would most certainly never find favour in any polite drawing-room?

"You are leaving the area soon, so I understand, Lady Jane," Mr Fairfax remarked as they came together in the set.

That he should be aware of this fact did not occur to her for a moment as strange. "Yes, I leave the day after tomorrow," she managed to respond before they separated again.

"But you are not returning to Kent, if my memory serves me correctly, but are journeying on to Bath."

Now, this knowledge of her intended movements did strike her as odd, until she suddenly recalled that she had divulged her intention to visit Bath to Lady Pentecost on the morning she had paid a visit to the Grange. Evidently the Dowager must have passed on this information. How else could Simon Fairfax have known?

"Yes, I'm paying a short visit to my aunt, Lady Templehurst, and shall be returning to Kent some time in April."

"Does that mean that you are intending to deprive us of your unrivalled presence during the forthcoming Season, my lady?"

"My plans are uncertain, sir, but it seems highly unlikely that I shall visit the capital this spring."

"All the young blades will be desolated by your absence. You have been one of the brightest lights for the past three Seasons."

My money is the glittering attraction, you

mean, Jane countered silently—the Simon Fairfaxes of this world not fooling her for an instant. How shallow they all were! How insipid their polite but meaningless utterances! She would far sooner endure Dr Carrington's hard-eyed disapproval and provocative remarks any day. Infuriatingly rude creature he might be on occasion, but at least he was honest!

The set came to an end and Jane was thankful for it, but her relief was destined not to last very long. She was afterwards partnered by a string of elegant young gentlemen, all equally proficient in making polite but faintly insipid small talk, and all equally well versed in passing the pretty compliment designed to raise a blush in a young maiden's cheeks, but not in hers; she had been on the receiving end of just such banal flattery too frequently in the past for it to have the least effect on her. The only one of her partners who didn't bore her to tears was Perry, who was a surprisingly graceful dancer, and someone who never attempted to make unwelcome overtures.

After he had returned her to her seat by the wall, he solicited Hetta's hand and Jane, pleased to hear Hetta accept at least this one request for her to dance, followed their progress down the large room for a few moments before transferring her gaze to the ample figure of their hostess, who was standing on the opposite side of the room, close to the long French windows. Lady Pentecost was conversing with a middle-aged matron who looked suspiciously as though she was made in a similar mould to the formidable Dowager. They had their heads together and their eyes were focused on the swirling dancers, but precisely who was the object of their no doubt spiteful remarks was difficult to judge.

Jane could only hope that it was neither Perry nor Hetta—could only hope, too, that Perry's new-found confidence didn't lead him into foolish indiscretion. For the time being, at least, it might be wise for them to keep their ever deepening friendship secret. Although Jane didn't doubt Hetta's ability to stand up to the Dowager, neither did she underestimate Lady Pentecost. Perry's darling mama could, and no doubt would, make things very uncomfortable for Hetta if she considered for a moment that there was the remotest possibility that Miss Dilbey, the niece of a person whom the Dowager no doubt considered an insignificant country squire, might one day become her successor.

"And what can possibly be causing you such concern, I wonder?" a deep voice unexpectedly remarked, making Jane start visibly.

"You could do a body a mischief, Dr Carrington, creeping up that way!" she snapped, which hid quite beautifully her underlying delight at seeing him, and which dispelled the growing suspicion she had been harbouring that he fully intended to ignore her as much as possible, just as he had done on the occasion of Caroline Westbridge's party, by remaining in the card room throughout the entire evening.

Without waiting for an invitation, he plumped himself down on the vacant chair beside her and astonished her further by asking, "Is it, perhaps, because you fear that a certain twosome might foolishly betray their feelings?"

Dear Lord, but wasn't he astute! Jane thought, smiling in spite of herself. His total refusal to dissemble was so very refreshing after the sickening string of platitudes and innuendoes she had been forced to endure since her arrival.

"Yes," she admitted with equal frankness. "But I must confess I'm rather surprised Perry chose to confide in you so soon over that particular area of his life."

"He didn't," he returned blandly. "But I've seen them together often enough when I've been called out to Squire Dilbey. One would have to be a simpleton not to have perceived the blossoming friendship."

"As yet, I think friendship is all it is," Jane confessed. "But I have high hopes, providing of course a certain someone doesn't succeed in throwing a rub in their way."

Tom's eyes moved fleetingly in the Dowager's direction, before his attention returned to the far more pleasing aspect of the delicately featured face beside him, with its straight aristocratic little nose and its softly rounded chin, which had the tendency to lift on occasions, clearly betraying displeasure. The muscles in his abdomen seemed to knot suddenly. Why did this occasionally haughty little madam have the power to affect him so?

"Yes, I can quite understand why that harridan might give cause for concern," he remarked, regaining control of himself with an effort. "Just as Richard's apparent absence tonight is causing me no little unease." He looked at her sharply, his disapproval all too apparent. "Never tell me you came here by yourself?"

"No, my maid accompanied me."

"Of course. How very foolish of me! A lady's maid—a most excellent deterrent to any would-be attacker!" He raised his eyes ceilingwards. "I don't know what Richard was about, allowing you to come unescorted!"

"He wished to accompany me, but I wouldn't hear of it," she responded in defence of a gentleman she much admired. "Poor dear, he was feeling quite under the weather. He's taken Elizabeth's chill. Besides which, the head groom and a stable-boy, well armed, I might add, offered ample protection."

The explanation did not satisfy him, and he remained at his most dictatorial. "You should consider yourself fortunate that I have no say in your behaviour, young woman, because I tell you plainly I would never permit you to go gallivanting about in such a feather-brained fashion. It's high time you had your wings clipped!"

It occurred to Jane, then, that she might well have bridled had he adopted such a high-handed tone with her even a few days before. Now, however, only a warm feeling of satisfaction glowed deep within her because he liked her well enough to be concerned over her safety, but she had no intention of admitting it.

"Tell me, Dr Carrington, did you prise yourself away from the card room and seek my company merely for the pleasure of pinching at me? If so, it might be best, all things considered, if you returned to your game forthwith," she advised in clipped tones, and he might have believed her genuinely piqued had his eyes, ever alert, not detected the slight betraying twitch at one corner of that delectable mouth of hers.

"No, I did not, you provoking little witch," he returned, making the far from flattering epithet sound more like an endearment. "I sought you out for the sole purpose of asking you to stand up with me. And, unless I'm very much mistaken, they are about to play a waltz."

Jane couldn't prevent a smile as he led her onto the floor. Not for an instant would it have occurred to him that she might not have been granted permission to perform this particular dance. Although he had, for reasons best known to himself, been less than pleased to discover that she had travelled here without a male escort, he would no doubt consider many of the other rules governing young ladies' behaviour ludicrous in the extreme and not worthy of consideration.

What a complex creature he was, to be sure! she

mused, taking a brief surreptitious glance up at him through her long, curling lashes as he began to swirl her quite expertly about the floor. She couldn't recall any other gentleman of her acquaintance who had the ability to affect her mood so easily, one moment annoying her unbearably, the next making her blissfully content. Although there was no denying he could be confoundly rude, it was, perversely, his no-nonsense attitude which attracted her. After all, what else could it possibly be? she wondered, trying desperately to ignore the gentle pressure of that shapely, long-fingered hand resting lightly on her waist while she continued the attempt to assess him dispassionately.

There was no denying that he possessed a fine physique, which was certainly displayed to advantage tonight in that same elegant evening attire he had donned for Caroline Westbridge's party the previous week, but his appearance, she suspected, would never be of any real importance to him. His cravat, though well starched, was plainly arranged; his shirt points were so low as not to be worth a mention, and his plain, cream-coloured waistcoat would no doubt be stigmatised as downright unimaginative by the fashion-conscious element in Society. There was nothing remotely ostentatious in his dress, yet she rather thought she preferred his elegant sobriety to the flamboyant styles affected by most of the dashing young blades in London.

Yes, all in all, he was a most attractive man, ruggedly good looking rather than handsome, she decided, and couldn't understand why, having all but attained the age of thirty, he had remained a bachelor.

A wicked possibility suddenly occurred to her and it took a monumental effort to suppress a chuckle. Outwardly appealing he most definitely was, but his peppery temperament would certainly be a little off-putting to those faint-hearted members of her sex. She doubted, however, that this was the main reason for his continued single state. No, it was much more likely that, totally dedicated to his profession, he hardly gave matrimony a single thought.

It would have astounded Jane, therefore, had she known just how frequently the subject of marriage and, more especially, thoughts of being married to her, had been occupying Dr Carrington's mind of late.

Tom would have been the first to admit that women had played only a very small part in his life thus far. Selfishly, he supposed, he had used them merely as a means to assuage his bodily needs, and had never been in the least danger of mistaking a natural masculine desire for anything deeper. Only Elizabeth and her grandmother, his kindly benefactress, had ever retained a place in his affections. Why, he had almost come to believe that he possessed a natural immunity to the more tender emotions, until the fateful evening, just three short weeks ago, when he had taken it into his head to attend that dinner-party hosted by his good friends, the Knightleys.

He had tried desperately to convince himself that the resemblance to his dear friend Elizabeth was what had attracted him to Lady Jane Beresford, but he hadn't been able to delude himself for long. The more he had come into contact with her, the more he had felt drawn to this aristocratic young woman who, against all the odds, had turned out to be something of a kindred spirit.

The muscles in his abdomen decided to twist themselves into yet another of those self-torturing knots. Ye gods! Hadn't he tried everything humanly possible to stem this ever increasing yearning to be near her? It was sheer madness to suppose that there could ever be any future for them. How could there be when they belonged in different worlds? The sooner they went their separate ways, the sooner his life would return to a semblance of normality, he knew, and yet he had felt he couldn't leave for Wiltshire without seeing her just one more time.

The mere thought that their paths were unlikely to cross again in the foreseeable future was sufficient to have an adverse effect on his concentration and he came perilously close to missing a step. "I must apologise," he said, after very nearly treading on her toes. "I'm afraid I do not dance very often and am a little clumsy."

"On the contrary, sir, for a tall man you dance with remarkable grace," she countered, relieved that he had spoken at last, for the awful suspicion that he intended to conduct the whole dance in stony silence had certainly crossed her mind. "It comes as no surprise to learn that you do not allow yourself the luxury of practising too often, and I can only wonder at what prompted you to come here tonight. I clearly recall your saying you would be journeying into Wiltshire."

He hesitated a moment only, before responding with, "My dear young woman, my nature being what it is, how on earth could I resist the temptation of seeing our esteemed hostess's reaction when I unexpectedly appeared before her? Believe me, I was very well aware that my belated invitation was not written in her fair hand."

Jane frankly laughed at this piece of devilment, causing several pairs of interested eyes to turn in their direction. "I hope you were not disappointed?"

"On the contrary. Her expression of astonished outrage was a deliciously mouth-watering moment that I shall savour for some weeks to come. Her one consolation, of course, was that should she have choked on the words of greeting she was forced to utter, then she would have had the very person at hand to administer to her needs."

His incorrigibility continued, keeping Jane in a high state of amusement as he cast aspersions on several other pillars of the community who were present that evening, and who didn't rate very highly in his estimation, and the dance, for her at least, came to an end all too quickly.

As he returned her to the chair beside Hetta's, Jane felt more than just mildly disappointed that he didn't ask her to stand up with him a second time. She followed his progress across the room, her disappointment swiftly turning into a far more unpalatable emotion, and one that she had experienced before in the not too distant past, as she watched him lead a very pretty girl, dressed very becomingly in a gown of lavender silk, onto the dance-floor.

More than a little bewildered by the resentment she was experiencing at seeing him dancing with another young lady, Jane took the opportunity, while Hetta was conveniently being held in conversation by two neighbours, to move quietly away. She felt the sudden need to be alone for a while, to try, if she could, to make some sense out of this sudden surge of jealousy gnawing painfully inside, and made a beeline for one of the tall French windows which had been left slightly ajar to counteract the heat given off by the hundreds of candles.

Her expensive silk shawl offered little protection against the coolness of the March evening, but she was not deterred. Making her way across the deserted terrace, she went down a series of stone steps to the garden. Gaily coloured lanterns illuminated that part of the path near the house for those guests wishing to enjoy a breath of air. Not that there would be too many willing to forgo the warm comfort of the salon—none except those, perhaps, troubled like herself, who preferred to be alone.

She had walked no more than a dozen yards away from the house when she thought she detected the sound of footsteps further along the path and took immediate action by concealing herself behind a sturdy tree. She hadn't even begun to unravel the tangled mass of conflicting thoughts whirling about in her head, and was unwilling to relinquish her solitude until she had. So she waited, expecting to see someone pass by, but surprisingly no one did.

Then she heard a further sound behind her and slightly to her right, quickly followed by an urgently whispered, "Are you sure you know precisely what to do and where to go?"

The voice was undoubtedly masculine, and the softly spoken "yes' in response most definitely feminine and, furthermore, vaguely familiar.

"Then we're almost home and dry, my little love. Just be patient for a while longer, and then we'll be together. Our problems will soon be at an end. By this time next week we'll be safe across the Channel, enjoying all the delights Paris has to offer."

Heavens above! Had she inadvertently stumbled upon a lovers' tryst? The planning of an elopement, perhaps? Her own concerns thrust aside for a moment, Jane suddenly felt very intrusive, but dared not move for fear of disturbing the evidently star-crossed pair. More murmured exchanges followed, none of which she could clearly hear, before there was the distinct rustling of clothing and low moans of pleasure floated across in the air.

Jane's upbringing might have been sheltered, but she was not so naive as not to have a fair notion of what was taking place a mere few yards from where she stood. The gentleman, obviously unable to retain control over his passion, had decided to take advantage of what he imagined to be an isolated spot, and the woman, evidently only too willing to oblige him, was uttering seductive words of encouragement.

With an embarrassed hue already flaming her cheeks, Jane couldn't bear the added mortification of being discovered now, and took the opportunity to tiptoe quietly away whilst the lovers were otherwise engaged. She had almost reached the house when her hopes of an unobserved return to the salon were dashed by a tall figure towering above her on the terrace.

For a few moments it was as much as she could do to stare up at him, then she managed to regain a modicum of self-possession and walked slowly up the stone steps. "Why, Dr Carrington! What on earth are you doing out here?"

"I might ask you the same question." His alert eyes scanned the darkened garden for a moment before turning to her upturned face. "Are you feeling unwell? You appear a little flushed."

Drat the man! He never missed a blessed thing! "As a matter of fact I was feeling a little warm earlier," she responded, quickly turning the lingering evidence of her acute embarrassment to her advantage. "That is why I stepped outside for a breath of air."

"You stepped rather further than just outside," he returned, regarding her much as an irate guardian might an erring ward. "This propensity you have for wandering about on your own really ought to have been curbed long ago."

"And what, pray, could possibly have befallen me by taking a short stroll in a private garden?"

Her airy response might have fooled most people, but certainly not him. Taking her chin in his warm fingers, he turned her face up to his. "I'm not sure… But something most certainly did."

All at once she didn't know or care particularly whether the amorous couple were still in the garden, perhaps now observing them. She was aware only of him; of those ever alert, but far from cold grey eyes holding her as securely captive as the strong fingers grasping her chin. She watched, almost mesmerised, as he transferred his gaze to her mouth, and closed her eyes in eager anticipation of what must surely follow, but fate had decreed that she was destined not to experience those perfectly sculptured and sensual lips on hers. The French windows were suddenly thrown wide and Hetta stepped out onto the terrace in time to see them, like a pair of guilty lovers, step hastily apart.

"Ah! So, you've found her, Dr Carrington. I thought I saw her go outside."

"Did you come in search of me for any particular reason?" Jane asked him, in a voice that sounded remarkably composed in the circumstances.

"Yes, I came to ask if you'd permit me to escort you in to supper," he explained, sounding equally unruffled, "and of course to partner me in the supper dance…"

"Which is just about to begin," Hetta informed them, leading the way back inside.

Evidently, in his typically arrogant fashion, he took her silence for acquiescence. Not that Jane minded particularly, for if the truth be known she was far too bemused by her totally uncharacteristic, almost wanton behaviour to concern herself about much else.

She really couldn't understand what had come over her. It most certainly wasn't the first time she had found herself alone with a member of the opposite sex who wasn't a close relative. On several occasions during the past three Seasons she had foolishly allowed herself to be inveigled into a compromising situation by some eager young gentleman, and others not quite so young, wishing to subject her to a display of masculine passion. A frosty glare had usually sufficed in dampening their ardour, but if that had failed she had never hesitated to administer a sound box to the ears or a sharp kick on the ankle, and her honour had remained intact.

Yet this time she had felt completely different. The most peculiar sensation, a strange combination of longing and apprehension, rippled through her, and she was forced to admit that she might have been in the gravest danger of losing that well-preserved virtue of hers had she found herself in a more secluded setting with Dr Thomas Carrington. She had experienced not the least desire to repulse any advances; in fact, the opposite was true. She had desperately wanted to feel those strong arms about her—had been eager to experience the pressure of those wholly masculine lips on hers. Would she have been satisfied with one embrace only or, like the woman in the garden, would she have been only too eager to encourage further intimacies?

With a supreme effort she tried to control the diverse emotions warring within her, and Tom, aware of it or not, did much to restore her composure by behaving like the perfect gentleman.

Throughout their dance together he kept up a flow of small talk, and when they went in to supper, joining Perry and Hetta at their table, he proved himself such an entertaining raconteur that even Perry, appearing completely relaxed, had his share of the conversation.

Tom didn't attempt to leave her side throughout the remainder of the evening, a circumstance noted by several of those present, and he even went so far as to escort her outside to Richard's waiting carriage when the time came for her to leave.

It might have been her imagination but she thought she could detect his hands shaking slightly as he reached for the fur-lined rug and placed it over her knees. There was definitely a slight tremor in his deep, attractive voice as he made his farewells, wishing her a safe journey to Bath and declaring the hope that they would meet again some time in the future if she should decide to pay another visit to Hampshire.

Strangely, though, he seemed disinclined to prolong their leave-taking, and gave her no time at all in which to respond. Closing the carriage door abruptly, he disappeared back inside the house, leaving her prey to such a wretched feeling of desolation that for the first time ever she was thankful for her maid's taciturn disposition, for she suddenly discovered that she could not have uttered a single word even had she wished to do so.

Chapter Eight

It was a commonly held belief that travel improved the mind. But Jane, making excellent progress on her journey to Bath, failed to see how this particular trip could improve the state of hers. Each mile that took her further away from Hampshire only succeeded in adding to her unhappy state. Even the excellently prepared luncheon which she had forced herself to eat at that very superior posting-house had failed completely to lift her spirits. There was no getting away from it—her despondency had reached an all-time low!

For almost a month she had been allowed to do more or less as she had pleased. Staying at the Hall had been like sampling blessed freedom after years of confinement. The Knightleys couldn't possibly have done more to make her feel welcome—which, to be fair, was no more than her sisters always did, but, unlike them, Elizabeth and Richard had taken excellent care of her without undue and suffocating attention. Was it any wonder, then, that she was very reluctant to leave a place where she had sampled the sweet taste of liberty?

A low moan succeeded in piercing through the ever increasing layers of gloom that were wrapping themselves around her, and Jane turned her head to look at her maid. "What is it, Latimer? Are you feeling unwell?"

"I do feel a little peculiar, my lady," she responded faintly. "I think it must have been something I ate back at the posting-house."

They had partaken of the same fare in the inn's private parlour, and Jane certainly wasn't experiencing any ill effects. "I should think that highly unlikely. I feel perfectly well, and we both sampled the same food."

"Except the game pie, my lady," the maid reminded her. "You didn't have any of that."

Jane watched, concern rapidly mounting, as Latimer slipped a hand beneath the serviceable cloak and placed her fingers gingerly against her stomach. Her colour was still good, but it appeared that she was in no little discomfort.

"Would you like me to stop the carriage? A few minutes in the fresh air might set you to rights."

As though it was an effort even to move, Latimer eased herself slowly forward in the seat and peered through the window. "I believe I know where we are. I travelled this route several times when I was employed by Lady Fairfax. Her carriage met with a slight accident on one occasion and we were forced to seek shelter at an inn not far from here—just off the main road, it was. I hate to be a nuisance, my lady, but do you think we could stop there for a short while?"

Jane didn't even take a moment to consider the matter. Pulling down the window, she called out. The carriage came to a halt and one of the post-boys appeared before her on the road.

"It be only a few miles to Calne, my lady. It might be best if we made straight for there," he advised, after listening to her request to pull off the main road at the next turning and find the inn.

"Oh, my lady, I really do not think I could remain in the carriage until Calne." Latimer placed a suddenly trembling hand to her temple. "I'm beginning to feel a trifle faint."

That settled the matter as far as Jane was concerned. There were few things more unpleasant than being forced to sit in a closed carriage for any distance when one's head was spinning and one's stomach threatened to expel its contents at any moment. Nevertheless, after travelling down a narrow and twisting country lane, only wide enough for one carriage, for what seemed a very long time, without seeing so much as an isolated barn, Jane began to regret her hasty decision.

"Are you sure there is an inn along this road, Latimer?" she asked, leaning out of the window in a fruitless attempt to catch sight of any habitation. "There appears to be only fields as far as the eye can see."

"I—I'm certain it's this way, my lady," the maid confirmed, peering out of the other window. "Oh, look! There is a house just up ahead. Perhaps we could stop and ask directions there?"

Against her better judgement, for she was now firmly convinced that there was no hostelry hereabouts, Jane complied. The red-brick dwelling, set a little way back from the road, was surrounded by farmland, but there was sufficient room in front of the few dilapidated outbuildings to enable the post-boys to turn the carriage and, from the smoke billowing from one of the chimneys, the place appeared to be occupied. If nothing else, at least she might be able to procure a glass of water for her maid, she thought, stepping down from the carriage.

Just as though they had been expected, the front door opened suddenly and a gaunt middle-aged woman came scurrying down the path like an excited child. "I heard the carriage and thought it were my master returning," she announced, with a forced smile which put Jane in mind of the Dowager Lady Pentecost. "We don't get many people travelling this way."

Hardly surprising as the road didn't appear to lead anywhere, Jane mused, subjecting the stranger to a swift appraisal. Judging by her attire, the woman was undoubtedly a high-ranking servant, possibly a housekeeper, but not a particularly conscientious one if the soiled apron was anything to go by. Nor did the house, on closer inspection, appear particularly well maintained. The paintwork on the doors and windows was cracked and peeling, and the small front garden was in urgent need of attention. The dwelling's isolation gave one to suppose that its owner was something of a recluse, who was, moreover, unwilling, or perhaps unable, to effect necessary repairs.

"Can you tell me if there is a hostelry nearby

where we could seek shelter for a while? My maid is feeling unwell."

"The nearest be a few miles further on, but it ain't the sort of place for the likes of you, my lady. It's nothing but a hedge tavern." The woman peered into the carriage and let out an exclamation of dismay. "Oh, you poor dear! Come along with me and lie down for a while. You look right poorly!"

Jane, on the other hand, thought Latimer, rosy-cheeked and bright-eyed, looked positively blooming in the circumstances, but looks, she knew, could be deceptive. Added to which, the maid had always been conscientious, not once neglecting her duties because of some trifling ailment during the whole time she had been employed by the Beresford family, so it would be unjust, not to say downright heartless, Jane thought, to deny her the time to recover suffi-ciently to continue the journey.

After instructing the post-boys to turn the carriage and await further orders, Jane entered the house to discover a thick-set man of middle age and average height awaiting her in the small, dimly lit hall. His large, work-roughened hands gave her every reason to suppose that he was not just employed in the house, but was expected to undertake a wide variety of duties, which in itself was not an uncommon practice. What did surprise her, however, was that the owner of such a neglected house could afford the luxury of employing two servants, given the fact that little or no money had been spent on the property for, she guessed, some considerable time.

"The missus 'as taken the young lady upstairs for a rest," he informed her, closing the door and showing her into a small parlour which smelt stale and unused, even though a good fire was burning in the grate. "Sit yerself down and mek yerself comfortable," he invited politely enough, but eyeing her in a way that made her feel uneasy. "The missus oughtn't to be long," he added, casting her one last furtive glance before leaving the room.

Jane was hardly given time to take stock of her shabby surroundings before the door opened again and the woman who she assumed was the housekeeper entered.

"How is my maid feeling now?"

"Still a mite poorly. Said it was something she ate." She moved across to the window and gave the faded drapes a twitch, sending a cloud of dust rising in the air. "Think we ought to do something about your carriage, though, ma'am. Can't expect the post-boys to stand twiddling their thumbs until you can be on your way again. Unfortunately there isn't room in the stable for the horses. Perhaps it would be best if the carriage awaited you at the posting-house in Calne. My master should be home soon. He's a kind-hearted gentleman who would be only too willing to convey you to The Bell in his own carriage once your maid's fit enough to travel."

"That's most kind, but I really don't think I can impose—"

"Not at all!" the housekeeper interrupted, her thin-lipped mouth curling into yet another of those untrustworthy smiles. "The master will be glad of your company, and, if it should turn out that your maid isn't fit to travel to Bath until tomorrow, I'm certain you'll get a room at The Bell."

Jane had no desire to remain in this house, but couldn't bring herself selfishly to desert Latimer unless she had no option but to do so. It wouldn't hurt to grant her maid an hour or so in which to recover, but if it became necessary she would seriously have to consider continuing the journey alone, leaving Latimer with sufficient funds to travel to Bath when she was able.

A sudden thought occurred to her, and she

looked at the housekeeper sharply. "How did you know our eventual destination?"

Only for an instant did the woman seem slightly discomposed. "Your maid must have told me, Lady Jane."

Latimer had evidently been in a rare talkative mood, for it seemed that she had also revealed her mistress's identity, Jane mused, deciding it might be wise in the circumstances to see her maid before she made any decision regarding the removal of the carriage to the inn at Calne.

Without the least hesitation the housekeeper acquiesced to Jane's request to be taken to her maid, and led the way out of the room and up the narrow staircase which, covered in a film of dust, was further proof that the servant was not overfond of work.

"In here, my lady," she said, opening the door at the very end of the narrow passageway.

Jane was granted only sufficient time to register that the room was unoccupied when she received a violent push, the force of which almost sent her sprawling to the floor. Before she could regain her balance someone grasped her from behind, a smaller hand relieved her of her fashionable bonnet and a gag was securely tied over her mouth, effectively stifling the terrified cry that rose in her throat. Then both her hands and feet were bound with a merciless disregard for her delicate skin, before she was finally picked up and virtually tossed down on the bed.

The speed with which the assault upon her had taken place left Jane breathless, and it was as much as she could do to raise her head a little. However, it wasn't the smugly satisfied expressions on the faces of the housekeeper and her husband that made her blood run cold, but the sight of Latimer, appearing completely unruffled as always, framed in the doorway.

"Well, we've done our part, Rosie, old girl. Now all we need do is await the master's arrival."

"Not quite, Mrs Talbot," Latimer countered, her steady gaze never wavering from the recumbent figure on the bed. "There's still the post-boys to deal with. You had better attend to that, Ralph." She waited until both husband and wife had left and then, just as though she was unable to break the habits of a lifetime, she bent to retrieve the discarded bonnet, and the reticule which had been dropped in the struggle, and carried them from the room without uttering another word.

Jane heard the key turn in the lock and listened

to Latimer's retreating footsteps. A few minutes later she clearly detected the sound of a carriage moving off and realised, with a sinking feeling in the pit of her stomach, that the post-boys were leaving, and with them any hope of an immediate escape.

Still unable to comprehend fully just what had happened, or why, she tried to ease herself into a sitting position. It took some time, but eventually she succeeded in her objective, and stared about the makeshift prison. Like the downstairs parlour, it was shabbily furnished and in urgent need of a clean, though the bedcovers at least appeared to have been recently laundered, no doubt in readiness for her visit.

There wasn't a doubt about it; her kidnapping had been well planned. But whose was the brain behind the abduction? Jane wondered. Certainly not Latimer's, although she was forced to concede that the wickedly deceitful creature had played her part well. Not until the housekeeper had foolishly mentioned Bath had it occurred to Jane that all was not as it should be, and even then she hadn't for a moment suspected that their arrival at this place had been anything other than a quirk of fate. What a fool she had been!

For several minutes she was forced to do battle with rising anger and a passionate desire to be avenged, but eventually she was able to regain control of her turbulent thoughts and began to wonder what lay behind her abduction. Monetary gain was the most obvious motive, of course, but why had her kidnappers put their plan into effect now? After all, it would have made more sense to carry out the abduction while her father could be easily approached with the ransom demand. Why wait until the Earl was out of the country? Her captors might need to keep her hidden away for several weeks before they received their ill-gotten gains. No, it just didn't make sense. More was wanted than mere money… But what?

She wasn't left wondering for long. The sound of a light carriage, a phaeton or curricle, she guessed, pulling up outside reached her ears. Then there came the sound of voices below, quickly followed by footsteps mounting the stairs. A few moments later the key was fitted back into the lock, the door swung open, and several things that had puzzled Jane during her sojourn in Hampshire suddenly became crystal-clear.

"Oh, my dear girl! My servants have been unnecessarily rough with you. Allow me to make you a little more comfortable."

With one judicious tug the offending gag was removed and Jane might have felt at least a modicum of gratitude if it hadn't been for the smug satisfaction she easily perceived on the handsome face looming above her. Anger threatened to return with a vengeance, but she succeeded in containing it and even managed to affect one of Lady Pentecost's fallacious smiles.

"The not so honourable Mr Simon Fairfax... I should have known!"

"Now, now, my darling. You mustn't be rude to your future husband."

His glib response confirmed her worst fears. The instant she had seen him, she had guessed what he had planned for her. Marriage, of course, would secure her entire fortune, and safe in the knowledge that her family would accept the forced alliance, rather than face a monumental scandal, he could continue to go into Society with his reputation intact. But first of all he would need to get her to the altar, and if he thought she would acquiesce willingly he had underrated his quarry.

Seating himself on the bed, he placed one perfectly manicured hand on either side of her and stared with evident appreciation at her far from friendly countenance. "God! You're even captivatingly lovely when somewhat dishevelled. I chose well when I decided upon you for my bride."

Refusing to be intimidated by his nearness, Jane made no attempt to press herself further back against the mound of pillows, even though he was so close she could almost feel the heat his body exuded. "You may have chosen, Mr Fairfax, but what on earth makes you suppose that I'll agree to be your wife?"

His self-satisfied smile did nothing to stem the ever mounting animosity she was feeling towards him. "My dear, a little time for calm reflection will force you to accept that you have little choice."

He then turned his attention to the cord binding her ankles and was silent for a moment while he dealt with a particularly stubborn knot. "I'm sure you'll be sensible and not make a bolt for the door," he continued in the same infuriatingly confident tone. "It would be futile to make the attempt, believe me. I would catch you before you had reached the stairs. I'm also sure that you'll soon see sense, and agree to my proposal. The only alternative, of course, is social ruin once it becomes known that you have spent several days…and nights…in my company."

"And you, of course, would ensure that it did become common knowledge," she responded, wondering how long she would be able to resist the temptation to raise one of her recently released feet and place a well-aimed kick on some part of his immaculate attired person.

"You do me an injustice, my lady. I should never stoop so low as to sully a fair lady's name. I cannot, however, vouch for the discretion of my servants."

Jane regarded him for a few moments in silence. Handsome though he was, he had never rated highly in her estimation, and he had now plummeted to an all-time low. He was quite simply despicable.

"And Latimer, I do not doubt, numbers amongst this small group of devotees," she couldn't resist remarking in a voice of thinly veiled contempt.

"Of course."

"In that case you are in my father's debt, sir. He has been paying your servant's wages these past three months."

"I'm certain that such an upstanding gentleman will not press for payment, in view of the fact that I'm shortly to be joined by marriage to his noble family."

"I wish," she responded, turning slightly to enable him to untie her hands, "you would rid your mind of this erroneous belief you harbour that I should consider marriage to you preferable to social ruin."

"And I sincerely hope you rapidly come to accept the fact that you really have no choice." His clipped tone betrayed clearly enough that her finely honed dart of derision had succeeded in piercing the veneer of unruffled reserve, but Jane's feeling of immense satisfaction was destined not to last very long.

"I have with me a special licence. Tomorrow you attain your majority and therefore can legally marry without your father's consent. You have until then to accept your fate with a good grace."

Rising, he moved over to the window. As he remained standing with his back towards her, Jane could only assume that, with his customary confidence, he retained no fears that she would escape. No doubt he had one of his degenerate servants posted in the hall in the event that she should be foolish enough to make the attempt, but she had no intention of doing so, at least not yet— not until she considered there would be a better than even chance of success.

"You shall not find me an unreasonable husband," he continued, and she forced herself to listen. "I shall make no unnecessary demands, but I do intend that ours will be a marriage in every sense. I should never wish to force myself upon you and am prepared to be patient—providing, that is, you do not compel me to use those very means in order to persuade you to agree to the union in the first place."

His meaning, although delicately phrased, was all too sickeningly clear. "So, you would even be loathsome enough to stoop to rape to attain your ends," Jane murmured, successfully concealing her rising fear, but not the utter contempt she felt.

"Not through choice, no, my dear." And for the first time there was an element of regret in his voice. "But needs must, as they say."

He came back across to the bed and stared down at her, but she could not now bring herself to look at him, although that was precisely what she would be forced to do for the rest of her life, unless she could somehow manage to extricate herself from this trap which, through a dogged resolve to achieve independence, she had helped set for herself.

If only she had listened to her brother and had

agreed to make use of one of the family's carriages, and to be accompanied by their loyal and trusted servants! If only she had accepted Richard's kind offer of his escort to Bath… But no, she had been foolishly determined to prove to all the members of her family, to everyone, that she was infinitely capable of making her own arrangements and more than able to look after herself. And just look where her stubborn pride had brought her!

She gave herself an inward shake. This was not the time to indulge in bitter self-recriminations. She had until tomorrow to find a way out of this mess, but certainly not longer. She didn't doubt for a moment that if she continued to refuse to acquiesce willingly he would ensure that she had no choice. So it might be wise in the circumstances to lull him into a false sense of security, by allowing him to believe that she was at least beginning to accept her fate.

It was an effort, but she forced herself to look at him again. "It would seem, sir, that you hold all the cards, but you cannot expect me to be enthusiastic over what life has in store for me. It is hardly flattering to know that you are coveted for your wealth alone."

"You underrate yourself, my dear. There are a number of heiresses brightening the *Marriage Mart* these days. One or two even more lovely than you, some might say. But you have always possessed a special something that sets you quite apart as far as I am concerned—grace, poise, charm—call it what you will. I have admired you for some little time, though I do realise, of course, that you have scant regard for me."

The knowledge didn't appear to trouble him to any great extent, as his next words proved. "I shan't lose any sleep over that, however, for it is my considered opinion that you have scant regard for most members of my sex. In all the years I've known you, I have never once seen you betray a preference for any particular gentleman's society."

A ruggedly handsome and frowning countenance, with penetrating grey eyes, suddenly appeared before her mind's eye, and the memory of a deep, attractive but disapproving voice commenting on her folly instantly erased those taut lines about her mouth. How she wished, now, that she had taken heed of Dr Thomas Carrington's sage advice about the sheer stupidity of travelling about on her own!

Simon Fairfax was not slow to perceive the

wistful expression that just for one unguarded moment flickered across her features. "Obviously I am in error—there is someone. Dear me," he remarked, with a flash of wry humour. "Am I likely to have some star-crossed gallant after my blood when the wedding has taken place?"

"No, you are not." She rose from the bed, and he made no attempt to stop her taking up his former stance at the window. "Would you be kind enough to leave me alone now, Mr Fairfax? As you perhaps can appreciate, I need to come to terms with what has befallen me."

"Of course, my dear. But first I must ask you to write a letter informing those concerned that you have no further need of a hired carriage. I shall then go to Calne to collect your trunks and deal with the necessary payments."

Knowing that it would avail her nothing to object, Jane seated herself at the small table upon which writing materials had been placed, and dutifully penned the letter he dictated.

"Thank you, my dear. I am so glad you have decided to be sensible. It makes everything so much pleasanter, don't you agree?" He read the missive through before slipping it into the pocket of his fashionable jacket. "I regret having to leave you in this deplorable house," he added, turning back at the door. "It isn't what you're used to, I know, but it's only for a couple of days. I inherited the place some months ago from a distant relative and installed the Talbots here when I thought up this little scheme. Mrs Talbot is very lax in carrying out many of her duties, but she is a fair cook. We'll dine when I return." And with that promised "treat' in store he went out, leaving her to chafe once again at what had befallen her.

She went across to the window, and it came as no great surprise to discover that it had been firmly nailed shut, no doubt in readiness for her confinement. The room was situated at the rear of the building. Below was a neglected garden, choked with weeds, with one or two ill-pruned fruit trees. Beyond the rickety garden fence were open fields stretching as far as the eye could see, with just the occasional small copse dotted here and there to break the monotony of the flat landscape.

More importantly, however, a small lean-to had been constructed along part of the back wall. It certainly couldn't be reached from here, even if it were possible to open the window, but there was every chance that access might be gained from the room next to this one. If she could manage to climb onto that sloping roof, then surely it would be a simple matter to reach the ground?

The sound of the key being fitted into the lock yet again interrupted her hopeful deliberations and she turned, unable to prevent a spark of hostility from brightening her eyes when the door swung open to reveal her visitor.

Oh, yes, she had been duped right royally! She had walked into the trap like a naive little fool, even though she had sensed from the beginning that there was something untrustworthy about Rose Latimer. Why, oh, why hadn't she acted upon instinct and been rid of the conniving wretch weeks ago? Well, that was yet something else to chalk up to experience, she supposed. And she would certainly make a point of choosing her own servants from now on, too!

"Mr Simon said I was to bring you this. It will be some time before you dine together and he thought you might like a little something to tide you over."

Latimer put the tray bearing the bowl of steaming broth down on the table beside the writing materials, and then turned, but didn't find it easy to meet her former mistress's unwavering and far from friendly gaze. She no longer considered herself a servant, but had agreed to continue acting the part until they arrived in Paris and she was rewarded for her part in Simon's scheme to acquire a rich bride. Then a totally different life beckoned, and one where she fully intended to issue the orders.

"Mr Simon has already left for Calne to collect your belongings. You'll no doubt wish to change for dinner. I'll help you, of course, should you require assistance."

Jane couldn't prevent a grudging smile at this. The woman certainly had an abundance of brass-faced nerve. "You may be sure I'll not require your services again, Latimer. You are, as one might say, relieved of all your duties. But just tell me one thing before you go," she went on, arresting the woman's progress to the door. "Did I prove such a difficult mistress? Did I treat you so unkindly that you felt the need to exact this kind of revenge?"

Rose lowered her eyes and stared blindly at a spot on the threadbare carpet. Not for the first time did she experience deep regrets over her part in Simon Fairfax's scheme to entrap the Earl's daughter, but what would the future have held for her if she'd refused to help him?

At the age of sixteen, when she had first given

herself to him, she had believed he truly loved her, but she was older and wiser now and had come to accept that there could never be any lasting future for her with him. The Simon Fairfaxes of this world did not marry servant girls; they chose, when the time came, from their own social class. Lord Fairfax's excesses had brought the family to the brink of financial ruin, and Rose really couldn't blame Simon for taking measures, unsavoury though they were, to secure his own future. After all, by aiding him in this cause, she had done no less herself. She had been offered the opportunity to be freed from a life of dismal servitude and had jumped at the chance.

To ensure a bright future she had been expected to do little more than keep Simon informed of Lady Jane's movements, so that when the right opportunity arose he could put his plan into action. She had suffered no real pangs of conscience over this. Lady Jane Beresford was a very lovely young woman, and she didn't doubt for a moment that Simon genuinely desired her. Added to which, it stood to reason that the Earl of Eastbury's daughter would marry one day, and she could do a lot worse than wed the Honourable Simon Fairfax. He was both handsome and charming, and although it was unlikely he would make a faithful husband Rose didn't suppose for a moment that he would make an unkind one.

This belief and the conviction she had retained that she wasn't doing the Earl's daughter any real harm had, up until the night of the Pentecosts' ball, continued to salve her conscience. Even when, under the cover of darkness, she had slipped out of the house to meet with Simon in the garden and, after their passionate interlude, had agreed to follow his instructions to the letter, she still hadn't experienced any feelings of guilt at the part she must play in the kidnapping. It was only later, when she and her young mistress were about to return to Knightley Hall, that everything had changed, in a matter of a few moments, and she had begun to experience tormenting pangs of guilt.

Lady Jane Beresford, unless Latimer was very much mistaken, was a young woman on the brink of falling deeply in love, though she probably wasn't aware of it herself yet. There had been that message in her eyes when she had watched the young doctor walk back into Pentecost Grange, a look that had shouted clearly enough, Don't go! Don't leave me! And that selfsame look had been mirrored in Dr Carrington's eyes, too.

But what hope was there for them? Lady Jane was every inch the refined and elegant aristocratic lady. She would be expected to choose a husband from the highest in the land, not some obscure country practitioner, who might not be precisely purse-pinched, but who certainly couldn't compete with her wealth. Why, they stood as much chance of making a suitable match as she and Simon Fairfax! She had done Lady Jane a great favour by ensuring that her path and Dr Carrington's wouldn't cross again in the foreseeable future… Or had she?

"No one, my lady, could ever accuse you of being less than a very considerate mistress," she said at last, and sincerely meant every word. She couldn't bring herself to add that she had made a determined effort not to become attached to her, and in part she had succeeded in this aim. Yet it had been impossible not to like and admire this warm-hearted young woman, who possessed that rare gift of being able to talk to those less fortunate than herself without making them feel in any way inferior.

"But I have always wished to better myself—had always hoped one day to be able to use my small skills for my own benefit. Simon offered me the chance of making my dream of becoming a milliner come true."

With my money, Jane thought bitterly, whilst experiencing at the same time a grudging admiration. If it hadn't been to her own detriment she would have genuinely wished Latimer well in her endeavours. "And where precisely do you propose to undertake this venture?"

"After…after the ceremony has taken place, Simon wishes me to accompany you to Paris. He suggested I make a fresh start there. He says the French lead the field when it comes to fashion."

What deep game was that wretch Simon Fairfax playing? Jane wondered. It was quite evident that his relationship with this woman was rather more than that of master and servant. It was quite evident, too, by the way she spoke his name as though it were a benediction, that poor Latimer was quite foolishly devoted to him, but whether he returned her regard was open to question. He must know that there was little chance of her making a success of her venture in Paris, so Jane could only assume that Latimer had made a very satisfying mistress and that Simon had no intention of dispensing with her services quite yet. Her eyes narrowed speculatively. Might now be the right moment to sow a seed of doubt in her former maid's mind?

"What he tells you is quite true. The French are very chic. But they have little affection for the people of this country. They welcome us with open arms when we visit their towns and cities, and are more than willing to encourage us to part with our money. Whether or not they would conveniently forget the many years our two countries were at war and patronise an establishment owned by an Englishwoman is quite a different matter, especially in view of the fact that they have superb modistes of their own. Believe me, Latimer, Mr Fairfax would be doing you no favour by helping you to set up a business venture in Paris. You would stand a far greater chance of making a success if you established yourself in one of our own rapidly growing cities in the Midlands or the north."

Latimer digested this sage advice in silence for several thoughtful moments, and then asked, unexpectedly, "You really don't like Mr Simon at all, do you, my lady?"

Jane knew little would be gained by lying. "In view of what he plans for me, it's hardly surprising, is it?" There was an unmistakable thread of sarcasm in her voice, but not a trace of bitterness now. "I vowed that I would never marry a man I could never love nor respect, but fate has decreed otherwise, it would seem. No, I do not care for him in the least, and in view of his recent actions I could never bring myself to trust him. And you would be extremely foolish to do so either. If you take my advice, you'll not let him out of your sight until he has rewarded you in full for your invaluable help. He could never have carried out his despicable plot without you, now, could he?"

"No, he could not," Latimer agreed, with a hint of regret. "You must hate the very ground I walk on. I just hope that one day you can find it in your heart to forgive me."

Jane resisted the temptation to wound with a pithy response, for strangely enough she couldn't find it within herself to despise this woman. She didn't even blame her for wishing to better herself. She just resented being the means by which her former maid hoped to attain her ends.

"I don't hate you, Rose," she admitted, calling her by her given name for the first time. "I just wish...I just wish we could have known each other better. I had already decided that it would be to our mutual advantage if you found yourself a new position. I'd sensed a deep resentment in you from the first."

"But not against you," Latimer hurriedly assured her.

"I'm glad of that, at least." It seemed to have become a time for confessions and Jane didn't have the least reticence in adding, "Had I been aware of your ambitions, I might have been in a position to help you embark on your new career, but I'll not insult your intelligence by pretending there's the remotest chance I would consider doing so now, at least not willingly. That doesn't mean, however, that I wish you ill-fortune in your endeavours. But you can hardly expect me to be overjoyed, knowing that your hopes for the future were made possible by the total annihilation of my own."

For several moments Latimer stood staring silently at some distant spot, and then, without uttering another word, left the room, leaving Jane to focus her thoughts once more on trying to find a means of escape.

Waiting for nightfall presented itself as the most sensible course of action. But could she afford to wait that long? Time certainly wasn't on her side. Furthermore, would the cover of darkness be of any real benefit? Reaching a sizeable habitation, where she could attain help, must be her goal, but, being totally unfamiliar with this part of the country, she might well find herself walking round in circles and run the risk of recapture.

It was all rather academic, anyway, she reminded herself, unless she could first escape from this room. The window, of course, was a non-starter, so the only way…

She moved slowly across to the door, silently blessing Simon Fairfax's relative for spending little money on the upkeep of the house. The door and its surround were excessively worm-eaten, which gave her every reason to hope that the wood might be easily gouged out to enable her to force the lock—if, of course, she could get her hands on something, a knife perhaps, to aid her. Dinner would offer an opportunity to purloin some useful implement, and then afterwards, when everyone had retired for the night, she could attempt to chisel away at the wood. It was a slim chance, perhaps, but likely to be her only one.

Examining the area around the lock more closely, in order to see what was involved, Jane placed her hand on the door-handle. Then the totally unbelievable happened: the door opened effortlessly. For several moments she was too stunned to think, let alone take advantage of her great good fortune.

Her eyes narrowed. Maybe luck had had precious little to do with it. Had Latimer inadvertently forgotten to lock the door behind her? Or had she quite deliberately given her former mistress a chance to escape? Jane wasn't certain, but she didn't intend wasting precious minutes pondering over the conundrum now.

Galvanised, she peered along the passageway. It was deserted, but that didn't mean that there was no one posted somewhere, possibly in the hall, vigilantly on guard. So, carefully closing the door, she tiptoed into the next room. It was much larger than the one she had been allocated and she suspected, from the fashionable male attire laid out neatly on the bed, that it was being used by Simon Fairfax, a circumstance which prompted her not to linger.

The window opened easily and, thankfully, with only the faintest protesting creak. As Jane had suspected, it offered easy access to the sloping roof below. Scrambling out and stepping down onto the slates proved no hardship. Unfortunately there was nothing near or leaning against the structure, not even a water butt, to aid her further descent. As luck would have it, though, it was no more than an eight-foot drop from the lowest point of the roof, although her recently injured ankle protested as she made the courageous leap down to the edge of what at one time must have been a lawn, but now could be best described as a weed-infested wilderness.

By the time she had scrambled over the rickety fence at the bottom of the garden she had forgotten her niggling hurts. Keeping close to the sides of the fields, in the hope that the hedgerows would conceal her flight, she put as much distance as she could between herself and her former captors. Only when she had reached the copse, three fields from the house, did she feel safe enough to rest for a while, but even then could not resist frequent glances over her shoulder just to ensure that there was no one following in hot pursuit.

Not a soul to be seen, thank goodness! So she could only assume that no one had yet returned to her room in order to collect her untouched broth. But it wouldn't be too much longer, surely, before her flight was discovered? It would take Simon little more than an hour to reach Calne and return with her belongings, and she guessed he couldn't be that far away from the house now. She might be granted a further thirty minutes before the search for her began, but certainly not longer.

Simon, she felt certain, would begin by scouring the lanes about the house. After all, he could hardly take his carriage across the fields. Which was some comfort, she supposed, but not very much. Who was to say that he hadn't one or two riding horses installed in that run-down stable? And how many male servants had he with him to offer assistance? She had seen only one man, Ralph Talbot, but she would be foolish to assume that he was the only one.

She still considered her best plan of action was to keep well away from any roads as far as she was able, and if she remained moving more or less in the same direction sooner or later, with any luck, she would come upon a village or hamlet where she could seek help. Simon could have no idea in which direction she was heading. He would realise, of course, that, on foot, she couldn't have got that far away, which was sufficient inducement for her not to tarry.

Leaving the relative concealment of the small clump of trees, she pressed onwards, doing her best to ignore the threatening clouds building up from the west, but unable to stop herself from dwelling on what recapture would mean. Simon Fairfax, yielding to what gentlemanly instincts he possessed, had not resorted to undue force, but she doubted very much that he would continue to behave in the same vein if he got her in his clutches again.

She would no doubt find herself severely restrained, making any further attempts at escape impossible. Not only that, she didn't doubt for a moment that he would resort to those vile extremes whereby she had no choice but to marry him. Surprisingly, the thought of being violated didn't induce a fit of the vapours, as it no doubt would have done in those faint-hearted members of her sex, but instilled in her a determination to outwit the villainous wretch.

Pausing to take a well-earned rest, she took a moment to look about her. Just how far she had walked she had no way of knowing, but she could perceive definite changes in the landscape: the flat arable land surrounding the house had given way to rolling pastureland, where sheep made the most of the fading light by grazing hungrily, barely giving her a cursory glance, and denser areas of woodland were now appearing on the horizon.

But for how much longer could she keep up this relentless pace? There was little point in trying to deny the fact that she was already experiencing the unpleasant results of the unaccustomed and lengthy exercise. Furthermore, unless she wished to add to her discomfort by spending the night in the open air, which certainly wouldn't be her first choice, then she would need to risk walking along a road in order to find some shelter.

She had already been forced to cross several byroads, but these had been little more than deeply rutted tracks, no doubt used by farmers to gain access to their various fields. She had experienced little fear in walking for a short while along any of these until she had found a gateway or a gap in the hedge wide enough to scramble through. But had she put sufficient distance between herself and that house for her to risk trying to reach habitation by keeping to a highway? Might Simon Fairfax have abandoned any search he may have undertaken by now?

Climbing through a gap in the hedge, she found herself standing on the even surface of a road. It was wider than any of those she had travelled along to Simon's house, and must surely ultimately lead to her goal: a town or village. But which way to go, left or right?

She was still debating over this when she distinctly heard the sound of hoof-beats. It wasn't a carriage, but a lone rider, she felt certain, but even so caution prevailed and she took immediate action by retreating to the gap in the hedge. There was always the possibility that it might be Simon or his servant, Ralph Talbot, and even if not, dared she chance begging assistance?

She risked a second glance along the road and, watching the lone traveller appear round the bend, could hardly believe the evidence of her own eyes. It couldn't be…

Tears of joy blurring her vision, she scrambled from her hiding place, waving and calling frantically and almost stumbling in her eagerness to reach the blessed protection of that gentleman's side.

Chapter Nine

It was market day and the town of Devizes was buzzing with life, its busy main streets rapidly filling to capacity with a variety of carriages and farm carts, with beast of varying kinds, and with people buying or selling, or merely watching the spectacle.

Tom, woken early by the first of the farmers herding his stock to market, quickly abandoned the idea of trying to go back to sleep, and for a while leaned out of his bedchamber window, watching the street below quickly become a hive of activity.

Market days were vastly important to the people of the town and surrounding area: occasions when they hoped to attain some financial reward for their hard labours, as well as times for festivity, when folk who hadn't seen one another for several weeks, maybe months, got together to exchange stories and gossip generally.

Shops and taverns did a roaring trade. Long before Tom had finished eating his breakfast, the inn where he was putting up was becoming crowded with the menfolk, many of whom had been up since daybreak, wishing to quench their thirst.

Tom spent the day exploring the town and viewing the wares for sale on the many stalls. There was much to see and a great deal to capture his interest, but from time to time he would catch sight of something—a girl with reddish hair, or a more affluent young woman decked out in her finery— that would revive a poignant memory. Unfortunately it had happened rather too often, each occasion leaving him slightly more depressed, so that by the time he was ready to leave to dine with Sir William Dent he wasn't looking forward to the evening ahead with any great enthusiasm.

"The horse be saddled and awaiting you, sir," the innkeeper's very obliging wife informed him as he descended the stairs into the coffee-room.

"Thank you, Mrs Pegg. I'm unable to say what time I'm likely to return, but I hope it won't be too late. You and your husband have already had a long and very busy day."

"Don't you concern yourself none over that, Dr Carrington. We always stay open till late on market days. There's always some who don't know when to stop celebrating. Mind, those with any sense won't leave it late before they start for home. The weather's changed for the worst during the past hour. The rain's keeping off for now, but I reckon it'll come afore the day's out, so if you decide to stay at Sir William's for the night I'll understand."

Although Sir William Dent's fine country residence was situated some five miles from Devizes, he was a well-known figure in the town. His hospitality was famed, and as he had three unmarried daughters, all as plain as pikestaffs, still residing under his roof Mrs Pegg couldn't see the eminent surgeon wishing to lose the company of such a personable young gentleman as Dr Carrington too soon.

"And don't be afraid I'll let the room if you've not returned by the following day, neither."

Assuring her that this was highly unlikely, Tom went to collect the hired mount from the stable yard and, following directions given by the innkeeper, left the town heading in an easterly direction.

The main road was still quite busy with people

making their way home, their arms filled with their purchases, and with their pockets and purses noticeably lighter, no doubt. By the time Tom turned onto the slightly narrower road which, according to Pegg's directions, would eventually lead him right past Sir William's door he had the highway virtually to himself, and his mind, as it too often did, began to dwell once again on Elizabeth Knightley's cousin.

How he had tried to fight that ever increasing attraction to her, but for all the good it had done he might as well have saved himself the effort. His mind might continue to assure him that he had been sensible in not trying to see her again before he had left Hampshire on the morning after the Pentecosts' ball, but his heart had continued to proclaim quite otherwise. He could ignore the all-too-painful truth no longer—he had for the first time in his life fallen deeply in love.

If the knowledge hadn't been so agonising he would have laughed at the absurdity of it all. The level-headed and conscientious Dr Thomas Carrington, whose dedication and no-nonsense manner had won the respect of the Hampshire community he served, had fallen victim to Cupid's arrow. Oh, yes, Venus's mischievous son had pinked him nicely; the potent dart was firmly embedded, and it would be some time, Tom felt sure, before the wound began to heal—if it ever did completely.

But life must go on and in the meantime he must throw himself into his work with renewed vigour. Yes—that was the best cure. Feeling sorry for himself and yearning for something far above his touch was no way to deal with the painful ache which rarely left him. It would be foolish to imagine that he would always successfully blot out the image of those beautiful, laughing eyes set in a finely boned countenance from his mind, so he must face the fact that for some time to come he would see something or someone that would ignite bitter-sweet memory.

As he rounded the bend in the road, it seemed as if fate, capricious wench, had decided to corroborate this conviction. A young woman, with reddish-brown hair cascading about her shoulders in some disarray, suddenly appeared from nowhere. He closed his eyes in an attempt to disperse the image, but a beloved and well-spoken voice calling his name forced them open again.

"Good God!" He stared down at her as she reached his side, still reluctant to believe the evidence of his own eyes. "Am I dreaming, or is it really you?"

"Well, of course it is!" She raised her arm and he automatically obliged by helping her into the saddle before him.

Still somewhat shaken by the great love of his life's miraculous appearance, he managed to enquire, "Would it be too much to ask what you're doing in this out-of-the-way place and..." he looked about him "...seemingly alone?"

"Would you believe it, Tom," she said, using his given name as though it were the most natural thing in the world, "I was abducted? Such impudence!"

Having the most desirable of creatures virtually sitting on his lap did little to ease his mounting confusion, but eventually the rather unbelievable explanation managed to penetrate the delicious feeling of euphoria doing its best to numb his thought processes. "Abducted? By whom, may I ask?"

"Simon Fairfax. Oh, do not let us tarry here!" she urged. "For all I know the wretch might be out looking for me at this very moment."

She had hardly finished speaking when they both heard the sound of a carriage. Moments later a curricle came bowling towards them, and there was no mistaking who was handling the ribbons.

"Oh, Tom, it is he! Quick, let us away over the field. He cannot possibly follow us there."

"Damn it, no! I won't turn tail and run. I'll confront the black... Here, what are you about, girl?"

Jane, seeing no sense in spending time arguing, took matters into her own hands, or more accurately the reins, and urged their mount through the gap in the hedge. Once in the field, she headed for the large area of woodland at the opposite end. She heard a shot ring out, and caught Tom's sharp intake of breath, but was unaware that there was anything badly amiss until she slowed the horse down to a walk in order to steer a safe path through the dense area of trees.

"They certainly can't follow us now," she remarked, experiencing a deal of satisfaction at the ease of their escape. Then, turning her head, she easily detected the lines of strain in Tom's face and a moment later noticed the blood oozing from the wound in his left thigh.

"Oh, good gracious! You're hurt!"

"I'm all right," he lied. "It's nothing but a scratch." He ground his teeth, though whether this was in anger or pain Jane wasn't perfectly sure. "If I ever get my hands on the villain who discharged that pistol, I'll…"

"Was it Simon?"

"No, the blackguard seated beside him."

"That was his servant, Ralph Talbot."

Jane watched him take a handkerchief from his pocket and knot it around his leg. By the ever increasing stained area on his breeches she knew the wound was not as slight as he would have her believe, but there was little she could do to help him now and she concentrated on keeping to as straight a line as possible. The wood seemed to go on for ever and beneath the canopy of dense branches it was quite dark and eerie. To add to their troubles rain began to fall, lightly at first and then with a vengeance. Then, if that were not sufficient ill luck, the horse decided to cast a shoe.

The gods, it appeared, were ranged against her, seemingly delighting in the endless string of misfortunes with which to plague a hapless damsel, but Jane steadfastly refused to become downhearted. She had escaped Simon Fairfax's infamous clutches yet again and, most satisfying of all, she now had the comfort of this highly dependable man's protection.

Tom, experiencing none of her optimism,

managed to assist her to alight, and watched in growing concern as she grasped the bridle and bravely led the horse onwards. It should have been he who eased the mount's burden by continuing on foot, but he was only too brutally aware that he would be foolish to make the attempt. He needed to conserve his strength in the event that they met up with Jane's abductors again, though just how much use he would be in any confrontation was open to debate. He was experiencing no feeling of dizziness as yet. But how much longer could he remain fully conscious if he continued to lose blood at the present rate? Experience told him not for very long.

At Jane's sudden exclamation of delight, he raised his eyes to see a large clearing a little way ahead and, more importantly, a cottage with several outbuildings. At least they could now shelter from the rain and, hopefully, find help.

When no one appeared at the front entrance in answer to Jane's summons, Tom gingerly eased himself down from the saddle, wincing slightly as he put his weight on his injured leg, and set up a shout, but still no one came. "Try the door."

Although she feared they might be mistaken for a pair of opportunist thieves, she was more concerned about Tom's condition and immediately obeyed the command by raising the latch. The door swung open effortlessly to reveal a large kitchen that was both warm and spotlessly clean. Tom took the initiative then and, brushing past her, was the first to enter the spacious room that appeared to function as the main living quarters. He noticed the table and benches placed against the far wall, but was more interested in getting the weight off his injured leg than taking stock of his surroundings, and made a beeline for the settle, which was invitingly placed close to the range.

He glanced across the room as Jane turned to close the door, and experienced a deal of regret at what he must ask of her, but knew he had little choice. "I'm afraid I'm going to need your help to get my boots and breeches off."

She hesitated, but only for a moment.

She saw him grimace as she pulled off his left boot, and he noticed her blush fiery red as she peeled away his breeches. A look of horrified fascination took possession of her features as her eyes became seemingly transfixed on a certain part of his anatomy. It was quite evident that she had never seen a man naked before, a fact that he found both infinitely gratifying and faintly amusing, but he resisted the temptation to tease her and succeeded in drawing her out of her entranced state by suggesting she fill a bowl with water.

Once most of the blood had been cleaned away, Tom was able to examine his injured thigh more closely. The wound in itself he didn't consider serious, but it was situated in such a position that he could not easily reach it to extract the lead shot. Without being told, Jane was very well aware of this fact too, and she went about the kitchen, opening the various cupboards and drawers, searching for what she would need to perform the unenviable task herself.

The extraction of the bullet was not easy or pleasant for either of them, but was achieved successfully and in quite a remarkably short space of time considering that Jane's slender hands were completely unskilled. The ordeal, not surprisingly, left Tom exhausted, and Jane didn't delay in completing her unpleasant task, binding the wound up deftly with strips torn from a linen sheet, and then helping Tom cross the kitchen and into the adjoining room which she had noticed earlier was a bedchamber.

Once she had coaxed him into giving her his slightly damp shirt and had him settled in the large and comfortable bed, she went back into the kitchen, returning a few minutes later with a glass containing a generous measure taken from the contents of a bottle she had found in the larder.

Tom disposed of the amber liquid in one large swallow. It wasn't very long before the brandy took effect, dulling the pain in his leg sufficiently for him to doze. He slept only fitfully at first, but then fell into a much deeper and more restful sleep. When eventually he awoke, it was to discover the room in darkness with only the faintest chink of light creeping beneath the door. It took a few moments for all his faculties to return, and with them a surge of panic.

Jane didn't delay in entering the bedchamber in response to his frantic shouts. "So you're awake, are you?" she remarked, looking and sounding as though she hadn't a care in the world as she went about the room lighting the various candles. "I was hoping you'd sleep through until morning."

"You shouldn't have allowed me to sleep at all, you foolish chit!" he ground out, and she couldn't prevent a smile. Scolding was so much a part of his nature, after all. "What would you have done if that blackguard Fairfax had found his way here, may I ask?"

"I would have been prepared," she informed him with infuriating calm. "But, as you have probably gathered by now, he didn't turn up. And neither, which is really disturbing, has anyone else."

Uninvited, she seated herself on the edge of the bed, betraying clearly enough her unease of mind. "I cannot help but feel that something must have happened to the owner of this place, Tom. I know it's not uncommon for country folk to go out leaving their doors unlocked, but not when they intend to be away for any length of time. I assume the man earns his living as a woodcutter, and he certainly wouldn't be working until this time of night. Why, it's almost ten o'clock! And where, I ask myself, is his wife?"

His brows rose at this. "And what makes you suppose that there is a wife?"

She regarded him as though he had taken leave of his senses. "Look about you, for heaven's sake! The place is spotless. I'm not suggesting for a moment that a man is incapable of keeping his home clean, but it would be a rare member of your sex who would concern himself with adding such touches as those," she pointed out, drawing to his notice the vase of wild flowers on the bedside table.

"No, I suppose not," he was forced to concede.

"I'm certain they meant to return long before now. No one who keeps chickens and ducks leaves them wandering about at night for the fox to get. And," she went on, not offering him the opportunity to respond to this, "soup had been prepared, no doubt in readiness for their supper—which reminds me, I'll fetch you a bowl. I've eaten my fill already. It's delicious."

She returned, carrying the broth and a large chunk of crusty bread on a tray which she set down on his lap once he had managed to ease himself into a more upright position. He discovered he was very hungry and, after sending her for a second helping, demanded in his rather blunt way a detailed account of precisely what had happened to her that day since leaving Knightley Hall.

"And that is what comes of gadding about the country unprotected, my girl!" he announced when he had learned all, his forthright tone betraying clearly enough his staunch disapproval, but concealing quite beautifully his intense relief that nothing worse had befallen her. "You are far too lovely to go careering about on your own!" Then, detracting from the compliment somewhat, he added, "It's a thousand pities you weren't blessed with the same degree of brains as looks!"

He shook his head as though at some private thought. "Thank the Lord that maid forgot to relock that door."

"Well, now, I've been pondering over that," she responded, not appearing unduly chastened by his scathing condemnation of her actions. "I think she deliberately left it unlocked to give me a chance to escape. We indulged in perhaps the longest conversation we'd ever had. Something I said must have pricked her conscience. Or maybe I made her realise that Simon Fairfax is a selfish rogue and not to be trusted. She's certainly excessively fond of him, but I don't think she's foolishly blind to his faults."

Tom was silent for a moment, digesting this, then remarked, "It sounds to me as if Fairfax had been planning your abduction for quite some time."

"Several months, I shouldn't wonder. His mother and mine have been friends for years, and ladies do tend to gossip. My mother must have informed Lady Fairfax that I would shortly be looking for a new abigail. No doubt Simon learned of this and told his mother to suggest Latimer for the post. Once she had been installed in our household, it was merely a case of waiting for the right opportunity to carry out his plans."

"I assume that to avoid a scandal you won't inform the authorities about what has befallen you…" Tom's suddenly grim expression boded ill for Lord Fairfax's son and heir "…but if I ever get my hands on him…"

"I must confess that it irks me to think he'll get off scot-free," she admitted, feeling no small desire to be avenged herself, "but there's little I can do. I don't wish to cause embarrassment to my family by making this day's escapade common knowledge. Besides," she sighed, "as you quite rightly pointed out, I've only myself to blame. If I had ensured that I had adequate protection, instead of foolishly striving to attain a little independence by loosening those constricting ties that have confined me since birth, none of this would have happened. Being an heiress is not all joy, Dr Carrington, believe me."

Up until that moment he had assumed that the highly privileged and pampered life she led, where, no doubt, the most arduous task she undertook in any one day was trying to find some pleasurable way to keep herself amused, suited her admirably. He ought to have known better.

During the short time he had known her she had proved herself to be a warm-hearted and level-headed young woman who cared deeply for her fellow man—her concern for her friend Lord Pentecost and her willingness to do all she could when young Ben had been injured were ample testament to that.

Had he needed more proof of how deeply he had misjudged her then he had been given it now. Most young women, no matter what their social class, would have succumbed to a fit of the vapours if they had experienced half of what she had been forced to endure this day. She was without doubt a rather exceptional young woman who, he now felt certain, possessed many hidden talents hitherto untouched and untried simply because of the many petty restrictions placed upon her by her highly privileged birth.

How frustrating it all must be to be forced to endure such a hidebound existence! He could quite understand, now, why she had striven to attain a little freedom, but knew it would be quite wrong of him to give voice to his thoughts and thereby possibly encourage her to take further risks in the future.

"Well, no real harm has come of it this time," he

remarked, turning his attention back to the delicious soup. "But you're not, figuratively speaking,
out of the woods yet. You may have escaped the
fiendish Fairfax's clutches, but you're now in
mine— A far worse fate, my dear, I assure you."

The only effect his evil leer had upon her was
to ignite a delicious gurgle of laughter. "Oh, no,
Dr Carrington, you cannot frighten me. I know
I'm perfectly safe with you. Simon Fairfax possesses all the trappings of a man of honour, whilst
he is anything but, whereas you…" she paused
for a moment in order to choose her words carefully "…you would never attempt to affect the
manners of a gentleman, though that is, funda-
mentally, precisely what you are."

"I'm not gentleman enough to give up this bed
to you for a start, my girl," he countered.

"In the circumstances I wouldn't expect you
to. I'm quite content to make shift with the comfortable chair in the kitchen." She went about the
room blowing out the various candles, leaving
just the one on the bedside table for him to extin-
guish when he was ready. "I'm rather tired, so I
shall bid you goodnight, and shall see you in the
morning, when I intend to have a good breakfast
awaiting you."

I don't doubt it for a moment, Tom thought, watching her leave. You have more than lived up to my expectations… I can only hope, my darling girl, that I possess the strength of character and am truly gentleman enough to live up to yours.

Chapter Ten

Tom awoke the following morning to the pleasant sound of melodious humming. He had forgotten what a lovely voice she had. But then, he reminded himself, everything about Lady Jane Beresford was quite above the norm. Even her ability to accept her present, unenviable situation with a kind of resigned optimism was much to her credit. What a remarkable young woman she was!

The delicious aroma of freshly baked bread suddenly assailed his nostrils, bringing a smile to his face and the inevitable pangs of hunger. Then he noticed his clothes, not only dried but pressed too, neatly folded over the back of the chair. He knew that his friend Elizabeth could, and often did, turn her hand to the most mundane tasks, but he had always considered her rather exceptional. Never had it occurred to him for a moment to suppose that there were other high-born ladies, having servants in abundance to pander to their every whim, who were capable of performing such basic tasks for themselves, let alone willing to do so. It appeared he had much to learn about the ways of the aristocracy, he mused, suffering only slight discomfort from his injured leg as he swung his feet to the floor and scrambled into his clothes.

The bedchamber door, kept well oiled, made only the faintest sound as he pushed it wide and stepped into the warmth of the kitchen to find Jane bent over the stove. From somewhere she had managed to lay her hands on an apron. She had the sleeves of her dress, businesslike, rolled up to her elbows, and those bared portions of slender arms were liberally splattered with flour. She looked so completely at home performing the task of preparing breakfast that it was difficult to believe that it was not a daily duty but a rare occurrence which, he supposed, by her continued cheerful humming, still retained the appeal of novelty.

She turned suddenly, as though sensing she was being watched, and that spontaneous smile which never failed to reach her eyes curled up the corners of her delectable mouth.

"Naturally I'm delighted to see you up and

about, but do you think you are being altogether sensible to exercise that leg so soon and risk re-opening the wound?"

"I've no intention of overtaxing myself, Jane. But if I remained idling in that bed, comfortable though it is, I would soon be like a bear with a sore head, growling and unapproachable."

The puckish streak in her nature couldn't allow this to pass without comment, and, all wide-eyed innocence, she looked across the room at him. "What…? More than usual, you mean?"

"Little baggage!" he muttered good-humouredly, appreciating the gentle sarcasm. "Am I such a bad-tempered boor?"

"You have been known to be, yes," she answered, with brutal frankness.

He couldn't help but admire her candour, even though it wasn't precisely to his credit. Yes, he had been grossly unjust to her on more than one occasion during their short but far from unevent-ful acquaintanceship, he was forced silently to admit. Perhaps it had been a defence mechanism triggered off by some innate masculine wisdom that had sensed from the first that this woman posed a real threat to his comfortable bachelor existence. If that was true, his armour had been woefully inadequate to cope with the onslaught of such formidable feminine weapons, for his defences against her were completely shattered now.

It would be grossly unfair, though, he reminded himself, to allow his feelings for her to surface. They were in a very precarious situation: together like this and completely alone. The last thing he wanted was to add to her mounting troubles by making her feel wary or remotely uncomfortable in his presence. She was in dire need of his support, and from the very complimentary remarks she had passed the previous evening it was quite evident that she trusted him implicitly. He was still far from certain whether he could live up to her expectations. After all, he was only flesh and blood and she, the gorgeous darling, was an exceedingly lovely young woman, totally feminine and infinitely desirable.

None the less, when she joined him at the table, bringing with her the fruits of her early morning labours, he managed, on this occasion at least, to control the strong urge to take her ruthlessly into his arms and subject her to a display of virile masculine passion. Instead, he encouraged her to tell him something of the life she had led at her ancestral home in Kent.

Conversation might have been the last thing on his mind, but he soon found himself absorbed in what she was saying. He had quite naturally assumed that, being a member of the privileged class, she had enjoyed a happy, carefree childhood, and to a certain extent his assumption had been correct. But as he listened to her recalling events in her past he gained the distinct impression that there had been numerous occasions when she had been a very lonely, somewhat isolated little girl, who had frequently sought the companionship of the servants below stairs. This, of course, went some way to explain her ability to converse so easily with people, no matter what their status, for he himself had noted on more than one occasion the gracious way she had always spoken to the Knightleys' servants.

"And your visits to the kitchen were certainly well worthwhile," he remarked, helping himself to more eggs and a third delicious roll.

The compliment drew a gratified smile to her lips. "Unfortunately we have a French chef now, who doesn't like sharing his domain with anyone. But years ago Mrs Blagdon reigned supreme in the kitchen. She was a dear soul, who was very indulgent and taught me a great deal about the art of cooking. I was never bored when I could escape from my governess and go down to the bowels of the house."

"Am I right in thinking that your brother and sisters are much older than you?" he asked when she fell silent.

"Yes. My mother produced four children in as many years. Then waited a further ten before bringing me into the world. My sister Clarissa is the nearest to me in age." Her smile was replaced by a slight frown. "I love them all dearly, but…"

"But you resent the way they still continue to treat you as though you were a child," he finished for her with quite remarkable perspicacity. "You must find that quite irksome. I know I should."

"Yes, I do," she freely admitted, while at the same time fervently wishing that she hadn't allowed increasing resentment at her family's almost claustrophobic protective attitude to lead her into taking such a foolishly ill-conceived stand. Really she had only herself to blame for her present predicament.

Not that she minded so very much for herself: sheltering in this cottage and having to do everything for herself made a refreshing change, and if the truth be known she was enjoying the experience hugely, but she had been suffering pangs of conscience over Tom's involvement. Not only was she responsible for getting the poor man shot, but she had unwittingly forced him into taking on the role of protector. Strangely, though, she could think of no one she would sooner have to take care of her than this sometimes infuriating man.

The realisation hit her quite forcibly, and it certainly didn't help to lessen her confusion to discover him regarding her rather keenly, those intelligent and highly perceptive grey eyes of his seeming able to probe the depths of her mind and read her every thought with uncanny accuracy.

"Well, that's enough about me," she announced, in a valiant attempt to give her bemused thoughts a new direction. "Tell me something about yourself." And although he obliged her readily enough she gained the distinct impression from the quizzical smile that he knew the precise reason for the swift change of subject.

She had learned something of his past, of course, from her cousin. She was aware that he had lost both his parents at a young age and that Elizabeth's grandmother, a lady for whom Tom had felt the utmost fondness and respect, had brought him up. She learned that his father had been an apothecary, and that his mother, of good yeoman stock, had come to the marriage with a dowry sufficiently large to enable her young husband to purchase business premises in the centre of Bristol.

When his mother had died Tom had continued to see something of her family, and kept in touch even now with his aunts and uncles and various cousins, but of his father's family he said not a word. Jane thought this rather strange and enquired whether his father had been an only child.

"Yes, he was. Both my paternal grandparents died before I was born."

"And was your grandfather an apothecary, too?"

"No, a clergyman. He was fortunate enough to attain a living on a large estate in Norfolk for a while before finding another, but far less lucrative one, in Gloucestershire." He regarded her for a moment in meditative silence. "I thought Elizabeth might have enlightened you."

"About what?"

"About my paternal grandparents."

By her ill-concealed puzzlement it was evident that she hadn't a clue what he was talking about, and he should have realised that she was completely ignorant of his family's history. Elizabeth was not a garrulous person, while Jane was certainly far from an inquisitive one and had no penchant for scandal. His grandparents' lives, and ultimately that of his father, might have been so vastly different if it hadn't been for the bigoted and unforgiving attitude adopted by his great-grandfather. It was a subject he rarely alluded to, but for some inexplicable reason he felt the need to hear Jane's views on the happenings which had occurred more than half a century ago.

"My grandfather, Percival Carrington, came from the professional classes. He was an intelligent man who chose a career in the church. As I've already mentioned, he was offered a living on a vast estate in Norfolk. He fell deeply in love with his benefactor's eldest daughter, and they married, but against the wishes of her father. He disowned her completely, and even went so far as to take his petty revenge by giving my grandfather's living to another. My grandmother had no further contact with any member of her family. She died shortly after giving birth to my father in what for her, a young woman accustomed to every luxury, must have seemed abject poverty."

Jane listened to this sorry tale in silence while she tried to bring to mind those amongst her many acquaintances who owned sizeable properties in the county of Norfolk. "What was your grandmother's maiden name?"

His white teeth flashed in a sportive smile. "Davenham."

One finely arched brow rose so sharply that it seemed as if she were being manipulated by some invisible puppeteer. "Well! I cannot say that I'm surprised you keep that connection very quiet. I'd not want it universally known, either, if I were related in any way to the Marquis of Fencham. The present holder of the title is the most self-opinionated, obnoxious little worm who ever drew breath, and his wife isn't much better—touched in the upper works, if you ask me, which tells you something of what their offspring are like. You may be sure, Tom, that I'll never breathe a word of the relationship between you and that family, distant though it may be."

That she had assumed that it was he who chose not to recognise his noble relatives, and not the other way round, left him totally nonplussed for several moments, and then he threw his head back and roared with laughter. If he had ever experienced any bitterness over his aristocratic relatives' complete indifference to his existence, he certainly felt none whatsoever now.

"You quite astonish me at times!" he told her when he was able.

"I'm sorry if I seemed rude, Tom," she responded with total sincerity, "but I don't care for that family at all."

"Don't apologise, darling girl. You're like a breath of fresh air." Then, realising he was in the gravest danger of losing that iron control he was exerting over himself and reaching out and taking her in his arms, he followed her example of minutes before by turning his thoughts in a new direction and focusing his attention on the contents of their temporary dwelling-place.

"I must say this is rather palatial for a wood-cutter's abode. There are not many hailing from the lower orders who can afford a kitchen range, let alone such an up-to-date one. And the furniture, although not precisely Chippendale or Hepplewhite, is extremely well made."

"Ah, yes! I've been meaning to tell you about that," Jane responded, reaching for the coffee-pot and obligingly refilling his cup before seeing to her own. "After I had let the chickens and ducks out this morning, I had a look around. There's a large outbuilding just beyond the hen-coop, and it's filled with all manner of things from cradles and toys to chairs, stools and tables. You name it—it's in there. He's not a woodcutter but a woodcarver. And a very good one, too. But just where he's hiding himself remains a mystery."

Tom shrugged his broad shoulders. It wasn't that he was indifferent, it was just that he had enough to concern him without worrying unduly about errant carpenters. "He'll turn up sooner or later."

"I hope you're right. I had a wander through the woods early this morning to see if…"

"You…did…what?" he thundered, regarding her as though she had taken leave of her senses. "Of all the feather-brained things to go and do! What would have happened if you'd met up with Simon Fairfax, may I ask?"

Betraying no outward signs of having taken offence at his sudden slide into a belligerent mood, Jane calmly took a sip of coffee before defending her actions by saying, "I'm not such a widgeon as to go abroad unarmed."

She then gestured towards the Welsh dresser upon which she had placed a dragoon's pistol. "I would imagine it's a souvenir from the war. Heaven only knows how our host came by it. It's in perfect working order. I spent some time cleaning and reloading it last night, as well as the rifle in the corner over there."

His expression changed dramatically, and he regarded her now with a mixture of astonishment and grudging respect. "Do you mean to tell me you're capable of handling such weapons?"

"Of course," she answered with simple pride. "You forget I enjoyed a misspent youth. My brother frequently took me out shooting with him—still does for that matter. My father's rather proud of the fact that he has at least one daughter who's not completely ignorant in the use of firearms.

"I'm sorry if that shocks you, Dr Carrington," she went on to say, after fortifying herself again from the contents of her cup. "I realise, of course, that you're in the business of saving lives. And, believe me, I wouldn't willingly shoot anyone, not even the infamous Simon Fairfax. But if I had come upon him in the woods this morning I wouldn't have hesitated in getting him into my sights. However, I never for one moment expected to run into him. He might be a loathsome, unprincipled wretch, but he's certainly no fool." She shook her head. "No, he's long since gone—with my money, all my clothes and my jewel box, I do not doubt. Which reminds me…"

Delving into the pocket of the borrowed apron, she drew out a small brooch, a dainty circlet of pearls set in a silver mounting, and placed it upon the table in front of him. "I found that beside the settle this morning when I was sweeping the floor. It looks quite old to me and worth something, I shouldn't wonder. Further proof that our host and hostess are not precisely purse-pinched."

"Well, actually, it's mine," he surprised her by admitting. "It belonged to my grandmother, a relic of her affluent past. Poor woman was forced to sell most of her jewels, but for some reason couldn't bring herself to part with this. Sometimes I wear it in my cravat if the mood takes me." His teeth flashed in a roguish smile. "I had a fancy to dazzle Sir William Dent yesterday with my finery."

This reminder of his intended destination forced Jane once more to concentrate her thoughts on the best way to get them out of their present predicament. Although Tom had been determined not to remain in bed, it would be foolish to pretend he could walk very far, or ride any distance, without reopening his wound, so it would be left to her to find the nearest black-smith in order to get the horse shod and then make her way to the nearest large town in order to hire a carriage.

Tom was very much against the idea of her going off on her own, but eventually she per-suaded him to accept that there was no alterna-tive, if they didn't wish to spend yet another night in the cottage.

All went well at first. The early spring sun, pleasantly warm, and cheering, shone down on her as she collected Tom's hired mount from the stable and walked along the narrow track which skirted the woods, and which eventually led to a narrow country lane. Fortune still favouring her, she soon came upon a local, walking in the opposite direction, who obligingly informed her that the nearest blacksmith's was in the village not two miles further along the road. Ill luck then decided to take its turn: upon arriving at the small habitation, she discovered that the blacksmith was out and wasn't expected home until lunchtime.

Accepting the set-back with a good grace, Jane left the hired mount at the smithy, and strolled round the village, passing the time of day with several inhabitants and inspecting the small church. She returned to the forge on the stroke of one, only to discover that the blacksmith had still not returned. His wife, however, being a kind-hearted soul, took pity on the pretty young stranger and promptly invited her to wait in the comfort of the house.

Jane needed no second prompting. Nor was she too proud to accept the kind offer of a bite to eat, and during the nourishing meal of cheese and crusty home-made bread, followed by a slice of delicious apple tart, she was regaled with a humorous account of life in the small Wiltshire village.

It transpired that the blacksmith's wife had lived in the village all her life. She knew most everyone residing in the surrounding area, and was related in some way to a great many of them.

"Then you are more than likely acquainted with the people living in that charming thatched cottage by the woods some two miles from here," Jane remarked, unable to let this golden opportunity of discovering to whom she owed a debt of gratitude for her comfortable accommodation the previous night slip by.

"Oh, you must mean Percy and Alice Price's place up by Bencham Wood!" the blacksmith's wife announced after a moment's thought. "Yes, I know them very well. He's a carpenter by trade. Very clever with his hands, is old Percy. It's a nice little place, but I shouldn't care to be stuck out there all by myself. They seem contented, though. Lived there for years, so they 'ave."

"Strange that there was no one about when I called this morning, don't you think?" The look Jane received in response to this, if not precisely suspicious, was certainly very thoughtful, and so, with scant regard for the truth, she hurriedly added, "I'm staying with friends who reside some few miles from here. It was such a lovely morning that I decided to go out for a ride. It was in the woods that my horse decided to cast a shoe, so I called at that cottage to ask the whereabouts of the nearest blacksmith. But as I've already mentioned the place appeared to be deserted."

The explanation seemed to satisfy the kindly woman. "Oh, they were probably out in the woods somewhere themselves. Alice often goes along to help her husband find a suitable tree to cut down. Except when they journey to Devizes on market days, or visit their daughter, who has a farm near the town, they never venture very far."

These snippets of information merely increased

Jane's fears that something must have happened to the Prices. It was so difficult to know what to do for the best. She didn't wish to raise the alarm, and instigate a thorough search of the woods, only to discover that the errant couple had merely paid a visit to their daughter and for some reason had delayed their return.

She glanced at the grandfather clock, solemnly ticking away the passing of time, in the corner of the room. She really ought to have been in Devizes herself by now, arranging for the hire of a carriage, but there was little she could do until the blacksmith returned. She only hoped he wouldn't be too much longer, otherwise Tom wouldn't only be concerned over the whereabouts of the Prices, but would be frantic over her long absence, too.

It just so happened that Tom, having just satis-fied his own hunger from the ample supplies in the larder, was not unduly worried as yet. He hadn't wanted her to go, it was true, but what choice had he but to capitulate? He was in no fit state to go himself, and wasn't foolish enough to suppose that the wound in his leg would have healed very much by tomorrow. None the less, if

Jane was unable to hire a carriage, which was certainly a real possibility at this time of year when many more people were inclined to travel, then he would ride over to Devizes with her first thing in the morning, injured leg or no.

Every hour she was alone in his company compromised her further. If she didn't realise that, he most certainly did. He hadn't saved her from Fairfax's infamous clutches only to force her into a union with himself. So, the sooner she reached the safety of her aunt's house in Bath the better, even if it meant her continuing the journey on the common stage.

The thought that he would be parting from her soon was a far from pleasant one. He succeeded to a certain extent in forcing it from his mind as he took a leisurely stroll outside, examining the exterior of the cottage and its several outbuildings, but his injured leg began to protest after a while, giving him little choice but to return indoors and patiently await Jane's return.

Although he had recourse to his pocket-watch on numerous occasions, it wasn't until the afternoon was well advanced, and she still had failed to return, that he began to grow uneasy. Clouds, darkly threatening, had been gradually building up from the west, and by early evening it was raining quite hard, adding to his ever increasing disquiet. He had just decided that he could bear the waiting no longer and, foolish though it might have been, had made up his mind to go searching for her, when he detected the blessed sound of a horse's hooves.

A few minutes later the door opened, a bedraggled and sodden Jane stepped over the threshold, and Tom's anxiety found release in a thundering tirade.

Jane could not recall being scolded so comprehensively in her life before, and she might have been suitably chastened if it hadn't been for the fact that she was in a rare ill humour herself. "Where the devil do you think I've been, you stupid creature?" she snapped back. "I've spent the whole day waiting to get that dratted horse shod. I never even went to Devizes. And how dare you lecture me in such a fashion?"

"You deserve more than a telling-off, my girl," he retorted, eyes glinting threateningly, but Jane refused to be cowed.

"If you dare say another word to me, Thomas Carrington, I'll…I'll throw something at you!"

She looked as if she meant it, too! Which, perversely, amused him, with the result that his own anger began to subside. He looked at her closely for the first time. Droplets of water running down the folds of the old borrowed cloak had already made a sizeable puddle about her sodden feet, and she was trembling, though whether this was from cold or temper he wasn't quite sure.

"Come and get yourself warm," he coaxed, and she responded instantly to the much gentler tone, leaving clear footprints across the flagstone floor as she moved towards the range. He managed to persuade her to give him the cloak and her pelisse, and to remove her calf-boots, but when he asked her to step out of her dress she regarded him as though he had taken leave of his senses.

"I'm not standing here in just my petticoats, Dr Carrington!"

"Quite right, m'dear. I want everything. And please don't argue!" he ordered, when she opened her mouth to do just that. "You're soaked to the skin, and I've enough to contend with without having you on my hands suffering a raging fever."

His voice might have sounded quite matter-of-fact, faintly bored, even, but there could be no mistaking the determination in his eyes, and she realised that if she didn't do as she was told he wasn't above undressing her with his own hands. She waited until he had disappeared into the bed-chamber before grappling with the hooks on her dress, and only just stepped out of its sodden folds when he came back into the kitchen, carrying a blanket.

"What? Not finished yet?" he remarked, with what she considered a tactless disregard for her acute embarrassment. "Need any help?"

"No, I do not!" she snapped, only just managing to suppress the urge to box his ears soundly. "And kindly turn your back. I've no intention of dis-robing with you looking on."

Tom cast her an impatient glance, but did as she asked. "Might I remind you that I am a physician, and quite accustomed to seeing members of your sex in a state of undress."

"I dare say," she responded, hurriedly stepping out of her pantalets and wrapping herself in the blanket, which he had obligingly tossed on the settle behind her, before seating herself close to the range, "but you are not my doctor. All right, you can turn round now."

Smiling in spite of the fact that he found the whole maidenly performance faintly ludicrous, Tom bent to pick up the discarded garments. After placing them over a metal rail near the stove, he knelt carefully on the floor in front of her, so as not to put too much strain on his injured leg, and, ignoring her squeal of protest, placed her slender feet on his knee and began to rub the circulation back into her frozen limbs.

Jane dared not put up any kind of struggle for fear of losing her grasp on the blanket, and tried her best to ignore warm hands that might have been rubbing vigorously enough to remove a layer of skin, but were, none the less, having a disturbing effect on her pulse rate as they moved up and down her legs from slender thighs to trim ankles.

"Right," he announced finally, rising again to his feet, but not before giving the top of her left leg an over-familiar and hearty smack. "I'll get us something to eat, while you stay precisely where you are."

The comfortable warmth of the kitchen was swiftly restoring her usual sunny humour, and his continuing authoritative tone no longer had the power to annoy her. She could even, now, smile at the fact that it wasn't precisely the way she had envisaged celebrating the attainment of her majority, and echoed her thoughts aloud.

"It's your birthday? Oh, yes! I recall your mentioning it when I last dined with the Knightleys. Why on earth didn't you remind me?"

"Surprisingly enough, the fact entirely slipped my mind until I was returning here in the pouring rain, feeling mighty sorry for myself," she admitted, taking the bread and cheese he held out and refraining from remarking on the fact that it was precisely what she had eaten at luncheon. It would have sounded so peevish, so ungrateful. And ingratitude was the last thing she felt towards this man, she decided, watching him search through the well-stocked larder, before walking back towards her with a bottle in his hand.

It wasn't precisely claret or burgundy, but Jane enjoyed the home-made wine all the same, and it did fortify her to a certain extent for his next very touching gesture—one that she was to remember and cherish until the day she died.

Delving into his breeches pocket, he drew out the exquisite pearl brooch and, reaching forward, placed it into her hand. "Happy birthday," he said simply.

It was a moment or two before she could swallow the obstruction blocking her throat to enable her to say, "Tom, I cannot accept this. It was your grandmother's—the only keepsake you have to remind you of her."

"I never knew her, Jane, so it holds little sentimental value for me. Most of the time it lies in a drawer, forgotten. I'm certain my grandmother would wholeheartedly approve of seeing it in its proper place—adorning the gown of a lady of quality.

"Now, you've had a long day, so it would be sensible to retire early," he went on, with an abrupt return to authoritative mode. "We'll need to make an early start in the morning if we're to reach Devizes with a reasonable chance of securing a carriage to take you to Bath. You have the bed tonight. I'll be quite comfortable here in this chair, with my feet resting on the stool."

Jane didn't attempt to argue. She was feeling weary, and still more than a little overcome by the generosity of his lovely gift. Remaining only for the time it took to collect and light a candle, she went into the bedchamber, and didn't waste any time in getting into the comfortable bed. Which was perhaps just as well as Tom, without so much as a knock, came striding in a few moments later to ask if she required a nightgown.

Yet a further example of how thoughtful he could be. What an enigma the man was! "I think

I shall be warm enough, thank you." She smiled a trifle ruefully. "Besides, we've taken enough liberties without my making free with Mrs Price's night attire."

"Price…? Is that their name?"

"Apparently so. The blacksmith's wife seemed to know everyone living in these parts." Jane's frown clearly betrayed her continuing unease. "Apart from the odd trip to Devizes, the Prices never go anywhere—which is rather worrying. I think we should inform the authorities tomorrow, don't you?"

"It certainly would be the very least we could do after making use of their home, but—" he shrugged "—I'm not unduly concerned, at least not now."

She didn't perfectly understand this. "Why? What do you mean?"

"Whilst you were out, I had a little look round the place," he explained, seating himself on the edge of the bed without conscious thought. "There are clear tracks—a cart's, I suspect—leading into and from that large stable. And there is evidence enough to suggest that they keep at least one horse. It was market day in Devizes yesterday, so I should imagine that is precisely where our errant benefactors were bound. The reason for their non-return, of course, remains a mystery."

She made no response to this, and Tom, who had been contemplating one ornately carved bedpost, wondering if it might not be an example of their host's fine workmanship, turned his attention back to her.

For several moments he stared into those beautifully coloured eyes, framed in lashes so long that they brushed against the delicate skin beneath, before transferring his gaze to the gorgeous russet-coloured locks, still slightly damp after her uncomfortable ride back to the cottage. Only a few feather-light tendrils caressed the unlined forehead, while the rest cascaded down to slender shoulders, perfect and white, rising above the bedcovers. Some detached part of his brain registered the tiny pulsating throb in the slender column of her neck, before he focused his attention on the gentle curve of her jaw and finally the perfect symmetry of a sweetly curved mouth.

He could feel his doctor's mantle slipping away and with it the iron control he had exerted over himself, allowing the virile male to surface and the raw, overwhelming desire he felt for this lovely young woman to take over. He lowered his head and his mouth captured hers, gently at first and then with a deepening hunger as he swiftly attained the response he needed to begin to satisfy this ever increasing longing for total fulfilment—which would be as new for him as it was for her, simply because it was engendered by love, not lust.

No thought of resistance had entered Jane's head. Her lips had parted instinctively and so willingly that she could no longer be deaf to the sweet message her young heart had been transmitting for days. She had fallen deeply in love. Now heart, mind and body were in such complete accord that when his lips left hers and began to explore the swell of her responsive breasts, and infinitely gentle fingers sought to caress and probe that softest of flesh between her thighs, she experienced no fear, only a desire for the increasingly pleasurable sensations rippling through her never to end, and an urgent need to caress and explore his body in return.

As her unpractised hands sought the lapels of his coat in a desperate attempt to ease it from him, he raised himself up and obliged her by shrugging his arms free and tossing the expertly tailored garment to the floor. His cravat and shirt quickly followed, offering her the unfettered view of magnificent shoulders and a broad and well-formed chest with its covering of dark, slightly curling hair.

Impatient to touch him, to feel that muscular strength beneath her fingertips, she reached out eagerly for the contact to begin, only to have her hand captured in a bone-crushing grip. His eyes, which only moments before had been devouring her every naked curve, were now fixed on the chest of drawers beside the bed. With his head slightly averted, she could no longer read the message their grey depths contained, but she sensed the drastic change in him, even before his every muscle seemed suddenly to grow taut.

Then, as though he could bear to touch her no longer, he thrust her hand aside, and rose from the bed. Quickly sweeping up his discarded garments, he stormed across to the door in three giant strides. "Don't dare to leave this bedchamber tonight for any reason," he rasped, before slamming the door closed behind him with a finality that left Jane devastated and with the wretched conviction that her eagerness to show her love had only succeeded in giving him a disgust of her.

Chapter Eleven

Jane woke to see a ray of bright morning sunshine filtering between the gap in the curtains. How she wished there were some way that warm shaft of light could melt the ice-cold misery encasing her heart, and penetrate the tangled, dark mass of conflicting thoughts in her brain! She might then be able to see, to understand what had wrought the sudden and drastic change in the man she loved, turning him in a matter of seconds from a gentle, considerate lover into a cold, unfeeling brute who seemed unable to look at her, let alone touch her.

It all seemed like some fiendish bad dream now, leaving her wondering whether she could any longer distinguish fact from fancy. Surely she had not misread the signs so badly? True—no words of love had passed his lips, but there had been such depth of feeling, such loving tenderness in his eyes before he had kissed her.

She shook her head, uncertain what to believe, but she refused to shy away from the very real possibility that whatever feelings he might have experienced were not strong enough to withstand the possible outcome of satisfying their mutual passion—were not sincere enough to prompt him to do the honourable thing and marry her… After all, what other possible explanation could there be?

The silent, bitter tears she had wept after he had left the room had in no way helped to ease the biting misery of total rejection, and she had no intention of giving way to such feminine weakness again. Thankfully, sleep, when it had eventually claimed her, had somehow managed to restore a modicum of self-esteem. She was Lady Beresford, the Earl of Eastbury's daughter, a young woman who had been taught from a young age to consider any display of forceful emotion as faintly vulgar, and for once in her life she appreciated this instilled doctrine. He had to be faced and, vastly humiliating though the prospect was, she fully intended to do it with dignity and with her head held high.

Without giving herself time to delay the inevitable a moment longer, she swung her feet to the floor, and noticed for the first time her clothes, placed neatly over the back of the chair. Just as she had done the previous morning, he had at some point slipped back into the room. She hadn't been aware of his presence, but then, perhaps, he had preferred it that way. No doubt he was looking forward to their next encounter with as little enthusiasm as she was herself.

She discovered him seated at the table when she entered the kitchen a few minutes later. The food on his plate appeared untouched, giving her every reason to suppose that either he had only just sat down, or his appetite had deserted him. There seemed to be a certain droop to his shoulders this morning, and, had she not been given a cruelly sharp lesson in the sheer folly of reading too much into a person's expression, she might have supposed that there was a look of complete desolation in those grey eyes of his. But she was wiser now.

He was possibly suffering from nothing more than lack of sleep because he had spent an uncomfortable night in the chair, she decided, joining him at the table, and not because he had been tormented with pangs of remorse over his behaviour. No, that wasn't fair, the voice of conscience told her. He wasn't an unfeeling care-for-nobody, and it would be grossly unjust to label him so. Of course he must regret what had taken place between them, must deplore his weakness in giving way to his baser instincts, but she refused to allow herself to indulge in the foolish hope that his air of despondency stemmed from anything more profound than that.

"Ah! Bread and cheese again," she remarked when he just stared at her across the table, not making the least attempt to converse. "I think when I've left this place I shan't choose to sample this particular fare again for some considerable time."

This brought a faint twitching to one corner of his mouth. "Yes, it certainly does become monotonous after a time, but I didn't wish to waste time cooking. It would be best if we made an early start."

Which was tantamount to telling her, of course, that he wished to be rid of her company as quickly as possible, she thought miserably. Not only had he thrust the knife in, but he was cruelly twisting it, too!

Once again the proud blood of her noble ancestors coursing through her veins came to her aid and, refusing to betray just how deeply he had wounded her, she said, sounding sublimely unconcerned at the prospect of their parting, "I'm in complete agreement with you. I must reach Bath today. Heaven only knows what my aunt must be thinking! Poor dear, she must be out of her mind with worry."

He regarded her for a moment in subdued silence, his eyes holding hers as though by some hypnotic force. "Janie, about last night—"

"I would prefer not to discuss what took place between us," she interrupted and, reaching for the coffee-pot, was appalled to see her hand trembling slightly. "It was most regrettable, and best forgotten."

"Yes, perhaps... But—"

"No, Tom!" she cut in more sharply this time, trying desperately to control the rapidly mounting hysteria. Why must he torment her like this? Dear Lord! Was he so insensitive that he didn't realise just how much he had hurt and humiliated her? Surely he didn't imagine that she was some light-skirt who bedded any man who happened to take her fancy?

She wanted nothing more than to run from him, and might well have done so had she not suddenly detected a noise outside. Seemingly Tom heard it too, for he rose to his feet at once.

"It looks as if the owners have at last returned,"

he said, reaching the window in time to see a lumbering cart come to a halt, and a middle-aged woman climbing down from the seat.

Jane wished the ground beneath her would open and swallow her up. She might have been spared the humiliation of having to discuss an incident she would far rather be allowcd to forget, but now it seemed she was to suffer the embarrassment of trying to explain her presence in this cottage. Life could be mercilessly cruel at times!

Tom, easily discerning the look of entreaty in her eyes, responded instantly to the unspoken cry for help and limped over to the door. Jane heard him say clearly, "Pray, madam, do not be alarmed," before he introduced himself, though the exchanges which followed were just a series of muffled sounds.

It seemed an eternity before the door was thrown wide again, and much of Jane's acute discomfiture disappeared at the sight of the plump, middle-aged woman, whose gait could best be described as waddling, entering the spacious kitchen.

"Oh, Miss Carrington, you poor child! What a terrible thing to have happened to you! Set upon by such rogues, and your dear brother injured, too!"

Not only was the stranger, who she assumed

was Mrs Price, a kindly soul, but very tactile, too. Jane rose from the table and instantly found herself encircled by a pair of fleshy arms for a few moments, which gave her just sufficient time to accept her surprising new identity. What else had her resourceful *brother* told them? Thank heavens he at least had his wits about him!

"Indeed, yes, ma'am. Vastly unpleasant! And I must thank you for your kind understanding at finding strangers making free with your charming home. But we had little choice, I'm afraid."

"Don't you give it another thought, my pet. I'm very glad now I did forget to lock the door. Though I didn't realise I'd done so at the time, of course. We left for Devizes in such a hurry on market day."

Jane cast a fleeting glance across at the afore-mentioned door, wishing fervently that Tom would return and offer some guidance as to the story he'd told. "I did learn that you might have gone to Devizes," she responded, feeling reasonably safe by continuing along this particular avenue. "I called on a blacksmith in a small village not very far from here to get the horse shod, and the lady at the forge seemed to know you quite well. Your name is Price, I believe?"

"That's right, my dear." She raised her eyes

heavenwards. "There isn't much the smithy's wife don't know. No doubt she kept you talking all day."

Jane couldn't help smiling at this. Evidently the blacksmith's wife had earned herself something of a reputation for gossiping. "I'm afraid she did, but that was because her husband didn't return until latc. I was hoping to ride over to Devizes myself to hire a carriage, but I'm afraid I never made it that far."

Mrs price gave Jane's arm a fond pat. "Well, don't you worry your pretty head over that. My husband will take you and your brother over to town when you're ready to leave, if you don't mind travelling in the cart?"

"And is that not kind of them, Jane?" Tom remarked, thankfully not delaying his return a moment longer. Their eyes met across the room—Jane's with a look of comical dismay, Tom's sparkling with devilment and just for a moment there was a resurgence of that wonderful rapport which had existed between them.

"I've just been telling Mr Price, here," he went on, gesturing to the man who was as lean as his wife was plump, "how we lost one of our horses during the attack, but managed to make it here just on my hired mount."

Jane merely smiled in response, deeming it safer to leave all explanations to her very inventive *brother's* fertile mind. They had at some point possessed a second horse... Now why was that? she wondered. She wasn't left in ignorance for long.

"I was escorting my sister to our aunt's house in Bath." Tom addressed himself to Mrs price who was regarding him with patent approval. "We spent the night in Devizes, and I suddenly took it into my head to pay a visit to an acquaintance of mine, Sir William Dent, but, as I mentioned outside, we fell foul of some ruffians, after my purse, I suppose, and never made it to our destination."

Jane realised that he had evidently considered carefully before mentioning Sir William Dent, believing, no doubt, that the Prices, although perhaps not acquainted with him personally, must surely have heard of the famous surgeon. The gamble paid off, for the Prices seemed to require no further explanations, or assurances that the young couple were perfectly respectable.

"And, naturally, I shall reimburse you for the provisions we've consumed whilst we've been here, Mrs Price."

"Pshaw!" She dismissed the idea with a wave of her plump hand. "What's a few victuals?

Besides, had it not been for you locking my chickens up at night, I swear the fox would have had most of 'em by now. That were the only thing that concerned me whilst we were away. But what could I do when our only daughter's first decides to come early?"

She had addressed her latter remarks to Jane, expecting a female to understand her dilemma perfectly, and she wasn't disappointed. Tom, however, fearing that the ensuing conversation on the joys of having grandchildren was likely to be a lengthy one, experienced no qualms in interrupting and reminding his *sister* that they really ought to be on their way.

Within a very short space of time Mrs Price, smiling broadly, stood outside, waving a last farewell to the delightful young couple, but as she went about her morning's work her round, normally cheerful face began increasingly to wear a very thoughtful expression. She grew impatient for her husband's return, and when he did eventually arrive home, in good time for his midday meal, she didn't waste a moment in asking whether the young couple were now safely on their way to Bath.

"I 'eard 'im ask about 'iring a carriage when

we arrived at The Swan. And he 'as been putting up there 'cause the landlady knew 'im. Funny thing, though..." He scratched his grizzled mop of hair. "She didn't seem to recognise the young lady."

"I knew it!" Mrs Price clapped her hands together in triumph. "Suspicioned as much right from the start!"

Her husband looked about the room in some alarm. "Don't tell me they really were thieves, Alice! Dear Lord! What's missing?"

"Nothing, you old fool," she responded lovingly. "They weren't no thieves... But they weren't brother and sister, neither, if I'm any judge. I reckon they were a pair o' runaways."

This pronouncement didn't appeal to the bewildered Mr Price any more than the idea that he might have been robbed. He tut-tutted. "Right rum goings-on, I must say. And in our 'ome, too!"

"Now, Percy, I'm not suggesting for a moment that anything of that sort's been taking place. In fact, I don't think it 'as at all. When I went into t'other room to change the sheets, I noticed only one side of the bed 'ad been slept in. And there was a blanket folded up on the settle, so I reckon the young doctor slept in 'ere."

He cast her a look of exasperation. "What the devil are you talking about, then, woman?"

Mrs Price betrayed no outward sign of having taken offence at her husband's impatient tone. In fact, she looked as if she hadn't heard him at all. She just sat staring across the room, gazing at nothing in particular, for several thoughtful moments before saying, "It was almost as if they were trying as hard as they could not to show their feelings…even to each other." Her eyes suddenly brightened with a triumphant glow. "But they didn't fool me. No, not for a moment! You'd need to be blind or just plain stupid not to see those two young people are deeply in love."

The passage of time might have taken its toll on Lady Augusta Templehurst's eyesight, but certainly not on her intellect. Her thought processes were as razor-sharp as they had been in her youth. Consequently, when her niece finally arrived at Upper Camden Place late that afternoon, it didn't take her very long to come to the conclusion that the explanation offered for the belated arrival was far from the complete story. Nor did she suppose for a moment that the theft of belongings by a disloyal servant was responsible for her niece's very melancholy air. Wisely, though, she chose not to pry further, believing that in time she would be regaled with a full account of the happenings during the eventful journey to Bath.

During the following few days Lady Templehurst concentrated her efforts on replenishing part of the stolen wardrobe. She derived much enjoyment from accompanying Jane to the fashionable shops, and gained a great deal of satisfaction in finding her niece a new personal maid, whose creative fingers and sunny disposition could not fail to please.

She never tired of her favourite niece's company, and in the normal course of events would have found much pleasure in their daily visit to the Pump Room and the evenings spent at the Assembly Rooms and at private parties, but her satisfaction was marred by the fact that she knew Jane was not obtaining equal enjoyment from her stay.

Lady Augusta's reputation as a formidable matron had been well earned. Her abrasive wit and knife-edged tongue, an awesome combination, remained potent enough, even in her declining years, to cut any presumptuous character down to size, but no one could ever have accused her of being vindictive or heartlessly cruel. None the less, she would have been the first to admit that she was not blessed with any degree of patience, and, after almost two weeks of being subjected to her niece's alternating moods of forced gaiety and despondency, what tolerance she happened to possess rapidly began to wane.

Things came to a head one morning at breakfast. Lady Templehurst had just finished reading aloud a letter she had received from her brother's son and heir, and looked up to find her niece in one of her ever increasing moods of abstraction, gazing aimlessly out of the parlour window.

"Well?" she prompted.

"Yes, I'm glad George is well," Jane responded vaguely. "I hope Matilda is, too."

Lady Templehurst raised her eyes ceilingwards. "I knew you hadn't been attending to a single word I said!"

The impatient tone had the desired effect, for Jane cast her aunt an enquiring glance. "Evidently you find your brother's missives as tedious as I do myself, dear, so I shan't risk boring you further by asking you to read it for yourself, but shall enlighten you again as to its contents."

After placing the letter down by her plate, she

gazed fixedly across the table, just to ensure she still retained her niece's full attention. "In his usual arrogant fashion my nephew has taken it upon himself to organise your life and include you in the small family party that intends travelling to Paris to meet up with your father who, it seems, has decided to leave Italy sooner than originally planned and remain for a short time in that gay city.

"George impertinently informs me that he is sending your father's carriage to collect you next week. In the normal course of events I would not have hesitated in ordering your father's coachman to tool the carriage, unoccupied, straight back to Kent, but in view of your present highly lethargic state I do not suppose for a moment that it is unduly important whether you are miserably discontent in Paris or Bath, or anywhere else for that matter."

Jane was one of the few people who never took offence at any of her redoubtable relative's pithy utterances. And in this instance she had to own that the biting sarcasm had been fully justified. She had tried so very hard to feign pleasure in a visit that would normally have afforded tremendous enjoyment, but she had to face the fact that she simply wasn't adept enough in the gentle art of dissimulation. Her character was far too open for that. All her efforts had been in vain. She had fooled no one, least of all the wily Lady Templehurst.

She cast her aunt a look of apology. "I've been abysmal company, haven't I?"

"Yes, my dear, you have," was the brutally honest response.

"I'm so very sorry."

"I do not doubt it for a moment, my love. Unfortunately, just an apology will not improve your present state of mind." Her eyes never wavered from her niece's lovely face. "But a truthful account of what precisely befell you during your journey from Hampshire just possibly might."

Jane regarded her aunt with a mixture of gentle affection and admiration. She might have guessed that the explanation offered for her belated arrival in Bath had been met with a certain amount of scepticism.

"What I told you before was not a complete pack of lies, Aunt Augusta. My former maid did pretend to be unwell, but we didn't stay over-night at an inn, and I did not awake the following morning to find both Latimer and my belongings gone. Nor did I remain a further day in order to inform the authorities and instigate a search for her," she freely admitted, before going on to offer the truthful account.

"You showed great presence of mind, Jane," Lady Templehurst remarked with an appreciative gleam, when her niece paused for a moment in her colourful recitation.

"I would not have escaped so easily, Aunt, if Latimer had not left the door unlocked. And I truly believe that was no accident on her part."

"Then it is much to her credit, and I can quite understand your reluctance to inform the authorities of her involvement. Though I must confess it grieves me to think Simon Fairfax will go unpunished. Like father like son, it would seem. I have always disliked Lord Fairfax intensely."

"Unfortunately, Lady Fairfax is a friend of Mama's, so you can appreciate my dilemma."

"Your mother has much to answer for, and not only in her choice of friends," Lady Templehurst responded with unbridled censure. "But, pray continue, my dear. We had reached the point where you had managed to escape from the house. What befell you next?"

All at once Lady Augusta perceived a change

in her niece. She seemed suddenly to grow tense, her eyes clouding with that far-away, almost desolate look all too often seen since her arrival in Bath, but she continued her story in a clear, unwavering voice.

"And this friend of the Knightleys—you think he can be trusted not to betray the fact that you spent two nights in his company?" Lady Templehurst enquired when at last she had learned all.

The answer when it came was succinct and decisive. "Yes."

"You seem very certain of that, Jane."

"I am. Dr Thomas Carrington is a man of honour."

Lady Templehurst's lips curled into a knowing half-smile. "A rare man, indeed." There was a significant pause. "But then, it would take a rare man to capture your heart, would it not, my dear Jane?"

The iron resolve finally crumpled. Lady Templehurst was out of the chair and beside her niece with quite remarkable speed for a woman of her advanced years. Gathering Jane into her arms, she allowed her to cry out her heartfelt misery unrestrainedly.

When at last the tears began to subside she said, with the honesty for which she was famed, "I

reserve the right to pronounce judgement when I have met this paragon of yours, Jane, and not before. Nevertheless, I shall not insult your intelligence by pretending that I am overjoyed with your choice of mate, although his station in life could hardly be described as contemptible. You may be certain of one thing, my child:
 if I do like him, and if I believe you would suit, then you shall marry your young doctor with my full blessing." She was at her most imperious. "And woe betide any member of the family who dares to prevent a union between you!"

Jane gazed up at her aunt with deep affection. "I do not doubt for a moment that you would make the staunchest of allies, but the need for your support will not arise." She couldn't prevent her lip from trembling, but managed to control the threat of more tears. "The reason I shall never marry Dr Carrington isn't because I fear my family's opposition to the match, but simply because Tom doesn't care for me deeply enough to ask for my hand."

Chapter Twelve

Tom reached for the quill and jotted a reminder in his diary to visit the rector's wife the following afternoon. Really, he was becoming quite forgetful of late. Important matters that once he would never have forgotten now seemed to slip his mind completely.

After sanding down the single entry in his bold, flowing hand, he was about to close the book, when his attention was drawn to the date printed at the top of the page, and he experienced yet again a resurgence of that distressing ache which, if the truth be known, never left him completely. Was it really just three short weeks since his return from Wiltshire? Dear God! It seemed like three years.

He released his breath in a sigh of doleful resignation. No man could have tried harder to put the past behind him and get on with life, but it was hopeless. Even his work, which he had thrown himself into with renewed vigour, had proved an insufficient remedy to heal a mind all too frequently tortured by images of a lovely aristocratic lady, whose indomitable spirit and ever lively sense of humour had captured his heart in a way that mere beauty never could.

The door opening intruded into his bitter-sweet reflections, and he looked up to see his housekeeper enter his consulting-room. "A visitor for you, Dr Carrington," she said, and a moment later Lady Knightley appeared before him.

Not even the sight of his dear friend could lift his spirits, but he did manage a semblance of a smile before inviting her to sit down. "By your healthy bloom I can safely assume that you do not require my professional services."

"Which is perhaps just as well," she returned, if not precisely sharply, then certainly with an edge to her normally pleasant voice. "I've a feeling I should need to be at death's door before you could bestir yourself to visit the Hall. You haven't called in to see us once since your return from Wiltshire."

Tom glanced away from eyes that reminded him too painfully of someone else's, and under the pretext of placing his diary back into the top drawer of his desk he averted his face. Elizabeth knew him better, perhaps, than anyone else, and she was an extremely perceptive young woman. It wouldn't do to give her an inkling of what was torturing him during his every waking moment.

"As you can imagine I've been extremely busy. My young apothecary can deal with most things whilst I'm away, but there are certain cases he cannot handle."

"I do know how hard you work, Tom. But you need to relax sometimes. You are becoming more and more antisocial. And I'm not the only person to remark upon it."

"I'm sure the local gossipmongers are very well aware that I was socialising only last Friday when I attended Margaret and Sam's wedding celebration."

Elizabeth opened her mouth to respond to this, but then thought better of it, and merely watched in silence as he rose to his feet and began to clear the papers from his desk.

"There's only so much time a busy practitioner has to himself. So, if there's nothing else, perhaps you'll excuse me?"

Elizabeth received her congé without so much

as a blink, but felt understandably hurt by this seeming indifference to her company. She knew Tom could be irascible at times and that his language was frequently blunt, but she had never known him to behave quite so uncivilly before, at least not to her. There was definitely something troubling him deeply.

She echoed her thoughts aloud when she rejoined her husband in his curricle a few minutes later. "I suspected when I bumped into him last week that something was preying on his mind," she went on to confess. "I thought at the time it might have something to do with Margaret Ryan's wedding, but now I'm not so certain."

She caught her husband's rather sheepish expression, and couldn't prevent a smile. "Oh, come, Richard! Surely you do not suppose for a moment that I'm naive enough to believe, simply because Tom isn't married, that he practises celibacy? He and Margaret Ryan have been much more than just friends for years. I do not doubt for a moment that he must have experienced some regret at losing such an obviously satisfying mistress, but I do not think it wholly responsible for his present subdued state."

"A lady of your quality oughtn't to know about

such things, let alone discuss them." Richard feigned shock before chuckling at the fulminating glance he received. "Yes, I too have noticed that Tom isn't quite himself these days," he admitted, serious once again. "But I've not the smallest intention of prying into his private affairs, if that is what you were about to suggest."

Elizabeth was sensible enough to realise that it would be pointless discussing the matter further. Richard was generously compliant over most things, but on some issues he was immovable, and interfering in other people's concerns just happened to be one of his particular taboos. He was perfectly right, of course, but that didn't prevent her from worrying, all the same.

She was still pondering over the possible reason for her friend's highly uncongenial state when Richard, with all the expertise of a nonsuch, tooled the curricle between the two solid stone pillars and into Knightley Park, and a minute or two later she saw an antiquated berline pulled up at the front of their house.

"Good heavens! Who on earth owns such an old-fashioned equipage? You haven't invited someone to stay and forgotten to mention it, have you, Richard?"

"I was about to ask you the same thing." Drawing his curricle to a halt behind the antiquated carriage, he watched two of his servants carrying luggage into the house. "Down you get. I shall be generous and allow you to have your curiosity satisfied first."

Elizabeth needed no second prompting. Leaving Richard to take the curricle round to the stables, she entered the hall to find it littered with a wide assortment of baggage, and her normally very efficient young butler looking slightly harassed.

"I apologise for the clutter, my lady, only the visitor has just this moment arrived, and as you omitted to inform me that you were expecting a guest I was in some doubt as to which bedchamber to give her."

Elizabeth swooped down on the butler's most significant disclosure. "Her, Medway?"

"Lady Augusta Templehurst, my lady. I've shown her into the drawing-room."

Although she refrained from uttering any exclamation of surprise, Elizabeth was quite naturally astonished to learn the visitor's identity, and, after issuing instructions for her aunt's baggage to be carried up to the green bedchamber, she didn't waste any time in entering the drawing-room to discover the relative she had not seen for almost ten years comfortably ensconced in a chair near the hearth.

"This is a most unexpected pleasure, ma'am!"

A wicked cackle answered this. "Shock, you mean. And a gross impertinence to descend on you like this without warning. I am fully sensible of it. Come here, child, and let me look at you."

Mistress in her own home Elizabeth most definitely was, but she found herself automatically obeying the imperious command, and even went so far as to demonstrate that she hadn't taken offence at being ordered about in such a fashion by placing a chaste salute on one of her aunt's satiny pink cheeks.

"Yes," Lady Templehurst remarked after scrutinising her niece's features closely. "You and Jane are most certainly the beauties in the family. The Beresford women were always either outstandingly lovely or muffin-faced—which tells you precisely just how highly I rate the looks of the other female members of the family."

Elizabeth was unable to suppress a chuckle at this outrageous remark, and realised that Jane had not overrated their aunt's outspokenness. She felt instantly drawn to this aristocratic lady and could only wonder why, as a child, she had been somewhat in awe of her.

"You must be wondering what on earth has brought me here," Lady Templehurst said when her niece had taken the seat opposite. "Haven't set eyes on you since the day of your dear father's funeral, and I have the unmitigated gall to invite myself to your home. My only saving grace, I suppose, is that I have always kept in touch with you by letter."

"Ma'am, pray rid your mind that your presence, unexpected though it is, is not very welcome. I'm delighted that you decided to pay us a visit."

Richard entered the room at that moment and Elizabeth did not hesitate in requesting him to add his assurance that Lady Augusta's arrival was a delightful surprise.

"Indeed, it is, ma'am," he obliged with remarkable aplomb. "Jane talks of you often, and always with affection. I am delighted to make your acquaintance at last."

"Graciously said, my dear boy." Lady Templehurst wholeheartedly approved of the handsome baronet whose charm of manner was famed. "I knew your father quite well. You resemble him greatly. He was a handsome devil, too! You are a very lucky girl, Elizabeth," she added, transferring her shrewd gaze to her niece. "I wish my Jane were so fortunate."

Richard did not miss the searching glance cast in his wife's direction, and felt certain that Lady Augusta had a very specific reason for her unexpected visit. However, after handing the lady a glass of Madeira, he merely asked how long they could expect the privilege of her company.

"Two days. Three at the most," she responded, after sampling the excellent wine. "I have no intention of inflicting my presence on you for any great length of time."

"You are welcome to remain as long as you wish, Aunt."

"That is very kind of you, Elizabeth, but I shan't impose on your gracious hospitality for long. I must reach Kent by the end of the week to stay with Jane." She took a further fortifying sip of Madeira before placing the glass down on the table by her chair. "My nephew George, the impertinent young jackanapes, had the temerity to request his sister's early return from Bath in order to accompany him and that feather-brained chit he married to Paris. Jane, being a young woman of superior sense, wasn't very enthusiastic at the prospect of spending several weeks in the French capital with her parents, her brother, eldest sister and their respective spouses. And who can blame her for that?"

Elizabeth frowned slightly. "Why on earth didn't she remain in Bath with you, ma'am?"

"Because I'm a selfish old woman, my dear. I rub along tolerably well with my brother. Much preferred your father, though. Never made any secret of that. Ten minutes in the Countess's company is more than enough for anyone. And with the exception of Jane, who's the best out of the lot of 'em by far, I'm not overly fond of their offspring, either. So I thought I'd take this opportunity, whilst the family is away, to visit the ancestral home one last time."

She paused for a moment to reach for her glass. "But, since Jane left Bath I've been thinking that I might like to take her to London. She seemed in a strangely subdued frame of mind whilst she was staying with me, and I thought a few weeks in London might be just the thing to cheer her up."

Richard regarded their visitor levelly, his expression giving nothing away, but Elizabeth displayed quite open surprise at this disclosure. "She seemed in excellent spirits during her stay with us, ma'am. I wonder what could have occurred to upset her? Although—" she turned to her husband "—she was somewhat concerned about her friend Lord Pentecost."

"Yes, she told me all about that." Like Sir Richard's, Lady Templehurst's expression gave nothing away, but inwardly she was delighted, for Elizabeth had unwittingly told her precisely what she had come here to discover: the Knightleys were in complete ignorance of what had befallen Jane after she had left the safety of their home.

"Never cared for Lady Pentecost," she admitted, without the least hesitation. "Odious woman! That's a further reason for visiting the capital. There's someone there I think it might be beneficial to see over that particular matter. You probably know him, Richard—Sir Bartholomew Rudge."

"I've met him, ma'am, certainly. Who hasn't? Plays too high for me. One of Prinney's set."

"Yes, he is, but then he always was a fool," she remarked in her usual forthright manner. "And he's never improved with age. But if you want to discover something, he's the one to ask. There isn't much that goes on that he doesn't know about."

After finishing off her wine, Lady Templehurst rose to her feet, with the aid of her ebony stick, and requested Elizabeth to show her to her room in order to change for dinner. "And on the way perhaps you would permit me to pay a visit to the nursery? I'm longing to meet those children of yours."

Nothing could have given Elizabeth greater pleasure. Lady Templehurst endeared herself even more by saying everything a proud mother could wish to hear about her offspring, and later, at dinner, proved herself to be an entertaining conversationalist, keeping Richard highly amused with her scathing condemnation of most members of the Beresford family.

After the meal was over they retired to the drawing-room to play a hand or two of piquet, and the evening continued to be a most enjoyable one until Lady Templehurst suddenly announced that she was not feeling well. At first she refused to entertain the idea of summoning a doctor, declaring that the discomfort would pass, but eventually acquiesced, and was comfortably tucked up in bed by the time Tom arrived.

It would have been difficult to say which of them subjected the other to the more searching scrutiny. Tom's eyes, as always, were penetratingly alert, and Lady Templehurst's gaze certainly never wavered from his direction as he entered the room and approached the bed with that smooth, long-striding gait of his.

She had never before heard her niece describe any gentleman as an ill-tempered, infuriating darling, yet she still couldn't help wondering whether Jane might not be in the grip of mere infatuation. Had Dr Carrington turned out to be a suavely elegant Adonis, she might have continued to doubt the true state of her niece's heart, but now, having seen him, she did not. Jane had fallen deeply in love with this ruggedly attractive man, whose light brown, waving hair was overlong, and whose attire, at best, could be described as casual.

"What seems to be the trouble, ma'am?" he enquired, and she discovered, quite surprisingly, that even at her age she was attracted by the throaty timbre of his voice.

"I experienced slight discomfort in my chest. Indigestion, I suspect. I do suffer from it. But Elizabeth would insist upon sending for you."

He did not respond, but seated himself on the edge of the bed and opened his medical bag to draw out a wooden cylinder about nine inches long.

"What in the name of heaven is that?" Lady Templehurst demanded to know.

"It's called a stethoscope, ma'am." He placed

one end to her chest and listened intently for a full minute. "It was invented by a French physician, René Laënnec. The story goes that he was consulted by a young woman who betrayed symptoms of heart disease. She was by all accounts a rather stout young lady, and in view of her age and sex he felt he could not resort to the usual method of examination by placing his ear to her chest."

A wicked cackle rent the air. "At my age I would be extremely flattered if a young man chose to place his cheek against my scrawny bosom!"

This ignited a spark of amusement in what she considered very attractive grey eyes. "I recall your niece remarking that you are something of a rogue, ma'am."

She was suddenly very much on her mettle. "I assume you refer to Jane. I doubt Elizabeth would ever be so impertinent." She could almost feel him stiffen, and the emotion which just for one unguarded moment flickered in the depths of his eyes told her much of what she needed to know. "May I take this opportunity, Dr Carrington, of thanking you for the care you took of my niece not so long ago? Yes," she added, in response to his all-too-obvious unspoken question. "She did inform me of precisely what befell her during her journey to Bath."

"I did precious little, ma'am." His tone was clipped—dismissive, almost. "But I'm relieved to hear that she eventually arrived at her destination without suffering further mishap."

Tom finished his examination without saying anything further, and then rose from the bed. "Your heart is fine, ma'am, but I'll leave you something to help you sleep. Tomorrow, I'll send over a draught which should help with any discomfort you may feel after meals."

After he had left, Lady Templehurst became lost in her own thoughts until there was a scratch on the door, and her maid opened it to admit Elizabeth.

"Tom informs me that there is nothing seriously wrong—thank goodness! How are you feeling now, ma'am?"

Lady Templehurst nodded dismissal to her maid, and then patted the edge of the bed. "Come here, child. I wish to speak with you." She waited until her command had been obeyed before confessing. "I had a specific reason for coming here, Elizabeth, which concerns my Jane."

"I recall your mentioning earlier that there was

something troubling her. I hope there's nothing seriously wrong."

"I'm afraid there is, my dear... She's fallen deeply in love. She's firmly convinced, however, that the gentleman who has captured her young but certainly not frivolous heart does not return her regard. But she is in error. Now, having met him, there is no doubt in my mind that he is as much in love with her as she is with him."

It did not take many moments before enlightenment dawned. "Tom!" Elizabeth exclaimed. "It's Tom, isn't it? I knew there was something, but I couldn't for the life of me think what could be making him so desperately unhappy. For that is precisely what he has been ever since he returned from Wiltshire."

"It is quite evident to me that he has confided in no one, which does that young man great credit, of course. But I think it is time you learned precisely what befell my niece after leaving the protection of your home."

Apart from the occasional exclamation of dismay, Elizabeth sat silently listening to an account of the event which had taken place during her cousin's eventful journey to Bath. When she had learned all, she said, "I can quite understand why Tom has kept silent. If that became common knowledge, Jane's reputation would be in shreds."

"Jane assures me that he did not seduce her." Lady Templehurst's rather wicked sense of humour came to the fore. "Personally, I should feel extremely aggrieved if I had spent two nights alone in the company of that wholly masculine young man and he hadn't attempted seduction!" She became serious again. "No, I mustn't laugh. It's wicked of me in view of the heartache those two young people are suffering. What I should like to know is why…? Why, if he does love her, and I'm firmly convinced that he does, has he not made an offer for her hand?"

Elizabeth was silent for a long time, and then said, "The reason may possibly be because he doesn't think he's good enough for her."

"In that case he must be brought to see the error of his ways."

"I'm afraid, Aunt Augusta, where Thomas Carrington is concerned that is far easier said than done."

Chapter Thirteen

Lady Templehurst didn't regret coming to London. After all, Jane could brood just as easily here in town as she could in Kent. She didn't regret, either, her decision in accepting Sir Richard's very generous offer of the use of his town house for the duration of their stay. It would, of course, have been perfectly possible to stay at the Beresford mansion in Grosvenor Square. Her brother, the Earl, was very generous and permitted any member of the immediate family to make use of his town residence, but, as Lady Templehurst had feared, one of Jane's sisters had already installed herself there with her husband.

It wasn't that she selfishly wished to deprive Jane of her sister's company—far from it, in fact. Unfortunately, though, her sister Lavinia was very like the Countess, needing the stimulation of continual company, and Jane was most definitely not ready, yet, to be thrust once again into the hectic social whirl most of her relations seemed to enjoy.

Raising her eyes from her embroidery, she stared across the room at her favourite niece, who was sitting in the window embrasure, staring down into the street. It would bc foolish to try to delude herself into imagining that this visit to the capital would set all to rights, but Lady Templehurst attained a modicum of satisfaction from knowing that Jane had gained some pleasure from their visit thus far. She had appeared to enjoy the few parties they had attended, and her spirits had certainly lifted whenever she had been in the company of Lord Pentecost and Miss Dilbey. However, Lady Templehurst could not be wholly content until her niece began to talk freely of the heartache she was succeeding in keeping hidden from the world at large. Not once had she mentioned Thomas Carrington's name since their arrival in town, and this, Lady Templehurst felt, was far from a good sign.

"You're very quiet, dear," she remarked, drawing her niece's attention to her. "What are you thinking about?"

"I was just wondering if you are right, Aunt

Augusta, that Hetta and Perry will make a match of it."

"All the indications are there for anyone to see, my love. I for one would applaud the match. From what you tell me the young Lord Pentecost has gained even more self-confidence since his visit to this London physician. Like his father, he will always require his periods of solitude, and I believe Miss Dilbey is very well aware of this. She's not only extremely pretty, but a very sensible young woman, and I think she'll make him the ideal wife."

She paused for a moment to set another stitch in the fire-screen she was embroidering. "I found his disclosures yesterday most interesting. His visit to the family solicitor to reacquaint himself with the contents of his father's will shows clearly enough, does it not, that he is thinking of the future? It is little wonder that he took precious little interest in his affairs after his father's demise," she went on, displaying the kind and understanding side to her nature that few people were privileged to see. "Not only was he grieving over the loss of a much loved parent, but he was battling with the added burden of believing he might one day go insane. Which is precisely why

I've asked my old friend Sir Bartholomew Rudge to visit us this morning to see if he cannot shed some light on that rather puzzling matter."

Jane remained sceptical. Although she was not well acquainted with the obese baronet, their paths had crossed from time to time during her three Seasons, but he had never struck her as a person in whom one could place much reliance.

"Sir Bartholomew may appear a buffoon," Lady Templehurst remarked, reading her niece's thoughts with uncanny accuracy, "but do not be fooled by that devil-may-care attitude he adopts. He possesses quite the most remarkable retentive memory. He can recall incidents from the distant past in minute detail. Also, little escapes his notice, and what he doesn't know about what goes on in society isn't worth knowing."

Jane's attention was once more drawn to the street below and the fashionable carriage which had just that instant pulled up at the door. "We'll soon discover whether your faith in him is justified, Aunt Augusta, for unless I'm very much mistaken, your old friend has just arrived."

Within the space of a few minutes the door opened and a rather portly gentleman, sporting a garishly coloured waistcoat, and the most preposterously large nosegay in the buttonhole of his fashionable jacket, entered the sunny front parlour. With his round face wreathed in smiles, and without uttering a word, he went directly across to Lady Templehurst and planted a smacking kiss on one of her pink cheeks.

"Couldn't believe it when I received your note, Gussie, old girl! Thought nothing would ever induce you away from that dashed watering place. Never could stand Bath myself! Must say, though, you're looking well."

"Which is more than can be said for you, Bart," she told him, with all the frankness of a long-standing friendship. "Do sit down and take all the weight off your feet."

Without betraying any outwards signs of having taken offence, he did as bidden, but made to rise again almost at once when he noticed Jane for the first time. "Sorry, m'dear. Didn't see you sitting there."

"Please don't get up, sir," Jane adjured him, fearing the procedure might prove a strenuous one for a gentleman of his size. "Might I offer you some refreshment?"

"No, thank you, m'dear. Never imbibe until after midday." He turned his attention back to

Lady Templehurst. "What a pleasure it is to see you back in town. But what the deuce are you doing here in Sir Richard Knightley's house?"

"He kindly offered me the use of it when I paid him a short visit not so very long ago, and I must say I find it infinitely more comfortable than the Beresford mansion, but that is neither here nor there. The reason I particularly requested you to visit, Bart," she said, coming straight to the point, "is because I believe you were well acquainted at one time with the late Lord Pentecost."

"And so I was," he didn't hesitate to confirm. "Considering we had little in common, we were good friends. We were at Eton together and then Oxford. Didn't see so much of him in later years, mind. Turned into something of a recluse. Still, who wouldn't," he added, "married to that harpy? Don't think he would ever have got himself leg-shackled if it hadn't been for his brother's death."

Lady Templehurst regarded him keenly. "What do you know about that, Bart? I've heard mention that the younger brother wasn't quite right in the head."

"What...?" He looked completely taken aback. "Utter rot! Don't know how these silly rumours get started. He was a quiet, reserved fellow, but a bruising young rider. Nothing wrong with the lad until he had that accident. Changed him completely, as I recall."

"What accident was that?" Lady Templehurst prompted, when her old friend fell silent.

"Oh, a very sad business. Happened during his last year up at Oxford." He shook his head as though at some private thought. "Remember it as though it were only yesterday. The late Lord Pentecost was paying one of his rare visits to London at the time. I was with him at White's when he received news that his brother had been hurt. Up to some lark, I shouldn't wonder, and went tumbling down a flight of stairs. Was unconscious for several days, if my memory serves me correctly. Recovered, but was never the same. Would fly off into almost insane rages, followed by moods of deep depression. Probably just as well that he died soon afterwards in that riding accident."

"Are you by any chance acquainted with the present Lord Pentecost?" Jane asked, after digesting these most interesting facts.

"I've met him. Strangely enough he puts me in mind of young Cedric—same build, same colouring. Noticed it at once when I came across the boy at my club t'other evening. He's even inherited his uncle's excellent seat on a horse, so I understand. Shame poor old Arthur only had the one son. He was fond of children."

"He may have been," Lady Templehurst remarked drily, recalling clearly what Perry had told them yesterday, "but that will he made certainly did his sole offspring no favours. Apparently, Bart, Peregrine cannot touch a penny of his father's private wealth, at least not the capital, until he attains the age of thirty or in the event that he marries, whichever comes first. The problem is that his mother must approve his choice of bride if he chooses to marry before he celebrates his thirtieth birthday, or the money remains in trust for the next holder of the title."

"Mmm. Bit of a rum deal, I must say," he was forced to concede. "Can only think that old Arthur must have been trying to protect his son from money-grabbing harpies."

"I believe the young Lord Pentecost has too much sense than to be beguiled by a pretty face. He has, however, become wondrous close with a young woman whom I should very much doubt would meet with his obnoxious mother's approval," Lady Templehurst announced, without the least hesitation, knowing that her old friend could be trusted to keep this information to himself.

He cocked one greying brow. "Shabby-genteel, eh?"

"No such thing! Good family. Related to the Devonshire Dilbeys. She has no money…at least, only what she can expect to inherit from her uncle. But in every other respect she would suit admirably. She's a very sensible young woman, and she's fond of him, too."

"If the gel's all you say she is, why do you suppose Sophia Pentecost would oppose the match?"

"I suspect," Jane put in, once again drawing the baronet's round, childlike eyes in her direction, "it's because she is unwilling to relinquish her position as mistress of Pentecost Grange. I do not think she would approve of any female Perry wishes to marry."

"Well, there's usually a solution to be found to most problems," he announced, after a moment's intense thought. "Merely need to spike her guns."

"And how do you suggest one goes about doing that?" Lady Templehurst asked, completely at a loss.

"Dear me, Gussie, old girl. Your years in Bath

have addled your wits!" His large stomach shook in response to the fulminating glance she cast him. He still had a soft spot deep down for the woman whom many years before he himself had considered marrying, but he had never repined when she had chosen Lord Templehurst. He had enjoyed the freedom of his bachelor existence.

"You are still someone, Augusta," he told her. "It's a simple matter, surely, of rallying enough of your old cronies to the cause? Get enough of 'em to approve the match, then Sophia Pentecost would look nohow trying to oppose it. Why, I might even lend you my support. I've never cared for the dragon-lady myself."

Lady Templehurst betrayed all the exuberance of an excited child. "By heaven, Bart! You might just have something there!"

Jane most certainly thought that he had hit on the very solution, and didn't hesitate in informing Hetta of the ageing dandy's most enlightening visit when she met her in the park that afternoon.

"It must have been this physical resemblance between Perry and Cedric that the late Lord Pentecost was referring to shortly before he died, and the fact that they were both intrepid horsemen.

Perhaps it was the fear that Perry, too, might also sustain a serious fall from a horse that concerned the late Lord Pentecost. Needless to say, had Cedric ended his days in a lunatic asylum it would not have been through any inherited defect."

Hetta, pleased to have the matter cleared up at last, nodded in agreement, and was on the point of disclosing some important news of her own, when she noticed Jane stiffen suddenly. A few moments later a curricle passed them and she watched her aristocratic friend give the briefest of nods in response to the driver's bright smile and cheerful wave.

"From your most unenthusiastic response, I can safely assume that you are not overly fond of the Honourable Simon Fairfax. I cannot say he made much of an impression on me when he visited Hampshire. Rumour has it that since his return from Paris he has been paying court to a wealthy cit's daughter."

"Then I wish her joy of him, for, as you surmised, I do not care for him in the least." She had no intention of explaining the reasons for her animosity and quickly changed the subject by asking Hetta what she had been about to say, and was utterly delighted to hear that Lord Pentecost had at last proposed.

"Perry would like the wedding to take place

this summer," Hetta went on to disclose, with a decided lack of enthusiasm, "but I cannot help thinking it might be better to wait."

Jane looked at her closely. "Why? You've no doubts, have you?"

"Not about our regard for each other, no. And I'm certain we would suit admirably. Although I'm more outgoing than Perry, I too like my periods of quiet relaxation, and do not wish to be forever socialising. Only…I know his mother would not approve his choice."

Jane slanted a look of comical dismay at her. "Both you and I know that the Dowager would not approve any choice."

"Perhaps not. But might it not be sensible to wait? When he's thirty he can marry whomsoever he chooses without fear of losing his inheritance."

"And are you both prepared to wait almost six years?"

"Perry doesn't wish to, and, truth to tell, neither do I. He says he would far rather be happy than wealthy, and I genuinely believe he means it. And as far as I'm concerned… Well, I know precisely what it is like to do without luxuries, so it would be no hardship." The tiny, heartfelt sigh betrayed her continued misgivings, even before she added,

"I just don't wish to be responsible for depriving him of what is rightfully his, even though I'm certain in my heart that without the money we would be perfectly contented. He has every intention of informing his mother when she arrives in town at the end of the week."

"Now, that I do consider would be a grave error of judgement."

"So you do think it would be better if we did wait?"

"In informing your future mama-in-law, certainly!" Jane experienced a surge of wicked satisfaction at the prospect of outwitting the Dowager Lady Pentecost. "I think it would be highly beneficial for you and Perry to have a talk with Lady Templehurst. Come to the house tomorrow morning. We have no plans to go out."

This was certainly true, but during Jane's absence Lady Templehurst had been forced to review certain arrangements, because of Lady Knightley's unexpected arrival in town. She saw no reason, however, for Jane to forgo the evening's entertainment in order to keep her cousin company, and encouraged her to dine with her sister Lavinia at Grosvenor Square as planned.

This suited Elizabeth very well, for, although she had every intention of spending a great deal of time with Jane, she was simply agog to discover how her cousin was going on, and didn't hesitate in broaching the subject the instant Jane had left the house that evening.

"She seemed in remarkably good spirits when she returned from her walk in Hyde Park. I suppose, though, that much of her cheerfulness was due to Hetta's most excellent news."

"Precisely, my dear Elizabeth. Jane is very happy for them both, but do not be fooled by that display of gaiety. Besides which, she was naturally delighted by your early arrival in town."

"Truth to tell, I simply couldn't stay away. I know the children will be well cared for in my absence. They have the most efficient and devoted nursemaid in the person of my former maid, Agatha Stigwell."

Elizabeth momentarily raised her eyes from her sewing to cast a shrewd glance in her aunt's direction. "Does Jane suspect that you might have confided in Richard and myself?"

"Suspect?" Lady Templehurst gave vent to one of her wicked cackles. "She knew without being told—knew the instant I mentioned that I had broken my journey to Kent by spending two nights at Knightley Hall. She might be emotionally damaged, but there's absolutely nothing amiss with the functions of her brain. She's no fool, Elizabeth. By all means speak of your friend Dr Carrington in her presence, for she will not mention his name. And I cannot help but feel that it would be far better if she did open her heart again to someone, instead of continuously trying to keep her misery from surfacing."

Elizabeth couldn't help but agree, though felt she could bring precious little comfort. Tom was virtually unapproachable these days—reclusive, almost. If it wasn't for his work she honestly didn't think that anything or anyone could induce him to leave his house.

So she would have been surprised, not to say astounded, had she known that at that precise moment her good friend was seated in the library at Knightley Hall, challenging her husband to a game of chess.

Richard had long since realised, even if his wife had not, that their good friend would not place himself in a situation where he might be forced to talk openly about his private concerns until he felt ready to do so. Richard had sensed, too, that

Tom would be reluctant to unburden his soul in front of Elizabeth, whose fondness for her aristocratic cousin was evident, and his judgement in this had not been at fault. No sooner had Elizabeth embarked on the journey to London than he had dashed off a note to Dr Carrington inviting him to dine that evening, and had received an immediate and favourable response.

During their meal Tom maintained a flow of pleasant conversation. Anyone observing him might have supposed that he hadn't a care in the world. However, as with Jane, the effort to maintain the display of light-heartedness soon became too much of a strain, and he succumbed to a mood of abstraction, his mind dwelling on events that he would have given almost anything to forget.

"You appear to have lost your concentration, old fellow," Richard remarked, his long-fingered hand swooping down to remove a hapless pawn.

Masculine eyes then met and locked above the chequered board. "You know, don't you?" It was more statement than question. "Lady Templehurst told you, I presume?"

Richard knew nothing would be gained by prevarication. "She confided in both Elizabeth and myself during her short stay here, yes. But I realised that you were falling in love with Jane even before you embarked on that eventful trip to Wiltshire."

This admission managed to induce a semblance of a smile. "I didn't realise I was quite so transparent, Richard."

"You forget, my friend, I have gone through much the same experience, except my sufferings were not, I think, as profound as yours."

Abandoning the game completely, Richard leaned back in his chair and sipped his wine, while he watched his companion down the contents of his glass and reach once again for the bottle. Tom was drinking heavily this evening— had been imbibing too freely for several weeks, Richard guessed—and it was beginning to show. His complexion was pallid, and his lacklustre eyes were darkly circled. The lack of concern he had always displayed over his appearance was certainly more marked. The waving hair, which he had always tended to wear long, now reached beyond the collar of his heavily creased jacket; and what purported to be a cravat looked nothing better than a crumpled rag that might have been used for a drying cloth before being abysmally tied about his neck.

"You cannot go on this way," he remarked, watching yet a further glass of wine being consumed with scant regard for its excellence.

Tom didn't pretend to misunderstand. "No, I know. I've been trying to drown my sorrows, but it doesn't work." Placing the empty glass down on the table, he made no attempt to refill it this time. "I've received a letter from Sir William Dent, inviting me to stay with him in London for a few days in order to attend several lectures he thought might be of interest to me."

"Then I would accept if I were you," Richard encouraged. "A change of scenery might be beneficial. I'm joining Elizabeth in town early next week. You could travel with me in the curricle."

"Why not?" Tom's sudden shout of laughter had a reckless quality. "I'd try anything if it helped me to forget."

"Is that what you want—to forget her?"

The response when it came was little more than a broken whisper. "No... But how can there be a future for us when she is what she is and I...? Oh, God, Richard! Of all the females in the land, why did I have to go and fall in love with her?"

Perhaps because it was meant to be, Richard answered silently.

He had realised from the first that Tom must have exerted the most formidable control over himself during the time he had spent alone with Jane, since he did not feel himself in any way honour-bound to marry her. And that he had not taken advantage of the situation was proof, surely, of the depth of his regard?

But what of Jane? Much depended on that young woman. If she loved him, and Lady Templehurst had given him every reason to believe that her niece did, then the situation was not hopeless. There might be some opposition to the match, but Jane would not let that deter her if her feelings for Tom went deep enough. Richard was extremely fond of them both, and thought that they would make an ideal match. He decided, however, for the time being, to keep his reflections to himself.

Chapter Fourteen

Richard would not have been in the least surprised to receive a note from his friend to say that
he had decided against a visit to the metropolis
after all. However, he had done him an injustice
to suppose for a moment that, even in his present,
eminently unhappy state, Tom was incapable of
coming to a decision and sticking to it.

Strangely enough, though, it was this single-
mindedness of Tom's—one might almost say this
dogged determination to stand by his principles—
that concerned Richard most of all, for it could well
prove in this situation to be Tom's downfall. Unless
someone, perhaps even Jane herself, a well-
adjusted female by any standard, could prove to him
just how misguided he was in this instance, there
wasn't the remotest possibility of a joyous outcome
to the present, most unsatisfactory state of affairs.

None the less, when his friend arrived at the hall, promptly at the pre-arranged time, Richard was delighted to see that he had taken his first step along the road to recovery. His appearance was much improved, and he had even gone to the trouble of having his hair shorn to a more acceptable length since the evening they had dined together.

They did not delay their departure. The morning was dry and bright—ideal, in fact, for travelling in an open carriage. Stopping only to change horses, and to partake of a light luncheon at one of the superior posting-houses, they made excellent time until they arrived at the outskirts of the metropolis, where Richard had, perforce, to reduce his speed because of the volume of traffic.

"I'd forgotten just how overcrowded it is in the capital," Tom remarked, viewing the congestion with avid distaste. "Unless my livelihood depended upon it, nothing could induce me to remain here for more than a short period."

"Yes, I know what you mean. Even though Elizabeth and I come here each spring, we are never sorry to leave the noise and stale air behind and return to Hampshire."

Tom frowned as a thought suddenly occurred to him. "Now I come to think about it, you are making your visit earlier than usual this year. Normally you arrive in town when the Season is almost over."

"Oh, didn't I mention it?" Richard looked mildly surprised. "I offered the use of my house to Lady Templehurst for the duration of her stay in London, and as Elizabeth hasn't seen anything of her aunt in recent years she decided she'd take the opportunity to spend a little time with her."

An uncomfortable, but thankfully short silence followed, before Tom said, "Is Jane residing there, too?"

"Why, yes!" The look Richard received would certainly have alarmed any craven member of his sex. "Now, see here, Tom. It was never my intention to deceive you, but you'll admit yourself we've seen precious little of each other in recent weeks, and to be honest with you it never crossed my mind to mention it before. I did, however, have the intention of taking you to the house first, but if you'd rather we went directly to Sir William's lodgings then I'll quite understand."

There was no response.

"You're bound to come face to face with her some time, old fellow," Richard continued, in an attempt to break the awkward silence. "Elizabeth and I were hoping to persuade her to pay a visit to Hampshire again some time during the summer, but we're not likely to meet with very much success if the poor girl suspects that her presence in our home will keep you away."

This contingency had not occurred to Tom before, and he was rather taken aback. "Good Lord! Yes, I'd not thought of that," he freely admitted. "I wouldn't wish to make her feel uncomfortable... ever. And you're right, of course. Yes, we'll call at your house first."

The decision had not been an easy one to make. Tom felt as though he were being ripped in two. He was nowhere near ready to come face to face with Jane again and couldn't hope to stand a better than even chance of keeping his feelings firmly under control. But, at the same time, the thought that, by not seeing her now, he might never again see her in the future was more than he could bear.

She might, of course, have no desire whatsoever to see him—a heart-rending possibility, but one much better faced. After all, he had not been given the opportunity to speak to her in private before he had journeyed with her in the Prices' cart to Devizes, and had seen her a short time later safely ensconced in the hired carriage to continue her journey to Bath. How could he have explained his behaviour of the night before while there had always been someone lingering nearby who might have overheard?

He knew in his heart of hearts that he had made the right decision in calling a halt to their love-making—that he'd been right not to have taken advantage of their situation—but there hadn't been a waking moment since when he had not desperately regretted not remaining with her throughout that unforgettable night.

It was in this highly confused state, where bitter regrets warred with the knowledge that he had behaved in the only honourable way, that he stepped down from the curricle as it was expertly drawn to a halt outside the Knightleys' fashionable London residence. Refusing to linger in the rear, he was smartly at Richard's heels as his friend threw open the parlour door. Two pairs of eyes, both sets betraying surprise and uncertainty in equal measures, turned in his direction, but it was into the third pair that he found himself staring...searching.

For several moments no one moved, no one spoke; then Jane, with all her innate grace and well-bred dignity—which afterwards Lady

Templehurst, with tears in her eyes, confessed to the Knightleys made her feel inordinately proud to be her aunt—rose from her chair and went towards Tom with her hand outstretched.

"It is delightful to see you again, Dr Carrington. I didn't know that Richard was bringing you with him to town."

He retained his hold on the slender, tapering fingers for as long as he dared. "Truth to tell, my lady, it was a last-minute decision on my part." Why was she being so formal? For that matter, why was he? "Sir William Dent invited me to attend some lectures with him on the improved treatments of certain disorders."

"All work, Dr Carrington!" Lady Templehurst remarked, finding her voice at last. "Do you never relax? I hope you will at least find the time to attend our party here on Thursday evening?"

"I'm afraid I cannot commit myself, ma'am, until I know what Sir William has planned." He certainly couldn't risk spending an entire evening in close proximity to Jane. Being near her now, and wanting nothing more than to take her into his arms, was sheer torture. How lovely she was!

"I trust my remedy did the trick and that you have not been experiencing further discomfort after meals?" he hurriedly went on, before anyone could force the issue of his attending the forthcoming event.

Jane transferred her gaze to her aunt and the message, *You broke your journey to Kent for the sole purpose of meeting him,* was clearly to be seen in her eyes.

"Yes," Lady Templehurst responded, as if to the unspoken accusation, before returning her attention to Tom's attractively masculine form. "It has worked wonders, Dr Carrington. I've had no trouble since. I must get you to make me up a further supply to take back with me to Bath."

Elizabeth then took command of the situation by offering the gentlemen some much needed refreshments. Richard, however, refused to prolong the agony for at least two of the people present, both of whom were making a sterling effort to maintain a flow of inconsequential chatter, but whose inner turmoil was like some tangible thing felt by all, and he did not delay long in taking Tom to Sir William Dent's house.

When he returned a short time later he discovered the ladies still in the parlour, busily making plans for the forthcoming party.

"You put me forcibly in mind of those three

crones in *Macbeth*. What the deuce are you all plotting?"

"I'm not so sure we should tell you after that piece of impertinence," his wife retorted with mock indignation.

There was a hint of wicked amusement in Jane's eyes, which was a relief to see after the barely concealed flicker of misery there for all to observe when Tom had taken his very formal leave of her. "I do not perceive how you can avoid telling him, dear Cousin, when it is he who will be making the announcement."

"And what announcement would that be, may I ask?" Richard demanded with all the suspicion of a man who was about to be persuaded into doing something he would far rather not.

"Oh, the most marvellous news!" Elizabeth exclaimed. "Perry has asked Henrietta Dilbey to marry him and she has accepted."

"I get the distinct impression," Richard remarked, eyeing the three ladies with patent suspicion, "that there is more to this than I have yet been told…I await an explanation from one of you."

As was his custom, Tom woke early the following morning. There were no lectures scheduled for that day, and as Sir William had arranged to visit some friends Tom was free to spend his time precisely as he chose. He was on the point of leaving the house to do a spot of sightseeing when Sir Richard unexpectedly arrived.

"Did we arrange to meet today?" Tom wouldn't have been in the least surprised to receive an affirmative answer. So much seemed to slip his mind of late. "If we did, I am entirely at your disposal. I hadn't planned to go anywhere in particular."

"In that case, how would you care to accompany me to my tailor?"

"Good Lord, Richard! Haven't you coats enough?"

"I have, but you haven't," was the caustic rejoinder, but Tom wasn't offended.

"I suppose you're right," he admitted, with a wry glance at the left sleeve of his comfortable but hardly fashionable jacket. "One or two new items of clothing wouldn't come amiss."

Richard, however, had other ideas. By the time they had left the shop Tom was the proud possessor of half a dozen fashionable coats and several pairs of unmentionables, plus new shirts and an ample supply of cravats, prompting him to ask whether his friend was trying to ruin him.

"You're not a pauper, Tom. Besides, you can wear that black coat to our party tomorrow evening."

"I could if I had any intention of attending, but I have not. And you must surely realise why."

In the years to come Richard was to look back on that moment as one of the most significant, if not in his life, then certainly in that of his friend. If he had chosen to explain that what had been originally planned as an informal party for no more than three dozen guests had been turned into a ball to celebrate the engagement of Lord Pentecost and Henrietta Dilbey, and had induced Tom to join in the celebration, the future might have turned out to be vastly different. For some inexplicable reason, however, he chose not to pursue the matter, and merely suggested that they repair to his club for some refreshments.

Society as a whole was accustomed to keeping late hours when in town and the rooms at White's at this time of day were virtually deserted. They seated themselves at one of the many vacant tables, and Richard was on the point of ordering a bottle and glasses when the door opened and in walked his good friend Viscount Dartwood.

The Viscount and his wife had visited Knightley Hall on several occasions, and knew

Dr Carrington well. There was much news to catch up on since the last time they had seen one another. Both the Viscountess and Elizabeth had given birth, thankfully, to healthy children, so the conversation tended to revolve around the joys of fatherhood, which wasn't of that much interest to Tom who began to take more notice of his exclusive surroundings. Consequently, he was the first to catch sight of the handsome, blond-haired gentleman entering the room, and by the time Richard perceived the red mists of anger in the young doctor's eyes it was already too late.

Tom was out of his chair and planting a fist full in the face of the new arrival before either Richard or the Viscount had a chance to intervene. Richard did, however, manage to prevent Tom from following up his advantage, by grasping him firmly by the upper arms.

"That's enough, Tom! You've floored him. Be satisfied with that." Richard didn't hesitate in requesting the Viscount, whose eyes betrayed more than just a hint of admiration for the flush hit, to escort their mutual friend outside, and then turned his attention to the waiter who had burst into the room to see what all the commotion was about.

"Nothing wrong. Mr Fairfax merely tripped and fell against the table. Fetch some brandy!"

"Damn it, Knightley! You'll not succeed in protecting your friend so easily. I'll call him out!" Simon Fairfax avowed, getting to his feet with his dignity far from intact.

"I was under the distinct impression that it was you I was protecting," Richard responded, with all the even-tempered control for which he was famed.

Setting the table to rights, he glanced in the corner at the only other occupant of the room, old Colonel Fitzpatrick, still dozing in the chair. "The incident will go no further. And you would be wise to forget it, too." He paused in order to take a pinch of snuff. "It would do you no good at all if the reason behind this slight altercation became common knowledge."

The younger man looked not in the least shame-faced. "So you know about that, do you? Then you must know that it wouldn't do the lady in question any good if the truth leaked out."

"Indeed it would not. But it would do you far more harm... I would see to that. So I would suggest that you listen very carefully to what I have to say."

It did not take many minutes for Richard to

push his advantage home and make Simon see sense. He then went out to the lobby to discover that only the Viscount awaited him.

"What the deuce was all that about, Richard? Can't say I care for Fairfax myself, but one doesn't indulge in fisticuffs in a gentleman's club. Tom will be barred even before he's made a member if he carries on like that."

"He had good reason for behaving as he did," Richard responded, "but as there is a lady involved I'd rather not explain." He glanced up and down the street. "Where is the young hothead?"

"I sent him to cool his heels in Hyde Park."

Oh, Lord! Richard groaned inwardly. Things were going from bad to worse. He felt certain that Jane had planned to go riding there with Perry this morning, and he could only hope that she didn't cross Tom's path in his present unpredictable mood.

Needless to say it was a forlorn hope. The park, too, at this time of day, was not crowded, for it was long before the fashionable hour when Society at large showed itself abroad. That was precisely why Jane enjoyed her morning rides; she could indulge in her favourite form of exercise without having to stop every few minutes to pass the time of day with her numerous acquaintances.

She was in the process of informing Perry, who had given his full approval for his engagement to be announced at the Knightleys' party, that everything was in hand for the ball the following evening, when she happened to catch sight of Tom heading across the grass in their direction. Had it been left to her, she certainly wouldn't have made her presence known, for even from that distance she suspected, by the tense set of his powerful shoulders and the impatient stride, that all was not well with him. Unfortunately, Perry, following the direction of her gaze, experienced no such qualms.

"Why, it's Dr Carrington!" he exclaimed, before hailing his new physician cheerfully.

Tom stopped dead in his tracks, and had little choice but to acknowledge the pair, one of whom he would far rather not have encountered again quite so soon.

"What, still in the capital?" he remarked to Perry as they brought their mounts to a halt beside him. "I understood you to say that you didn't care for town life, Lord Pentecost."

"I have been enjoying this particular visit,

which in part is due to you, Dr Carrington. I did go to see your colleague and his opinion was the same as yours. And I have since discovered, thanks to Janie and her aunt, that my late uncle's mental disorder was the direct result of an accident he sustained."

"I'm pleased the mystery has been solved," Tom responded, doing his level best not to stare in Jane's direction, but aware that those lovely eyes of hers were firmly fixed on his physiognomy. "How much longer do you intend remaining in town?" he asked, not out of any particular interest, but in an attempt to converse only with Perry.

"Not very much longer. A week at the most. Mama's arrived in town now."

Jane could almost hear Tom saying, Then I'm not surprised you're leaving it, and quickly turned her betraying gurgle of mirth into a cough, which succeeded in drawing his attention. Their eyes met, but she was afraid to try to interpret the silent message in those grey depths. She desperately wanted to believe that he loved her, but she needed the answers to several questions before she dared trust her instincts again.

An awkward silence followed, and she was just steeling herself to ask whether they would have the pleasure of seeing him at the Knightleys' ball the following evening when a sporting carriage bowling along the driveway towards them succeeded in capturing her attention. There could be no mistaking the portly royal figure who handled the ribbons with such flair, and Jane was just wondering whether Tom had ever seen their future king at such close quarters before when bouncing across the vehicle's path came a bright red ball, quickly followed by its young owner, eager to retrieve his precious toy.

Above her own gasp of dismay Jane heard the mother's terrified scream, and saw the Regent trying to take evasive action by swerving to the left. The next instant, Tom, with lightning speed, threw himself in the path of the carriage to sweep the child up in his arms. Just how they escaped being trampled beneath the startled team's hooves Jane couldn't imagine, but both ended up lying on the grass, the little boy frightened, but otherwise unharmed.

Perry dismounted and hurried to help Tom to his feet. The mother, gathering her young son in her arms, was sobbing out her grateful thanks, and the Regent, having managed to draw his spirited horses to a halt a few yards away, handed the reins to his groom and came towards the small group.

"By Jove, Dr Carrington!" Perry exclaimed, eyes brightened by the excitement of it all. "That was an excellent piece of work."

"Indeed it was, sir! Indeed it was!" His Royal Highness agreed, looking rather shaken by the near catastrophe as he mopped his sweating brow with a fine piece of silk.

Jane decided it was time to offer her help, for she could see that Tom was far from gratified by all the attention he was receiving, and, dismounting, she forced her way through the ever increasing group of onlookers who were gathering around to discover what had occurred.

"Lady Jane Beresford, sir," she said, reminding the Regent, even though they had met before on several occasions, of her name. "The Earl of Eastbury's daughter."

"Of course! Yes, I remember you very well, my dear."

Jane doubted it, but wasn't offended. Given the number of people introduced to him each year, he could hardly be expected to recall every single one. She turned to the naturally distraught mother and very gently suggested that she take her son home to recover, and then introduced Perry and Tom to the Regent.

"A pleasure to make your acquaintance Dr Carrington," he said, shaking him warmly by the hand. "Dashed brave thing you did, sir! Wouldn't have had that happen for the world! Dear me, no! Glad you sent the mother away, m'dear," he went on, turning to Jane. "Shouldn't bring children here. Much better to let them play in Green Park. Much quieter there."

"I might suggest, sir, that you could do with some peace and quiet yourself," Tom remarked, after casting a professional eye over the future sovereign. "The unfortunate incident has natu-rally distressed you greatly. I think a short rest would be most beneficial."

"Yes, very sensible, Dr Carrington," he agreed, and remained only for the time it took to offer his sincere thanks once again.

The crowd of onlookers quickly dispersed after the Regent's departure and Jane, sensing that Tom had no desire to remain, would have taken her leave, but Perry forestalled her by saying, "You will be coming to the Knightleys' ball tomorrow evening, won't you, Dr Carrington? We'd very much like you to be there to celebrate our happy news."

"I'm afraid not, sir. I've other plans," he replied, and with the briefest of farewells he walked smartly away.

"Pity he has made other arrangements for the evening," Perry remarked, drawing his eyes away from the doctor's rapidly retreating form. "If it had not been for him—and you, of course—I wouldn't be the happy man I am today."

He cast Jane a surprisingly penetrating stare. "You must realise, just as I do myself, that my mother must have known the truth about Uncle Cedric all along. It was most unkind of her to keep the facts from me. That in itself is not unusual—she has, after all, not been particularly kind to me throughout my life. But I shall never permit her to be unkind to Hetta. And that is why I agreed to your aunt's suggestion of keeping our intentions secret from her. Once the engagement is officially announced, there is little she can do. And I'm so glad you'll be there to celebrate the moment with me, Jane... I just wish Thomas Carrington could have been there too. I have a deal of regard for that man."

He raised his eyes in time to see the doctor disappearing round a bend in the path, and a sudden thought occurred to him. "You don't think I've offended him do you, Janie? You don't think he's annoyed because I chose to consult that London physician after he had told me I had nothing to worry about?"

"No, Perry, I do not," she responded, making a supreme effort to control the threat of tears. "I think his decision not to attend the ball has rather more to do with me."

Chapter Fifteen

Jane didn't regret leaving the party early, but now that she had arrived back at the house she didn't relish the prospect of retiring, either. She wasn't in the least tired, merely heart-weary, something which both her aunt and Elizabeth understood quite well. Neither had made the least attempt to persuade her to remain at Lady Cossington's drum, and she had been grateful to them for that.

After handing her velvet evening cloak to the Knightleys' excellent young butler, she made her way across the hall, but checked at the foot of the stairs. It was unlikely in her present frame of mind that she would succumb very quickly to sleep, so it made sense to provide herself with something to pass the time.

The library here, like the one at Knightley Hall, was well stocked, and she felt certain of finding something to her taste. She did not, however, expect to find the master of the house sitting quite alone in his sanctum, and didn't attempt to hide her surprise.

"Why, Richard! I understood you to say that you were going to your club this evening."

"That had been my intention, but then I decided I should prefer a quiet evening at home. I have since discovered, however, that one can soon grow tired of one's own company, so can I not persuade you to remain with me for a while?"

She needed no second prompting, and made herself comfortable in the chair on the opposite side of the hearth, while her cousin's charming husband procured her a glass of wine.

"By your early return I can only assume that you gained little pleasure from the evening's entertainment?" he remarked.

"No, I did not," she freely admitted, seeing no reason to deny the fact. Although Richard had not once broached the subject of her eventful journey to Bath, she felt it safe to assume that he was in full possession of all the relevant facts.

"Truth to tell, Richard, had it not been for Lady Templehurst's desire to visit the capital, I would have been content to remain in Kent. I am, however, for obvious reasons, very much looking forward to the ball here tomorrow evening. Perry's happiness means a lot to me, and I cannot express my thanks strongly enough for allowing my aunt to hold such a large party in your house."

"You are a devious young woman!" he told her with mock severity, before handing her the wine and resuming his seat. "Do you feel no pangs of conscience over your part in the subterfuge?"

"Quite frankly, I cannot say that I do," she responded, truthful to the last. "I do not think Lady Pentecost deserves any consideration." She sampled the contents of her glass while her mind wandered back over the years. "I cannot forget the way she treated Perry when he was a boy. He could never do anything to please her. It is little wonder that he reached adulthood with no self-confidence, although he is much improved now. She did little to make his childhood happy, Richard. And I for one will not idly stand by and allow her to ruin the rest of his life if I can do something to prevent it."

His attractive mouth curled into an appreciative smile. "You are a very determined young woman, I see."

"I can be if I believe in something strongly

enough. And I do sincerely believe that Hetta will make Perry happy."

"I'm inclined to agree with you on that," he responded, holding her gaze steadily. "Very few of us meet the ideal mate, Jane, and when we do we should not let the chance of true happiness slip by." He saw the slender fingers tremble slightly. "He does love you, you know."

"Does he, Richard?" She saw little point in trying to dissemble, and betrayed her feelings clearly enough in a long-drawn-out sigh. "If only I could be sure of that."

He found the slight catch in her pleasantly melodious voice heart-rending. "What makes you doubt it?"

"He never once attempted to make contact with me before he came to town, not even by letter. And now, when he has the opportunity to see me, to be with me, he deliberately keeps himself at a distance." She wanted nothing more than to cry out all the hurt that she had buried deep within for so many weeks, but it seemed she had no more tears left to weep. "He isn't even going to attend the party tomorrow evening."

"No, I know. I saw him this morning." His lips curled into a rueful smile. "I made the mistake of taking him to my club. And who should also decide to pay a visit at that time of day…? None other than Simon Fairfax."

This briefly turned her thoughts in a new direction. "I knew the wretch was in town. I saw him a few days ago when I was in the park with Hetta."

"Blackguard!" Richard muttered. "He had the cursed temerity to inform me that he never meant you any real harm, and that he had been put to a great deal of trouble for no reward. Apparently, when he returned to his house, after having searched for you, he discovered that your maid had departed with what money you had in your possession, and your jewel box. He journeyed to Paris in the hope of discovering her whereabouts, but found no trace."

"Really? How very interesting." Jane experienced a deal of satisfaction at learning this. "I wonder if she took my advice, after all?"

She then went on to inform Richard of her former maid's wish to become a milliner. "The jewellery I had with me, although not my best pieces, might have been sufficient for her needs. And strangely enough I cannot find it within me to begrudge her the booty. If it hadn't been for her, I might never have escaped the infamous Simon's clutches."

"If it hadn't been for her," Richard countered, unable to fathom, even with all his vast experience, the workings of the female mind, "you wouldn't have found yourself in that predicament in the first place. However, if it's any consolation, at least one of the miscreants involved in the despicable affair is now sporting a fine black eye."

"Ah, yes! Now you come to mention it, I did hear a rumour circulating at Lady Cossington's party that someone had planted Simon Fairfax a facer." She discovered that, even in her most unhappy state, she had not lost her sense of humour, and laughed. "Whom have I to thank for it…? You, Richard?"

"Sadly, no," he was forced to admit. "It would have given me the utmost pleasure to have obliged you, my dear, but not in a gentleman's club. Tom, however, experienced no such qualms."

He regarded her in silence for a moment, watching her amusement quickly fade, then said, "I shall not attempt to make any excuses for his current behaviour, except to say that he doesn't consider himself good enough for you. And you cannot deny that there is every likelihood that you would come up against some fierce opposition from certain members of your family."

"Do you think I have not considered that, Richard? Of course there would be bound to be some, but I know my father well enough to be sure that he would soon come round, once he realised what a dedicated and intelligent man Tom is." This time her shout of laughter was mirthless. "It is ironic, is it not, that I always feared being coveted for my wealth alone, and yet when I do eventually meet the man with whom I could happily spend the rest of my life it is precisely that wealth, if what you tell me is true, which has proved to be the bar?"

"It does not have to be so, Jane."

"It should not be so!" There was a hard and determined edge to her voice now, one he had never detected before. "And believe me, Richard, if I could be certain that Tom truly loves me, I would move heaven and earth to make him see reason. But how can I know for sure when he can hardly bring himself to look at me, let alone speak to me?"

Although Richard himself had no doubts, he could quite understand her uncertainty and, deciding that it would not benefit the state of affairs to comment further at the present time, very tactfully changed the subject.

After she left him a short time later, he

remained staring down at the empty grate, his mind deep in thought, until the other ladies arrived home, and Elizabeth came in to see him before retiring for the night.

"Did you have an enjoyable evening?" he enquired politely, but knew what the answer would be even before she responded.

"It is difficult to attain any great pleasure, my dear, when one knows how desperately unhappy Jane is. The poor girl tries so hard to go on as normal. She certainly doesn't lack courage."

"No, she certainly doesn't lack that." He focused his attention once again on the empty grate. "I spoke to her tonight about it for the fist time. She never attempted to avoid the issue—nor did she attempt to subject me to a display of feminine tears. She would make Tom the ideal partner. And I'm now firmly convinced that she is as much in love with him as he is with her."

Elizabeth was not able to duplicate her cousin's admirable control, and unashamedly had recourse to her handkerchief. "Oh, Richard, is there nothing either of us can do?"

He was silent for so long that she thought he would not respond, but then he astonished her by announcing, "That, my love, is still far from certain. But I am now prepared to break my golden rule—because I damn well mean to try!"

After attending the first of the lectures the following afternoon, Tom returned to Sir William's hired house. His host had planned to go on to his club, and, although Tom had received an invitation to accompany him, he thought it wisest, given the events of the previous day, if he maintained a low profile at White's for the time being.

For a while he toyed with the idea of filling the time until Sir William's return by going for a walk, but then decided against it, just in case he should happen to come face to face with Jane again. Not that it signified to any great extent if this were to happen: her image rarely left his mind's eye in any event.

He settled in the end for going through the notes he had jotted down during the lecture, and had only just made himself comfortable in the front parlour when the butler announced Sir Richard.

"Good heavens! I never expected to see you today. I would have thought you would have been far too busy with last-minute preparations for your event this evening to pay afternoon calls." His teeth flashed in an engaging smile of welcome. "Needless to say, though, it is good to see you. Take a seat. Can I get you a glass of wine, or something else, perhaps?"

"No, thank you, Tom. As you say, I've much to do, so I cannot stay long. I've left the ladies back at the house arranging the last of the flowers." He paused for a moment to study the shine on his Hessians before adding, "I know I'm here on a fool's errand, but I did promise to make one final attempt to make you change your mind and join us this evening."

Tom made not the least attempt to suppress a deep sigh. "You know why I can't, Richard."

"Yes, sadly, I do know. But Jane especially wished you to be there to share her joy in the occasion. I am to make the announcement at about eleven."

"Announcement?" Tom betrayed more than just a modicum of interest. "What announcement?"

"Well, I know they both wanted to keep it secret until tonight, but I'm sure neither of them would object to my telling you. I'm to announce their engagement. Jane, naturally, is delighted, and it goes without saying that Perry is over the moon at having captured the affections of such a lovely young woman."

The look of astonished incredulity on his friend's face was almost Richard's undoing, but the knowledge that much depended on his performance now, if there was to be the remotest chance of a joyous outcome to this little subterfuge, helped him to retain his rigid control and not give way to mirth.

"You're hoaxing me!" Tom announced, finding his voice at last. Then he recalled the encounter in the park, and Perry mentioning something about a celebration. "It cannot be true," he added, but with far less conviction.

"Afraid it is, old boy. And I must say both Elizabeth and I think they'll make a charming couple. They're very well suited, after all."

"Well suited…? Richard, you cannot possibly be serious!"

He rose abruptly to his feet and began to pace the room, putting Richard in mind of a caged animal: confined, perhaps, but none the less dangerous and demanding respect, and Richard certainly had the utmost respect for his friend's intelligence. Fortunately, though, Tom, at the present time, appeared to be allowing his feelings full rein, and was not thinking clearly, which, of course, was all to the good.

"Thanks to Jane, I've begun to view Perry in a completely different light. He's an intelligent young man who holds sensible views on a great number of serious topics. He's spent a couple of evenings with me at the Hall, as it happens... Damned good chess player. Nearly beat me on the last occasion."

"Chess?" Tom stopped his pacing to run decidedly unsteady fingers through his hair. "What the hell has that to do with anything? She doesn't love him... You know she cannot possibly love him."

"That I could not say." Richard experienced more than just a fleeting disquiet. He hated putting his friend through this, but doggedly stuck to his task. "You must remember that members of my social class do not in general marry for love. Mutual regard usually suffices. There are exceptions, like Elizabeth and myself. But most marry to unite families, and enlarge their estates."

Tom's only response was a flashing look of disgust, before he resumed his angry pacing, and Richard thought it best to leave before his conscience got the better of him and he told his friend the complete truth.

"I'd better be on my way now. As I mentioned earlier, I've much to do." He went over to the door, but turned back to add, "May I at least pass on your felicitations to the happy couple?"

"No, you bloody well can't!" Eyes hard and resentful, Tom glowered across the room. "Richard, you can't let this happen. You must prevent it! Make her see sense, for pity's sake!"

"I...?" Richard managed to raise his brows in exaggerated surprise. "What the deuce do you suppose I can do?" He held his friend's angry gaze levelly. "Oh, no, my dear friend—I'm not the one to prevent it."

"Then I damn well will!" Tom announced with steely determination. "She'll marry Pentecost over my dead body!"

Well, that seems to have done the trick, Richard mused with intense satisfaction, and promptly left the room as Tom resumed his angry pacing.

Chapter Sixteen

As Sir Bartholomew Rudge had remarked, Lady Augusta Templehurst remained a personage of some standing. Although her removal to Bath ten years before had succeeded in placing her outside the cream of Society's field of vision, her popularity had been such that just her signature at the bottom of the invitation cards had proved sufficient inducement to persuade many to cancel previous engagements in order to attend the Knightleys' ball.

Sir Richard and Elizabeth, too, had a wide circle of friends, most of whom had been only too pleased to put in an appearance, and, by half past ten the two large adjoining salons on the upper floor, more than adequate to accommodate all the guests, and beautifully decorated for the occasion, were rapidly filling.

Needless to say the joint hostesses were well pleased with the results of all their efforts. It had been no mean feat to organise the ball in so short a time, but the sight of Hetta, charmingly attired in a gown of pale primrose silk, and looking so deliciously happy as she danced with her future husband, made all the hard work well worthwhile.

Since the arrival of the Dowager Lady Pentecost in town a few days before, Perry and Hetta had, in an attempt to avoid rousing the formidable matron's suspicions, very wisely seen less of each other. Evidently their tactics had worked, for although Lady Pentecost was certainly glancing in their direction she didn't appear to be taking an undue interest in either of them, no doubt believing that her son had been merely courteous enough to stand up with the niece of a close neighbour.

Which was possibly just as well in view of what was to take place in less than half an hour's time, Elizabeth mused, drawing her eyes away from the dancing couples to welcome yet another late arrival.

The Dowager Lady Fitzwarren, a matriarch of no small consequence, had just reached the entrance to the first salon, and was about to exchange a few words with her host and hostesses, when there was a slight commotion below.

The next moment a tall young man, whom she would have considered strikingly attractive had it not been for the ferocity of the frown darkening his brow, came bounding up the stairs. He brushed past her so forcefully that the Dowager almost cannoned into Sir Richard.

"Where the devil is she?" he rudely demanded to know.

"About halfway down on the right, talking with her sister," Richard responded, completely un-ruffled—which was more than could be said for most of those who followed the new arrival's progress across the floor, and watched him clasp one slender wrist and haul the aristocratic young lady behind him from the room.

Lord Peregrine was definitely momentarily startled, but then became thoughtful. "I say, Hett, did you just see that?" he asked as they came together again in the set.

"Yes. I expect most everyone noticed. Very odd behaviour, don't you think?"

"No, not really," he surprised her by responding. "Thought there was something wrong. I might never say a great deal, Hett, but I do notice things. Felt there was something amiss with Jane—not been quite herself since she arrived in town. And yesterday, when we met up with Dr Carrington in the park, I realised why… She's in love with him, Hett—I'd stake my life on it. And it wouldn't surprise me at all if he feels exactly the same way about her."

Hetta was rather taken aback to hear this, but then cast her future spouse a glowing smile of admiration. "Perry, you're quite remarkable! That would never have occurred to me. But now you mention it—yes, I do believe you're right. My, my! That will cause a few brows to be raised."

Lady Fitzwarren, still standing by the door, was most certainly looking startled by such unconventional behaviour, and had recourse to her lorgnette as she continued to follow the couple's progress back down the stairs. "Upon my soul! Weren't that Eastbury's gel…? Your niece, Augusta?"

"Indeed, it was," Lady Templehurst responded in a level tone as she tried to control the exhilaration she was experiencing at Dr Carrington's totally unexpected, but wholly gratifying, arrival.

"Well, ain't you going to do something about it, Knightley?" Lady Fitzwarren demanded. "He looked like a fiend! He may do the gel harm."

"Oh, I shouldn't think so, ma'am," Richard replied, still completely unperturbed. "Lady Jane

Beresford is a most redoubtable girl. She's more than capable of handling the situation."

He might not have been quite so certain had he been standing in his library at that precise moment to witness his wife's cousin being so ruthlessly shaken that she was in the gravest danger of losing the spray of artificial flowers nestling in her beautifully arranged hair.

"Oh, how dare you?" she managed, more than a little breathless from the ordeal. "How dare you drag me in here and treat me in this odious fashion? It is not to be borne, sir!"

"Don't you adopt that haughty tone with me, my girl!" Tom growled through clenched teeth, and only just managing to suppress the strong urge to repeat the punishment. "I'll not permit you to go through with it, do you hear? I didn't put myself through hell just so that you could retain your virtue, only to have you throw yourself away on the first sprig who asks you to marry him."

Jane studied his angry features in silence for a moment. She was still more than just a little indignant over his rough treatment, but she had heard his every word, even if she didn't perfectly understand as yet precisely what he had meant.

"Would you mind letting me go, Tom?" she

asked softly, and instantly he released his hold, though, like some vigilant predator, he watched her every move as she wandered over to seat herself in one of the chairs. "I think you had better explain your reason for coming here this evening," she added, after subjecting him to a further searching stare, and seeing clearly the continued anger, but also the deep hurt, in his eyes.

"You know quite well why I'm here." His tone was more impatient than angry now. "You must not permit the engagement to be announced!"

Her brows rose. "Why ever not?"

"You can sit there and blithely ask me that? Ye gods!" He took a threatening step towards her, and for one dreadful moment she thought she was in the gravest peril of being shaken again, but then he seemed to check himself.

"All right, perhaps I shouldn't be here at all. Perhaps I have no right to interfere. Just answer me one question… Are you in love with him?"

"In love with whom?"

"Pentecost, of course!" he snapped, swiftly coming to the end of his tether, but her next words proved his undoing.

"No, I'm not in love with Perry, Tom… I'm in love with you."

"God, Janie, don't!" It was if the words had been torn from him, so painful did they sound. "Don't you think I feel the same way? Don't you realise that the mere thought of your marrying Pentecost—of your marrying anyone—tears me apart?"

Tom both looked and sounded as though he was in the depths of despair, but Jane most certainly wasn't, and could hardly contain her elation. He loved her. She was certain of that now. And nothing and no one, she silently vowed, would prevent them having a future together!

"But I have no intention of marrying Perry," she told him, in a voice as clear as glass.

He glanced at her then, uncertain. "But Richard informed me earlier that he was to announce the engagement tonight."

Jane was beginning to see a chink of light. She had noticed Richard return to the house late in the afternoon, and he had looked mighty well pleased with himself. If he had been instrumental in prompting Tom to come here, then she would love the wickedly conniving devil for the rest of her life.

"Yes, he certainly is to announce the engagement," she responded, slightly unsteadily. "An engagement between Lord Peregrine Pentecost and Miss Henrietta Dilbey."

For a moment it seemed as if he had not heard, then very slowly he turned to face her squarely, his eyes suddenly probing and dangerously alert. "But I understood Richard to say…" His features adopted that same fiendish look that had so discomposed Lady Fitzwarren. "By heaven! I'll have his liver and lights for this!"

"Oh, I think not," Jane said, with all the calm assurance of one in full command of the situation. Her course not quite clear, and emboldened as she was by the fact that she knew for sure that her future was destined to be at this man's side, she didn't hesitate to enquire, "When did you fall in love with me, Tom?"

The direct question took him completely off guard. He would have given almost anything to be able to deny it, but it was rather too late for that now—his actions alone this night had betrayed him.

"I'm not sure, Janie," he replied softly, and went over to the fireplace to stare down at the empty grate. "I think I knew for certain that day I showed you round my friend's house in Melcham, remember?" He waited for a response, but none was forthcoming. "You jokingly remarked that the house would not be too large once I had a wife and family… The trouble was that I could only envisage you as mistress of that house. You seemed so right there."

A soft, reminiscent little smile hovered about her mouth. She remembered that day so well. "You were far quicker than I to realise in which direction the wind was blowing, Tom," she admitted. "I didn't know until the second night in the cottage, but then…"

Her smile faded. There was not a doubt in her mind that he loved her, but there were still things she needed to know. "Why did you behave as you did that night? Why did you leave me that way, making me feel rejected, too loathsome to be touched? Why did you never once try to contact me during these past weeks? And why, since your arrival in town, have you made no attempt to see me alone before now?"

For several long moments he continued to stare down at the hearth, then, raising his hand, he gestured in the vague direction of the beautifully embroidered bodice of her gown. "Because of that."

Slightly puzzled, she glanced at her firm young breasts rising from the *décolletage*. "Are you trying to tell me that there is something wrong with my figure?"

"What?" He looked totally nonplussed for a

second or two. "Of course not, you foolish creature!" he snapped, with an abrupt return to peevishness. "You're perfect." He groaned. "That's just the trouble."

"Then what in heaven's name are you talking about?" she demanded, not in the least deterred by his brusque tone.

"That confounded brooch I gave you." He experienced more than just a little resentment as he focused his attention on the silver circlet encrusted with pearls that adorned the bodice of her dress, and recalled all too painfully the last time he had seen it. "You left it on top of the chest of drawers that night. I happened to notice it lying there, and remembered, you see." But her puzzled expression was proof enough that she didn't understand at all.

"I informed you that it had once belonged to my grandmother," he went on to explain. "Perhaps what I omitted to mention was that she swiftly came to regret her hasty marriage to my grandfather. She became bitterly resentful, and even went so far as to blame him entirely for ruining her life."

"I see," Jane responded, perceiving clearly now precisely what he had feared. "And you imagined that I would one day come to resent it, if you had not called a halt to our lovemaking and we had been obliged to marry."

She didn't bother waiting for a response. Eyes brimful of loving reproach, she rose from the chair and moved slowly towards him.

"Some might consider that very noble of you, Tom. Personally, though, I consider it damnably foolish, not to mention arrogantly presumptuous. What makes you suppose for a moment that just because I come from the same social class as your grandmother I am likely to behave in a similar fashion…? That my nature resembles hers in any way? And what makes you suppose," she went on, once again not waiting for a response, "that just because you are prepared to make yourself desperately unhappy you have the right to make my life desolate, too?"

He reached out to her then, and ran one finger gently down her cheek before taking her into his arms. "Have you been miserable, my Janie?"

"Dreadfully," she assured him, and all his noble intentions crumbled beneath the strength of her love mirrored in those lovely grey-green eyes. He could exist without her, but knew he'd never be happy.

He kissed her gently at first, almost tentatively, and then, at last finding some blessed release after weeks of suppressing his emotions, with an urgency that left her breathless and in little doubt of his desperate need of her.

"Darling, this is madness," he murmured, in a half-hearted attempt to regain a modicum of control and make her see reason. Burying his face in her hair, he clung to her, like a man in peril of drowning and holding fast to his only means of survival. "What of your family? You know they would not approve."

Loath though she was, she disengaged herself from his loving hold. He needed reassurance, and if she stood the remotest chance of convincing him how wrong he was, he must not only hear it from her own lips but see confirmation of what she was saying in her eyes.

"I shan't try to pretend that there will be no opposition, Tom. My mother and sisters have always harboured the foolish notion that I would one day acquire the title of Duchess or Marchioness. But my father is more level-headed, and I know he will like you. Besides which, you already have a very staunch ally in Lady Templehurst."

This brought some comfort, but he was very well aware that there were other considerations to take into account, not least of which was the difference in their financial situations. "I am not precisely a pauper, Jane, I could afford to keep you in comfort, but there isn't the remotest chance that I could maintain you in the style to which you are accustomed. I know you are a woman of substantial means and if…" his lips curled into a wry smile of resignation "…when we marry your money will come to me, but I shall not touch so much as a penny of it, Jane," he vowed. "As far as I am concerned, that money will always be yours to do with as you wish."

She did not think that now was the most appropriate time to discuss her inheritance. He was a proud man, and would naturally wish to feel that he alone was capable of supporting her. There would no doubt be occasions in the future in which to broach the subject again, and maybe suggest that her money be used to educate their children, and provide any daughters they might have with reasonable dowries. After all, not all men were as stubbornly proud as the one with whom she had chosen to spend the rest of her life.

"I do not want a life of luxury, Thomas Carrington," she assured him softly, "only one at your side. So now will you stop searching for difficulties where none exist and, instead, prove to your future wife just what a loving husband you intend to be?"

Unlike her, he could still foresee turbulent waters ahead, but he did not doubt that together they would master the currents and find a safe haven. He had known almost from the first that there was something very special about this young woman, and he had realised that at long last he had found someone with whom he could quite happily spend the rest of his life. Their love had transcended all social barriers, and would remain strong enough to bind them, no matter what tribulations lay ahead.

So he gave himself up to the pleasurable task of proving to her just how sensible she was to place her future happiness in his caring hands, and would have been quite content to verify this conviction many times over had not the library door suddenly swung open to reveal the tall figure of their host.

"There are several persons upstairs in some concern over your welfare, my dear Jane," he remarked, sauntering towards them, the epitome of a man of fashion. "Your sister, to name but one, is quite naturally distraught after witnessing your forced departure."

He cast his friend a look of mild reproach. "Really, Thomas, you cannot continue to indulge in such behaviour… Brawling at White's, and abducting fair damsels from ballrooms…" He paused in order to inhale a pinch of snuff. "Remind me to instruct you some time in how to comport yourself."

"And remind me some time to plant you a facer!" was Tom's threatening response. "What the devil do you mean by telling me that Jane was to marry Pentecost?"

Sir Richard's expressive brows rose. "I know I am a few years your senior, Tom, but there is nought amiss with my memory, and I can therefore state with certainty that I never told you any such thing."

Jane thought it prudent to intervene and, disengaging herself from her still aggrieved future husband's arms, she went over to Richard. "Well, I for one neither know nor care what you did say, precisely, but whatever it was I thank you, sir, from the bottom of my heart. You have made me the happiest of females."

He did not need to hear this: the proof was in her eyes for anyone to see. "Then it is well." He transferred his gaze to his friend to see the same blissful expression on his face, too. "Now, all I need to know is am I to announce one engagement tonight…or two?"

Tom gave a shout of laughter. "You might be an unscrupulous dog, Knightley, but your wits aren't addled… What do you think?"

Richard couldn't prevent a broad smile of satisfaction. "Then might I be the first of many, I'm sure, to offer you my sincerest congratulations? You have succeeded in capturing a pearl beyond price, and I hope you will have the good sense to cherish her always."

"That is my intention," Tom responded softy, slipping his arm gently round his love's shoulders.

Richard continued to regard them in gratified silence for a moment, but then bethought himself of his duties. "Loath though I am to play propriety, but in view of the fact that I am in honour bound to protect this fair lady's name in the absence of her father, I must ask you both to accompany me back upstairs."

Many pairs of eyes turned in their direction as Richard led the way back into the crowded salon. Lady Templehurst took one glance at Jane's blissfully happy expression, and the rather proud look in the eyes of the man by her niece's side, and unashamedly drew out a wisp of silk.

Richard waited only for the set of country dances to come to an end, and succeeded in gaining the attention of all the guests by asking the quartet of musicians hired for the occasion to strike up a chord.

"It gives me the greatest pleasure," he said, his deep, clear voice reaching the furthest corners of the room, "to make an announcement—in fact two announcements—this evening."

An unexpected commotion by the door forced him to pause. The next moment there was a general murmur of excitement and several of the guests who had gathered round began to move apart to enable two portly and flamboyantly attired gentlemen to approach their host.

"I do believe we have interrupted something, Rudge," the larger gentleman remarked in a jovial aside. "Sir Richard, are we *de trop*?"

"On the contrary, Your Royal Highness," he assured him, once again successfully raising his voice above the excited whispers. "Your arrival is most opportune. I was on the point of announcing the engagement between Lord Peregrine Pentecost and Miss Henrietta Dilbey. And...no less gratifying…the engagement between my good friend Dr Thomas Carrington and Lady Jane Beresford."

For several moments there was a stunned silence, then, "Carrington, did you say…? Carrington!" The Regent's plump face beamed with pleasure. "But I know him! Excellent fellow! Oh, by Jove, yes!"

He led the way in what became rapturous applause and hearty congratulations to both couples. "Love weddings. Didn't like my own, of course. Dear me, no," he remarked in an undertone to a young lady regarding him in awestruck silence, before he turned once again to his companion. "Where are the happy couples, Bart? Must offer my personal congratulations."

Sir Bartholomew left the future king to ease his way through the throng, and went in search of his old friend Lady Templehurst, who, surprisingly, was amongst the few not to leave their chairs in order to join the crowd of well-wishers congregating down the far end of the room.

"Well, Gussie, old girl? How has the wicked Dowager taken the news?" he asked, raising his glass to scan the throng for a glimpse of Lady Pentecost. "Don't seem able to locate her."

"You won't. She fell into a swoon and had to be helped from the room." She gave vent to one of her wicked cackles. "Oh, Bart, you could not have timed it better! And bringing the Regent, too! Now she'll never dare to oppose the match. What a complete hand you are!"

"Told you, m'dear, I'd lend you my support. Didn't expect the second announcement, though. Who's this Carrington fellow? Never heard of him, myself, but Prinney seems to know him, right enough." He regarded her tear-filled eyes in silence. "Eastbury's daughter and a doctor, eh? Come as a bit of a shock to you, has it, old girl?"

"I would say, rather, an extremely satisfying surprise," she admitted, astounding him. "He's the very one for my dear Jane. He loves her too."

"Be that as it may, I rather fancy it will cause something of a stir."

"I rather fancy it already has," was the prompt rejoinder. She then gave vent to yet another of those famous wicked chuckles. "Now the Regent himself has openly countenanced the match— both, in fact—there isn't a soul who would dare to oppose either! What an evening this has been! I cannot thank you enough for what you've done,

Bart. Why, I'm almost tempted to show my appreciation by marrying you myself!"

"Now, now, old girl. Don't let's be hasty," Sir Bartholomew advised, suddenly finding his cravat had grown uncomfortably tight. "Very fond of you, and all that. Always have been. But two engagements in one evening are more than enough to be going on with!"

* * * * *

millsandboon.co.uk Community

Join Us!

The Community is the perfect place to meet and chat to kindred spirits who love books and reading as much as you do, but it's also the place to:

- **Get the inside scoop from authors about their latest books**
- **Learn how to write a romance book with advice from our editors**
- **Help us to continue publishing the best in women's fiction**
- **Share your thoughts on the books we publish**
- **Befriend other users**

Forums: Interact with each other as well as authors, editors and a whole host of other users worldwide.

Blogs: Every registered community member has their own blog to tell the world what they're up to and what's on their mind.

Book Challenge: We're aiming to read 5,000 books and have joined forces with The Reading Agency in our inaugural Book Challenge.

Profile Page: Showcase yourself and keep a record of your recent community activity.

Social Networking: We've added buttons at the end of every post to share via digg, Facebook, Google, Yahoo, technorati and de.licio.us.

www.millsandboon.co.uk